Hayes eased a finger be[...]
The Sharps was resting a[...] [...]
keeping the upper crate from moving. When he angled
his eyes downward, he had a difficult time seeing his own
chest, legs, or feet, thanks to the shadows and the dark
clothes he wore. As much as he wanted to ease his other
hand toward the pistol at his side, he was certain that
much movement would give away his position.

"Take a look around the corner," Mose said. "Could
be someone heard us out here."

Wes drew his pistol and stalked toward the corner.
Actually he drew Hayes's pistol. The nickel-plated .45
filled his hand, causing Hayes to choke back the impulse
to rush forward and reclaim it. As Wes approached the
corner, he moved dangerously close to the crates where
Hayes was hiding. So close, in fact, that Hayes thought it
impossible the outlaw hadn't seen him yet.

A few more steps took Wes past the salesman's position. Hayes got a good enough look at Wes's face to see
that his eyes were fixed on the front portion of the building. There were more scraping steps, followed by the
brush of a shoulder against the wall.

The next several seconds passed in silence.

Both outlaws held their ground with guns drawn.

Ralph Compton

STRAIGHT
SHOOTER

A Ralph Compton Novel

by Marcus Galloway

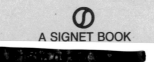

A SIGNET BOOK

SIGNET
Published by the Penguin Group
Penguin Group (USA) Inc., 375 Hudson Street,
New York, New York 10014, USA

USA | Canada | UK | Ireland | Australia | New Zealand | India | South Africa | China

Penguin Books Ltd., Registered Offices: 80 Strand, London WC2R 0RL, England
For more information about the Penguin Group visit penguin.com.

First published by Signet, an imprint of New American Library,
a division of Penguin Group (USA) Inc.

First Printing, June 2013

Ⓓ REGISTERED TRADEMARK — MARCA REGISTRADA

ISBN 978-0-451-24004-0

Printed in the United States of America
10 9 8 7 6 5 4 3 2 1

PUBLISHER'S NOTE
This is a work of fiction. Names, characters, places, and incidents either are the
product of the author's imagination or are used fictitiously, and any resemblance
to actual persons, living or dead, business establishments, events, or locales is
entirely coincidental.
  The publisher does not have any control over and does not assume any respon-
sibility for author or third-party Web sites or their content.

ALWAYS LEARNING   PEARSON

THE IMMORTAL COWBOY

This is respectfully dedicated to the "American Cowboy." His was the saga sparked by the turmoil that followed the Civil War, and the passing of more than a century has by no means diminished the flame.

True, the old days and the old ways are but treasured memories, and the old trails have grown dim with the ravages of time, but the spirit of the cowboy lives on.

In my travels—to Texas, Oklahoma, Kansas, Nebraska, Colorado, Wyoming, New Mexico, and Arizona—I always find something that reminds me of the Old West. While I am walking these plains and mountains for the first time, there is this feeling that a part of me is eternal, that I have known these old trails before. I believe it is the undying spirit of the frontier calling me, through the mind's eye, to step back into time. What is the appeal of the Old West of the American frontier?

It has been epitomized by some as the dark and bloody period in American history. Its heroes—Crockett, Bowie, Hickok, Earp—have been reviled and criticized. Yet the Old West lives on, larger than life.

It has become a symbol of freedom, when there was always another mountain to climb and another river to cross; when a dispute between two men was settled not with expensive lawyers, but with fists, knives, or guns. Barbaric? Maybe. But some things never change. When the cowboy rode into the pages of American history, he left behind a legacy that lives within the hearts of us all.

—*Ralph Compton*

Chapter 1

Iowa, 1887

Wes Cavanaugh robbed banks.

Even when he was a child, that was all he'd ever wanted to do. When his cousins would pretend to be soldiers fighting great battles or knights from fairy tales slaying dragons, he was always pretending to force innocents to reach for the sky as he held them at gunpoint and took all of their hard-earned imaginary cash. While growing up, he was a likeable enough young man. That changed once all of the hard work in his daddy's field and barn granted him the muscular bulk that allowed him to truly assert himself. When he was able to knock Larry Drangle onto his back with one punch to the jaw, Wes realized his dream to become a bad man.

After that, he learned to shoot, honed his riding skills, and listened to everything his uncle had to say about tracking. His family didn't much appreciate the turn their boy had taken, which was why so many of them tried to steer him in another direction. But none of them were a match for the one true skill Wes was given at birth. He was a natural-born liar. Wes's ability to appear earnest as he was taught how to ride gave his father hope when, in actuality, Wes was planning on riding away from the law in a rush. When his uncle taught him the fine art of tracking, Wes stored the knowledge away so he wouldn't slip up when he was the one being tracked by a posse or two. When he was being taught to shoot . . . well . . . there was no way even he could hide the joy that rushed through him when firing a pistol.

Once he had what he thought he needed to put his childhood dreams into motion, Wes stole his father's .38, saddled his horse, and struck out on his own. He was seventeen and full of beans, but that didn't stop him from attempting to rob the first general store he could find.

It was a disastrous affair that began with Wes storming in and talking tough. The shopkeeper played along until he could get to his shotgun, and when he fired a barrel at Wes, the young man's true education began. He barely escaped with his life, but his thieving instincts were strong enough for him to snatch a blanket and a handful of stick candy on his way out simply because they were the only things he could reach.

On that day, Wes learned what it felt like to truly have his neck on the chopping block. He also learned what happened when a man left the comfort of his family's land and strayed from the light of the law. It was cold in those shadows, which was why he quickly learned the value of gathering other like-minded souls as partners. Although the small group immediately thought of themselves as a gang, it took some time to prove themselves as such.

A string of botched robberies and a handful of small successes funded their ride. But even if he hadn't stolen a penny in those days, Wes would never have looked back. It was too late for that. His course was set and he took too much pride in his chosen profession to abandon it so easily.

And so, after putting eleven years of theft under his belt, Wes Cavanaugh might not have been as notorious as some but he was prosperous enough to keep riding the trail he'd set himself upon when he first galloped away from his daddy's barn. However, riding in a large gang wasn't necessarily a good idea. More men meant more loose ends when things took a turn for the worse. On those occasions when a gang had to scatter and lie low, more men meant better odds for the law to find one and make him talk about the others. Also, having fewer men meant splitting the profits of a job into fewer shares. Any one of those things was a good enough reason for Wes to trim down the gang and be more selective in his company.

When he rode across Iowa in the fall of 1887, Wes did so with a man who called himself Mose Robins. Wes never asked if Mose was his proper name or if it was short for something else because he didn't care. Mose was tough enough to stand firm in a fight, he could shoot straight, and he wasn't smart enough to double-cross his partner with any degree of subtlety. Most important, Mose was as loyal as a dog. He also had the same number of fleas living in the thick mass of coarse whiskers sprouting from his chin and upper lip. Although Wes didn't exactly tend to his appearance by doing any more than running an occasional hand over his close-cropped brown hair or splash some water on his face to keep the thick sideburns in place, he looked like a dandy compared to Mose.

Where Wes was lean and muscular, Mose was thick as a bear preparing for hibernation. Where Wes looked as if his sturdy frame and scarred face had been chiseled by the harshness of life spent on the trail, Mose looked as if he'd been put together like a hastily thrown pile of clay. Mose had it where it counted, however, and could throw a punch or fire his pistols without fail. Together, the two of them had cobbled together a nice little partnership.

It had been days since the men had seen a hint of civilization. Being that they were riding across the thick belly of Iowa, that was no surprise to anyone. It was early in the fall, which meant the winds were becoming a comfort rather than a hot blast against sweaty brows. As one cool breeze rolled across a field of corn, causing hundreds of stalks to sway to and fro, Wes lifted his nose to it and drew a deep breath.

"Feels good!" he declared.

Never one for excessive expression, Mose looked around and shrugged. "Feels the same as yesterday," he grunted. "And the day before."

"What's got into you?" Wes asked. His voice reflected a touch of the Irish brogue from his mother's side that he'd never been able to shake.

Mose's voice, on the other hand, was a dull, grunting baritone dredged up from the backwoods of the Appalachians. "Ain't nothin' got into me. Nothin' but the last of that jerked beef and chicory coffee."

"You going soft on me?" Wes asked as he leaned over to give the bigger man a good-natured swat. "A few nights sleeping under the stars and your soft little rump is aching?"

"You best watch yerself."

Wes sat easy in his saddle and placed both hands on the horn in front of him. "You're right. I take it back."

"Good."

"I was completely wrong. There's nothing little about your rump."

Anger flashed in Mose's eyes but quickly died down. Shifting uncomfortably to find a better position, he grunted, "If ye're studying me from that angle so much, I'd say you need to get to a saloon more than I do."

"You want a drink? I have some whiskey from that bottle left. Enough for a swallow or two, anyway."

"I ain't talkin' about goin' to a saloon for drinkin'. I'm talkin' about finding me some company other than you. Somethin' wrapped up in a fine dress with long hair and a sweet smile."

"Still the ladies' man, eh?"

"Born and bred!" Mose said with a wide, yellowed smile.

"You should have plenty of soiled doves to choose from when we get where we're going."

"And where is that, exactly?"

That was another thing Wes liked about Mose. After days of riding across some of the flattest land he'd seen in a long while, Mose was just now getting around to asking why they were trudging across so many fields.

"Ever been to Cedar Rapids?"

Mose scrunched his face into a fleshy mess. He pondered for almost half a minute, mulling the question over as if it pertained to one of the mysteries of the universe. Finally he grunted, "Can't say as I have."

"You'll like it just fine. Plenty of saloons. There's even a mighty big theater where you can catch a show with some pretty dancing girls."

"I like saloon girls better. Besides, there was plenty of saloons in Illinois. Why'd we have to leave there?"

"We had to leave on account of the two posses that were chasing us."

"Oh yeah." Letting out a huffing breath, Mose said, "We could'a gave them the slip without crossing the state line. They weren't so tough, anyways. I bet we could'a made our stand and burned them down."

"What would have happened when those posses met up and decided to ride together?" Wes asked. "It was only a matter of time before that happened, and I doubt taking a stand against all of them boys would have been so easy."

"I guess that's right. Still, I don't like ridin' across this damn state. Ain't nothin' but tall grass and corn. This trail is so flat and dull I could tie off my reins and go to sleep all day without missing a thing."

"Perhaps you should do just that. It'd give my ears a rest."

After a few quiet moments passed, Mose shifted again and asked, "Where did you say we was headed?"

"Cedar Rapids."

"What's in Cedar Rapids?"

"Man I know lives there," Wes replied. "We spent some time locked up across the state line in Nebraska."

Mose shuddered. "More cornfields and flat plains."

Ignoring the other man's grumbling, Wes said, "He went out that way to scout out some train stations, stagecoach stopovers, and the like. All around the border near Omaha is all kinds of places like that that're ripe for the picking. Folks coming through bound for Oregon, Colorado, not to mention rich folks going California way."

Mose gazed about as if he could see the lines of a map etched into the terrain spread out in front of him. "Are we getting close to Omaha? I hear there's lots going on there."

"Cedar Rapids is a ways off from Omaha, but the man I'm looking to meet up with can tell us the best way to get there and all the plum spots to hit once we arrive."

"Train stations?" Mose asked.

Wes nodded.

"What about banks?" the big man asked.

"Could be places better than banks," Wes told him. "That whole area has people comin' and going, day and night. This time of year should be the best because folks will be making the mad dash to cover as much ground as they can before the snow starts to fall. There will be valuables being shipped, payrolls going out to all them workers. Plenty for us to pick from, and this friend of mine scouted it all out."

"What's this friend's name?"

"Jimmy Stock."

"Never heard of him."

"That's what makes him a good scout," Wes replied. "Nobody knows who he is and they don't notice him poking around to see what's what."

"He must be a real good friend if he's going to part with so much valuable information. Will he be riding with us?"

Shrugging as he swatted at a fly that had landed upon his neck, Wes said, "Perhaps calling him a friend is a bit of a stretch. More of a friendly acquaintance. As for him parting with that valuable information, that's how he makes his living. We'll be paying for the information we get, and he won't be riding with us."

Mose made a face as if he'd just accidentally swallowed the fly that the other man had shooed away. "Why couldn't we do our own scouting?" he asked.

"Because Jimmy knows where to look and he knows who to ask for things like when certain shipments are coming through or what route a stagecoach carrying a fat lockbox is taking. Trust me, I've worked with him before and Jimmy's never led me astray."

"Then how come I ain't never heard you mention him before?"

"Because his ain't the kind of work that a man can do very often. He's got to disappear for months at a time, scrounging around for whatever it is he looks for, hunting down the men he talks to, and then finding ways to get them to say the sorts of things men like us need to hear. Last time I met up with Jimmy was two winters ago, and the spring that followed was one of the most profitable I've ever had."

Despite the gleam of greed that shone in one of Mose's eyes, the big man still scowled. "Wish you would'a told me about this sooner."

"I'm telling you now."

"And what if I didn't wanna work with this Jimmy?"

"Then you'd be a fool," Wes snapped. "You'd also be a man who don't like money, and I know you're not that sort of man at all."

The aforementioned gleam returned to Mose's eye. "How much money are you talking about?"

"Enough to pay for the company of all the soiled doves you can handle for the next year."

"That's a tall order," Mose said wistfully.

"Well, I can't say for certain how much money we're talking about, but I did get word that Jimmy is in Cedar Rapids. If he's stuck his head up and is letting men know about it, that means he's got information to sell."

Suddenly Mose did some thinking. Wes could tell as much because the big man got a vaguely pained expression on his face before asking, "How much does he sell his information for?"

"Could be upward of two hundred dollars."

"Two hundred?" Mose pulled back on his reins as if he meant to snap the leather straps in half. His horse raised its head and stomped fretfully before coming to a halt. "That's more than we got in our last job! We'd best get plenty of good information for that kind of money."

Bringing his horse to a stop as well, Wes made sure he was a good distance from his partner with one hand close to his holster when he warned, "That's the price for one bit of news that he found. We'll be in the market for more than that once we get to Cedar Rapids."

"Upward of two hundred for just one of his scouting

stories?" Mose bellowed. "What kind of fool would pay that much?"

"It's an investment!" Wes said. "We spend a little money to make a whole lot more. We'll be coming out ahead when it's all said and done! Can't you see that?"

Mose cocked his head to one side and bared his teeth like a dog that was getting ready to pounce. "You're talkin' to me like I'm stupid. I ain't stupid."

"I know that."

"And we're already ahead! After the work we did in Illinois, we're ahead close to three hundred dollars, and I won't have you toss it away just to hear some man talk about what he saw when he was out scouting!"

"Those jobs were fine, but they were small potatoes."

"We nearly got killed," Mose reminded him. "I don't call that no small potatoes!"

"You're right. We did nearly get killed. That's because we were on our own, working blind and scrounging for what we could get. In case you've been asleep for the last few months, you might have noticed it's been slim pickings lately. We've lined our pockets, but it hasn't been easy. Having someone point us in the right direction can make things a whole lot easier."

Squinting as if he was seeing his partner in a new, mostly unfavorable light, Mose said, "You chose the wrong line of work if you wanted easy."

"You think I don't know that? I've been in this line of work since I was in short pants. All I'm saying is there ain't no reason we can't use our heads a bit more and line up some jobs that could go a little smoother or at least pay off enough for us to sit back and enjoy ourselves for a while. And when I say use our heads," Wes quickly added, "I didn't mean to call you stupid or anything of the like."

Mose slowly nodded, turning his eyes toward the trail

ahead of him even though that trail hadn't changed since they'd crossed the state line. "How much of our money are you looking to . . . invest?"

"I figure we could do well if we can line up two or three jobs." When the bigger man snapped his gaze over to him, Wes quickly added, "I'd make up the difference with my own money. And for that . . . I'm gonna expect a bigger cut until that investment is paid back."

Normally, broaching the subject of taking a bigger cut would be enough to put a twitch into any outlaw's face. This time, however, Mose swallowed it down like bitter medicine. "Suppose that's fair," he grudgingly admitted. "You really think we'll get a line on some good work?"

"I wouldn't pay good money if I didn't."

"What kind of things can this fella tell you that we couldn't figure out on our own? We been doing this for a good, long spell. We ain't wet behind the ears where robbin' is concerned."

"You got that right," Wes said. "That's how I know the two of us can pull off these jobs when most outlaws would need a whole gang. What we don't know is where the prime work is or when a place will be unguarded or where a certain stagecoach will be taking on supplies so it's not guarded or . . . I don't know what else. It's that sort of thing that we need. We might be able to find out some of that with some scouting of our own . . . if we're lucky and happen to be in the right spot at the right time. But if we get what Jimmy is sellin', we don't have to do that end of the job. We do what we do best because Jimmy did what he does best."

They rode for another couple of minutes in silence. Mose chewed on what he'd been told as if the words were tough, stale bread. When he'd finally digested them, he asked, "How long you known this Jimmy?"

"Long enough."

"Do his scouting stories really pay off that good?"

"Why do you think I'm willing to put up so much money just to hear what he's got to say?" Wes asked. "And why else would I be willing to ride across this flat bunch of nothing just to hear him say it?"

Mose looked around at the land surrounding them. It wasn't particularly ugly terrain, and it sure wasn't difficult to navigate. In fact, after he'd taken in everything his partner had to say, a small, contented sigh leaked out of him as he admitted, "This really ain't so bad. I suppose it couldn't hurt to keep riding and give your friend a chance."

"I knew you'd see it that way."

"But I'm warnin' you," Mose added. "If I don't like what he has to say, I ain't about to hand over any money that should be mine. I should still be angry that you were about to spend both of our shares without askin' me first." Suddenly the bigger man scowled. "You really were plannin' on spending all that money. That means you had to spend *my* share as well."

"It's for the greater good," Wes said.

"What if I refused to hand it over?"

Without missing a beat or sparing the time it took to look over at his partner, Wes replied, "Then I would have gunned you down and taken it from you."

The ugly scowl remained on Mose's face for a few seconds before it was shattered by a wide grin followed by a laugh that rumbled up from his belly and shook his entire body. When he was through, Mose flicked his reins to get his horse moving faster and said, "You would've tried! I can get the drop on you any day of the week and twice on Sundays."

"That don't matter. You'll like what Jimmy has to say," Wes assured him. "And if you don't, we can always do some scouting of our own. There's plenty of work to be

Chapter 2

Cedar Rapids

Tennison's was a saloon on the outskirts of town that was filled with enough noise and activity to make both outlaws forget about the days of tedious riding it had taken for them to get there. Not only was there a stage at the back of the house where a trio of dancing girls flapped their skirts to the music provided by the piano and banjo players sitting to one side, but there was a smaller stage in a rear corner where a fourth girl did a little dance of her own. That stage wasn't much larger than a card table, but the men sitting around it whooped and hollered as if it was the greatest show on earth.

Wes and Mose took a moment after stepping inside to soak it all in. As with most everyone else, their attention was immediately drawn to the stages. After that, Mose looked toward the long bar that stretched from the front of the saloon on the right side of the house all the way to the back wall. Well over a dozen men stood at the bar, and there was room for several more. Wes, on the other hand, was more attracted to the games of chance being played on the left side of the large room. Three faro tables were closest to the door, and two roulette wheels spun farther back. Poker was being played at several tables as well as some other games going on in the shadows at the farthest end of the room, which Wes couldn't quite make out from where he stood.

"I like this place," Mose said.

Wes nodded. "Me, too. I think I see Jimmy."

"Can't we get a drink first?"

"Go right ahead and get me one, too. I've got business to tend to."

Being well accustomed to letting his partner dive in to the business dealings first, Mose made his way over to the bar without a complaint about being handed the simpler tasks. He was more than happy to smile at the working girls scattered throughout the saloon and gab with the barkeep while Wes made a straight line to one of the smaller tables situated near the periphery of the poker games.

The man at that table wore a simple white shirt with his sleeves rolled up to expose arms that looked like cords of tightly knotted leather. His skin was deeply scorched by the harsh sun and elements from every kind of terrain known to man. His eyes were narrowed to slits that seemed incapable of opening fully. A battered hat sat on the table to his left, a constant companion more cherished than any human soul. In front of him, playing cards were splayed into a solitaire game, each of the painted faces showing just as much wear as the man who dealt them.

"Howdy, Wes," the grizzled man said before Wes had a chance to say a word.

Removing his hat and setting it on the table as well, Wes pulled out the only other chair and took a seat. "Been a while, Jimmy. You're looking good."

Glancing up from his game, Jimmy studied the other man's face. He must have known all too well that he looked like something that had been dug up from a poorly tended garden because he discarded the compliment along with the next three cards from his deck. "Didn't think I'd see you again."

"I've been busy, that's for certain. You must have heard that I was all the way down in Arkansas for most of last spring."

"No. I thought you'd be dead by now."

"Oh," Wes said with a few quick blinks. "I suppose that sort of thing can work to my benefit. Keeps the law off my tail for a spell."

"Sure. Whatever you say. How'd you know I was here?"

"I crossed paths with Dave Mustaine while in Illinois. He told me you crawled out of the woodwork and set up shop out here in the middle of nothing at all."

Once again, Jimmy looked up. He even placed his cards down so as to pay full attention when he asked, "How is Dave?"

"Dave's . . . well . . . Dave. Got into a fight about three minutes after I shook his hand. Punched some cowboy in the nose for touching his horse. Turns out it was the cowboy's own horse he'd touched after all."

When Jimmy grinned, it wasn't pretty. He was missing one out of every three teeth. The ones that remained were brown as dirt and chipped into sharp, jagged angles. "That's Dave, all right. I sent him to Illinois to check in on a rich fella owns a jewelry store out that way. How'd that pan out?"

Wes leaned across the table so he could be heard when he whispered, "Dave flashed me a wad of money thicker than his fist. Told me he caught that fella bringing his shipment in during the middle of the night just like you saw him do in Missouri. That merchant would have snuck all that pretty stuff right in if Dave didn't know he was comin'. Dave was so drunk that it crossed my mind to relieve him of some of that cash, but . . ."

"But that wouldn't have been very wise," Jimmy said with a knowing grin.

"No," Wes said. "It wouldn't at all. Not with Dave bein' Dave and all." After contemplating the money he'd lost by not stabbing that particular friend in the back, Wes asked, "So, what have you got left to sell?"

Getting back to his game, Jimmy shrugged. "Not a lot. I been sitting here for a while now. Plenty of men have come to pay me a visit. Only reason I'm still here at all is that I like this place."

Wes looked around at the games being played, the festivities on and near the stages as well as the socializing at the long bar, and wasn't impressed by any of it. "What do you mean you're just here because you like this place?"

"You heard me. What ain't there to like? You should try the beer."

"You don't have nothing left to sell?" When he didn't get a response right away, Wes slammed a fist onto the table hard enough to mess up the solitaire layout. "My partner and me rode across this whole damn state as well as a part of Illinois to get here."

Jimmy collected his cards and started shuffling. "That ain't my concern."

"The hell it isn't! We dropped everything we were doing, turned down jobs on account of the promise that you had better ones for sale."

"If you had jobs to do, you should've done them. Just like I'm doing mine. If I want to sit here and play my cards before crawling back into the woodwork, that's my affair."

When Jimmy dealt another game of solitaire, Wes couldn't stomach it. He slapped his hand onto the table again and this time swept the cards off in a single angry motion. "You'd best think twice before you talk to me that way," Wes warned. "I've killed men for less."

"You wanna go down that road?" Jimmy asked in a voice that sounded like rusted iron being dragged across wet slate. "I see worse than you on my best days, and I'm still alive and well. Plenty of them can't say as much. I don't guarantee anything to the men who ask to hear what I seen, but I can guarantee you one thing. If you so much as twitch toward that hog leg at your side, I'll cut yer throat and leave you to bleed out where you sit."

So far, nobody in the immediate vicinity took notice of the cross words being exchanged. Everyone else had better things to do and probably wouldn't stop doing them until they were forced to defend themselves. More than any of them, however, Wes was concerned with the scout sitting directly across from him. Jimmy's features were uneven lines slashed into sunbaked flesh. His eyes betrayed not a single reservation about making good on his threat or taking a bullet in the process. Wes knew that if he drew on Jimmy, he'd have to put him down with one shot because there wouldn't be a chance to fire another.

Wes slowly let out a breath and did his best to ease back into his chair as if he was doing a favor for the scout instead of thinking twice about his own course of action. By the time he'd placed both hands flat on the table to prove they were empty, Mose ambled over to drop a pair of mugs down to splash dark foamy liquid in every direction.

"I know you prefer whiskey, but this beer is some of the best I've had in a while!" Mose said. "Took it upon myself to bring you one."

Jimmy wiped off his cards. "You won't be disappointed."

"This yer friend?" Mose asked.

Wes nodded and made quick introductions. His patience was clearly wearing thin by the time the other two had shaken hands, which did nothing to speed Mose up as he found another chair and dragged it over to the table. "Now that we got all that out of the way," Wes said, "can we get back to business?"

"He's always goin' on about business," Mose said before taking a healthy gulp of beer.

Jimmy smirked and fixed his eyes on the larger of the two men as he said, "There is one bit of information I picked up that could be of some use."

"That so?" Mose grunted. "You pick that up while scouting and such?"

"I do my fair share of scouting, but I also have friends who tell me things. I sell those things to earn my keep."

Mose used the back of his hand to wipe some foam from his mouth. "So I been told."

"There's a train due to leave Omaha," Jimmy explained. "It'll be picking up a load of money that's to be used to pay all the men laying down the new Union Pacific tracks along that whole line. Them Chinese may not earn much, but there's a whole lot of them. Same goes for every other poor soul driving spikes into the ground. Then there's the foremen and bosses. They've got pay coming as well, and a good portion of it will be carried on that train."

Wes straightened up. "You mean one train is gonna carry enough money to pay all them workers?"

"Not all of them," Jimmy said. "The train will make stops along the way to pick up funds from banks across the country, but it will be starting with a sizable amount when it leaves Omaha."

Mose let out a belch that was loud enough to catch the attention of the players at a nearby poker game and put a foul stench in the air drifting past Wes's face. The big man didn't care about any of that, although he did seem to catch a whiff of the scent because he waved it away as if it were smoke. "Sounds like a pretty valuable piece of information," he said.

Jimmy nodded once. "It is."

"Then how come you still got it?"

"Shut your mouth and let me do the talking," Wes said impatiently.

"No," Mose said. "If he's saying anything about it to us, it means that it must still be for sale, right?"

"That's right," Jimmy replied.

"And if it's still for sale, that means ain't nobody seen fit to buy it yet."

"Or," Wes said hopefully, "it could be that he just came across it in the last day or two."

Mose conceded that point with a shrug before pouring some more beer down his throat.

Reluctantly Wes asked, "How long have you known about this?"

Keeping his eyes on Mose, Jimmy said, "I heard rumblings about it a few months ago when I was coming down through the Badlands. I rode with a tribe of Sioux while in that neck of the woods, and they watched the iron horses very carefully. Some of their scouts told me about one train in particular that caught their eye because of all the soldiers riding along with it."

"Soldiers?" Wes asked.

"Told ya," Mose grunted. "Ain't nothing that sweet is gonna be taken easy. There's gotta be plenty of gun hands riding on a train like that. That is, if there really is some load of railroad money in some boxcar."

"Oh, there is," Jimmy said. "I can assure you of that. If I was in the habit of leading men like yourselves on wild-goose chases, I wouldn't have survived this long to talk about it."

"You got that right," Wes snarled. Despite all of the effort he put into sounding as menacing as possible, neither of the other men at the table appreciated it.

"So, what's the hitch?" Mose asked.

Jimmy raised an eyebrow. "Hitch?"

"There's gotta be a hitch. Always is."

"I suppose you could say there are hitches, but nothing that you wouldn't expect for such a job." Glancing back and forth between Mose and Wes, Jimmy spoke in a voice that issued from him like a gurgling current bubbling up from an oily pool. "This train is guarded well. Upward of a dozen armed men onboard and even a few men on horseback who ride alongside the tracks to watch for robbers or any other sign of trouble."

"How many men on horseback?" Wes asked.

"Don't rightly know, but the Sioux said there were enough to warrant keeping their distance. That's saying a lot for Sioux." Jimmy poured the cards from one hand into another and back again. "There's plenty of men who talk about this train. When it rolls down the track with an escort that size, it's hard to miss. But it ain't trying to sneak anywhere. It's just doing its job and it does it well. Ask any of a dozen men who work on the railroad at those stations and they'll tell you plenty of stories."

"How do we get at that money?"

"There's no telling what the money itself is kept in. I've heard tell that it's in a safe so thick it takes extra coal shoveled into the engine just to get it moving down a track. Could be held in lots of smaller safes, but however it's stored it's got to be tough to crack."

After taking a swig of beer, belching, and wiping his mouth on his sleeve, Mose said, "Them are some mighty big hitches."

"I like him," Jimmy said with a chuckle.

"Yeah," Wes said. "And he does bring up a good point.

If you've been sitting here as long as you were saying before, why is it you've still got this little piece of information under your hat? You've known about it for some time."

"It's been something of a pet project of mine," Jimmy replied. "Didn't seem worth my time at first. After all, you don't need someone like me to tell you there's a fat load of cash sitting in a federal reserve. Anyone with eyes in their head can see that train is hauling something valuable when it rolls by with all them guns protecting it."

"So what have you got to offer?"

"I can tell you what the inside of the train looks like, for one."

Wes looked over to Mose, and the big man nodded appreciatively back at him. Noticing the bigger man wasn't looking directly at him, Wes realized his partner was actually admiring one of the dancing girls on the large stage. He left Mose to his simpler pleasures and leaned forward with both hands pressed flat against the table. "How'd you get inside that train?"

"I have my methods," the scout replied. "Let's just say it's one of the reasons men like you pay to talk with me over drinks. Speaking of which, I'm getting parched."

"Mose," Wes snapped. "Get the man a beer."

Happy for any reason to go back to the bar and brush against some more working girls along the way, Mose excused himself.

"I can tell you what car the money is in," Jimmy explained. "I can also tell you the best time and place to get it."

"When exactly is the train due to leave Omaha?"

"That's another little tidbit you'll need to pay to find out."

"All right," Wes sighed. "How much do I need to pay?"

"Five hundred."

"Five hundred dollars?"

"It sure ain't pesos," Jimmy said.

"I don't have that kind of money."

"That's too bad. I imagine you'll at least triple your investment even if you don't get around to opening one of the large safes."

Wes's mouth almost started to water. "Is that price why you haven't sold this yet?" he asked.

"Partly. I've told this same story to a few others recently, but they didn't have the money, either. Told me they'd be back as soon as they got it, though, so I figured I'd make myself comfortable in this here town until they arrive. Reckon it won't be too much longer before I can move on."

"How much will it take for you to stay here and keep your mouth shut?"

"Why, keeping silent wouldn't serve me very well, being in this particular line of work and all," Jimmy said.

After a prolonged sigh, Wes said, "I want to buy the rest of that story. That is, if you can guarantee it's true."

"I don't guarantee much, but what I say is as close to gospel as you can get. If you didn't know that already, you wouldn't have come so far to buy me my drink."

Speaking of which, Wes could see that Mose had paid for the drinks and was making his way back to the table. Wes wanted to get some more discussion in before the bigger man came along to ruin it as he had before. "All right," he said. "I can pay you a hundred now and the rest after I get it."

"A hundred may be good enough to hold me over most of the time, but I'm itching to get moving again. You'll have to do better."

"Don't you have anything else you can part with for a cheaper price?"

"No."

There was no way for Wes to know if Jimmy was being forthright in that regard or merely reeling in the fish that was already on his hook. Either way, Wes did know he couldn't exactly force the scout to part with anything he wasn't willing to give him. Closing his eyes as if he were about to sacrifice his firstborn, Wes said, "Make it two hundred."

"Two fifty."

Glancing toward the bar, Wes saw that his partner was now talking to a woman in a red dress who was either one of the saloon's working girls or mysteriously attracted to oafish bears in desperate need of a bath. Turning back to Jimmy, he said, "Fine, I can pay half now, but I want something more than just your word."

"What else can I give you?"

"Give me at least part of what you were gonna tell me. For this much money," he added while removing a bundle of cash from his pocket and showing it to him, "it had better be more than some tale about your Sioux friends."

For the first time since the conversation had started, Jimmy seemed to take him seriously. "That sounds reasonable." He squinted for a few moments and then leaned forward. "Hand over that money."

Gritting his teeth, Wes gave him the roll of money.

After turning the wad over in his hand, Jimmy said, "Your best bet is to hit that train at a particular time while it's at a station. I won't go into any more than that, but you'd be wise to be a ways off when you do it."

"What's that supposed to mean?"

"It means you'd need either a whole lot of men or an aversion to drawing breath if you were going to take a run at that train head-on. If you had someone who could fire at a few specific points from a distance with a good rifle, it'd make that job a whole lot closer to manageable. The larger caliber you can get, the better because you'll only get one shot to put your men down."

"That could make this job manageable enough for two men to pull it off?"

"I told you I wasn't going to part with it all," Jimmy warned.

Knowing better than to argue, Wes said, "If this ain't a job that I can pull off with what I got, I can't use whatever you do want to part with. You've always been on the square, Jimmy. At least let me know if I'll be able to put any of this information to use."

Jimmy thought long and hard before nodding. "Two men should be able to come away with a good amount of money if they do it right. Not all of the money, but enough to put smiles on their faces. That one with the rifle had better be a real straight shooter, though. Otherwise, both of you are dead."

"Don't worry about that," Wes said. "Just be sure to keep the rest of this story under your hat until we come up with the rest of that money."

"I don't control when men come along to have a word with me. If someone has enough to pay my price, then I'll tell them what I know. If that happens, you can have most of your money back."

"Most?"

"Well, I already told you more than you knew when you walked in here," Jimmy said as he calmly pocketed the two fifty. "That's worth somethin'. All you gotta know is that the rest of what I got to say is worth a whole lot more."

"You've got a lot of my money," Wes snarled. "And I'm not the sort who likes to just hand it over for nothing."

"You'll be getting a lot more than nothing. We both know that much."

"Just so long as you don't give it away to anyone else that comes along."

Mose approached the table with a beer in each hand. He set one down in front of Jimmy and hoisted the other to his mouth.

Jimmy took the beer and held it aloft. "I'll give you two days."

"It's a deal," Wes said.

Mose sat down and showed them a drunken grin. "Whatever deal you made, I'll drink to it!"

Chapter 3

There was a steady stream of folks walking down the busiest street in Cedar Rapids. Many of them were paired up, talking to husbands, wives, or children. Some were in larger groups. Proper families. Aldus Bricker watched them extra close so he could avoid being tripped up by some little kid who stepped into the street or wandered in front of someone with someplace they needed to be.

In his younger days, Aldus didn't think very highly of children. He understood parents were proud of their young'uns, but, not having any of his own, Aldus only saw most children as noisemakers in short pants and frilly hats. He would never be cruel to a child, but he wouldn't spare much time to comfort one, either. That was in his younger days. Now that Aldus was hip deep into his thirties, he saw things a bit differently.

He smiled at the two little girls who scampered in front of him when he crossed the street and even offered a quick "Watch yourself, now," instead of looking past them as he might an insect buzzing around his head. When they made it to the boardwalk on the other side, he kept watching for a second or two to make certain they didn't trip or fall. The mother of those two girls was hot on their heels, and she gave Aldus a quick smile before wrangling her children. He didn't get another glance from any of them, which suited Aldus just fine. The ladies weren't being rude. They were just being like most everyone else.

Aldus wasn't a handsome man. He stood just a bit shorter than the average fellow with the stocky build of a boxer and the face to match. While he did have his share of scars, they blended in almost completely with his rough features and weather-beaten skin. The beard covering his chin was just thick enough to be considered brushy, but not overly so. His hands were thick with calluses and his fingers were swollen after years of being balled up and knocked into other boxers' chins. He'd spent years in the ring. Some fights felt as if they took years in themselves. Now, his nose a worn crooked line and his ears puffed and misshapen, Aldus was forging another path.

He didn't need to know street names or intersections as he turned at the next corner and continued on. Aldus knew Cedar Rapids the way he knew several other towns. The places he needed to go were etched into his memory like so many tracks laid down in his head. He walked the track to the post office now, opened the door, and tipped his dented bowler hat to the bespectacled gentleman sitting behind a short counter.

"Fine mornin' to you," Aldus said.

"That you, Mr. Bricker?"

"It is. You got anything for me?"

The fellow behind the counter had thinning gray hair and a hooked nose that was almost long enough to make contact with his upper lip. He stood up, pushed his spectacles up as far as they would go, and went over to a row of pigeonholes on the wall. "There's a few letters for you. All arrived in a bunch." Picking up a small bundle, he flipped through to the last one, examined the number scribbled on it in pencil, and nodded. "Yep. Looks like they were sent on the twenty-seventh of last month."

Standing at the counter, Aldus drummed his fingers expectantly. "Uh-huh. That's good to know."

"Just a bit more than two weeks ago, I reckon," the other man said as he squinted toward the ceiling and tapped the corners of the letters against his chin. "Fifteen days, actually."

"Thanks for—"

"I'm sorry," the man quickly said. "Make that sixteen days." Now that he'd solved his mystery, the man gladly handed over the letters. "Do you have anything that needs to be delivered?"

"Not yet, but I will before leaving."

"When will that be?"

"Shouldn't be long," Aldus replied. "Less than a week. That is, unless things go better here than they did the last time."

Tapping a finger to his temple as if he were tipping an unseen hat, the man said, "You know where to find me."

"Sure do. Thanks!"

As the man behind the counter got back to the bit of nothing he'd been doing before, Aldus wished he knew the postal worker's name. While he could remember a lot of things, names seemed to escape him most of all. He could blame that on the amount of traveling he did and the vast number of faces he saw along the way, but in the end it didn't really matter. Aldus knew what he knew and he accepted the things he didn't know. It was a simple system, too simple for some, but it worked for him just fine.

There were four letters in the bundle, and Aldus couldn't help himself from looking at each in turn while he walked down the busy street. Each was addressed with a familiar, flowing script that was just as neat and uniform as newsprint. The handwriting didn't have the cold, blocky shapes of a newspaper's articles, but each letter was crisp and precise. He smiled widely and squinted at the letter until his name took shape.

Aldus knew how to read for the most part, although he couldn't just pick something up and see what had been written the way most folks could. When he'd been in school as a little one, he used to whine that reading made his eyes ache, and when his father cursed him for being weak, he complained that he didn't like being cooped up in a room with the teacher and all them other children. His eyes wandered from the blackboard simply because it took so much effort to make sense out of what was there.

It took a fairly long spell before he could recite and recognize the alphabet. Even then, reading didn't come as easy to him as it did for everyone else. Sometimes the words made sense. Sometimes they didn't. Sometimes they looked the way they were supposed to. Other times they were a jumble of nonsense. By the time he gave up on schooling altogether, Aldus could make just enough sense of written language to get the general idea of what it meant. Normally such a thing was a chore that he avoided through a series of simple tricks and halfhearted explanations. Those were the times when it worked in his favor to look like a piece of meat that had been gnawed on and spit out. Folks weren't too surprised when they had to explain things to a man who looked like him. When he picked up his letters, however, Aldus couldn't help remembering the taunts from his father cursing him for being a common idiot.

He was retracing his steps down the street when he spotted a post supporting the awning of a store with folded blankets and sundries in the window. He leaned against the post, took the first letter out, and carefully placed the rest in his back pocket. The paper he unfolded was crisp and clean. He lifted it to his nose, hoping for a scent more provocative than ink, but was pleased well enough when he caught a hint of sweetness. It could have been his imagination or a scent from some other store nearby, but he liked to think it was a small sample of the hand that had written those perfectly formed words.

He recognized his name at the top of the letter, and his heart swelled.

He couldn't help looking all the way down to the bottom of the page where the name Bethany stood out like a splash of color in an otherwise drab world.

When he went back to the body of the letter, much of what had been written appeared as just a bunch of pretty lines. After a bit of careful scrutiny, however, he made out a few portions of sentences and then a batch of words here and there. She was doing well and hoped he was doing the same. There were some troubles with one of the children. She was almost done with the quilt she'd been working on. One of her children was sick.

Aldus stopped when he got there and reread that part several times. The harder he stared at the letter, the more irritated he got. Soon the letters seemed to dissipate before his eyes like so much smoke being scattered by a passing breeze. His temper flared and the muscles in his forearm flexed, but he stopped himself before making a fist. If he damaged that letter in any way, he'd never be able to forgive himself. Knowing it was a lost cause to try reading any more at this point, he folded the letter and eased it back into its envelope.

The frustrations faded quickly, shoved aside like the pains he felt in his knuckles or the twitches plaguing his back from time to time. Every one of them was no pleasure to bear, but they were a part of him and he was no longer the crying little boy who was too weak to carry on beneath their weight. Besides, all he needed to do to put those particular frustrations behind him was find a quiet spot where he could study the letters and soak up what they had to tell him. Hearing from Bethany was like that for Aldus. No matter what else was going on at the time, seeing her sweetly written words was like feeling a gentle hand brushing against his battered face.

He smiled at that thought. The smile didn't falter in the slightest when he heard a gunshot crack through the air in the distance. Aldus quickened his pace toward the sound of gunfire until he could spot two wagons parked in a lot at the town's northern perimeter. The first wagon was about half as tall as a stagecoach and built up on both sides with stacks of wooden cases and a narrow space down the middle that was accessible by a set of steps that folded down from the back. The second was a covered wagon similar to the ones driven by any number of folks heading west for better lives.

The wagons were parked beside another structure that was twice as long and much more attractive to the eye. Constructed of a simple wooden frame, the structure had no roof or even any complete walls. Instead, the front portion was erected near the wagon while the rear section was set up approximately ten yards away. The side walls were nothing more than support beams adorned with colorful advertisements that Aldus could recite from memory. The front consisted of a waist-high counter with notches carved into a thick rack where four rifles could be propped with their barrels pointing toward the structure's farthest end. That back wall was something that Aldus never got tired of looking at.

There were three wooden beams crossing the back wall. The lowest was about as high as a saloon's bar and was a simple shelf where bottles and Mason jars could be

arranged in a row. The second beam had round targets
nailed in place. Each target was made of tin and had
numbers painted on it along notched vertical and hori-
zontal lines. The uppermost beam was actually a thin
pole, situated at about eye level, that was threaded
through five specially made targets. Those targets, crafted
from iron, were cast in the shape of a duck on top with a
heavy circle hanging below, which was heavy enough to
always keep the ducks upright no matter how many
times they spun around that pole. Fixed to the smallest
pieces of wood that were mainly there to give the structure its shape and hold up some of the brightly painted
banners were dozens of clay pipes and smaller circles, no
bigger than fifty-cent pieces, pasted onto short sticks.

Another gunshot cracked through the air, followed by
a familiar voice that was just loud enough to be heard
over the voices of the rifles and the ringing of ears.

"A fine shot, sir!" the voice proclaimed. "No doubt a
mixture of natural-born talent and fine craftsmanship."

The man who spoke would have been tall enough to
spot from a distance even without the top hat he wore.
His body was lean and wiry as if it had been specially
made to maneuver within the cramped confines of the
wagon parked nearby. His long face was beaming and
expressive, marked by a perfectly trimmed goatee. Thick,
unruly eyebrows bobbed up and down as he spoke in a
quieter tone that Aldus couldn't make out from where
he stood. After easing past a small cluster of folks standing a few paces away from the wooden structure, Aldus
crossed his arms and listened closely to the words he
could now hear a little better.

"What you're holding there is one of my finest models,"
the man in the top hat proclaimed. "It fires a forty-two-
caliber round with exceptional accuracy."

"How reliable is it?" The man who asked that ques-

tion examined the rifle in his hands. He stood at the front
of the wooden structure, and when he sighted along the
top of the rifle at the far end, he waited several seconds
before pulling his trigger. The only sound came from the
rifle itself, and Aldus smirked when the man held the
rifle in front of him and said the same thing most men
did when they missed what they'd been aiming at.

"This damn thing isn't any good," the man said an-
grily. "Barrel must be crooked."

The man was a muscular fellow with coarse brown
hair. At first, it seemed the other, bigger man standing
nearby was just another onlooker admiring the finely
decorated shooting gallery. But the bigger man's amuse-
ment didn't come from the finely crafted targets or the
attractive arrangement of the clay pipes lined up like so
many little flags frozen in motion. He chuckled and
slapped the first man on the shoulder while saying,
"That's it, Wes. Must be the rifle."

Much of the crowd dispersed, leaving Aldus somewhat exposed since he remained where he'd been standing. At least, he might have been exposed if either of the
two other men seemed the least bit interested in him.
Instead, they were intent on selecting another rifle.
When Wes handed back the one he'd just fired, Aldus
could see the holsters strapped around both men's waists.
It wasn't unusual for men to wear a gun, but he didn't
like the look of those two. Instincts honed from being in
a boxing ring for so many years made it easier for Aldus
to sniff out other fighters, and those two were definitely
more than simple customers looking to buy a new hunting rifle.

"I need something that'll be accurate from a distance," Wes said.

The man in the top hat took the rifle from him before
it was tossed away like so much trash. "Any rifle is good

from a distance, my good sir. The real question is how much distance do you need to cover?"

"Let's say . . . a hundred yards."

"I'd say this rifle could cover that distance quite well."

"Enough with that rifle!" Wes snapped. "Show me something else. Something with more kick."

Aldus could tell the salesman was getting nervous. Although the fellow in the top hat didn't make it known outright, he took a bit more time than usual while selecting another rifle from the rack hanging off the exterior of the wagon. Those rifles were displayed on a side panel that could be closed up when the wagon was prepared to roll again. The man in the top hat glanced around, spotted Aldus, and let out a breath.

"Here's a good one," the salesman said while sliding a longer rifle from between the metal rings attached to the panel. "A specially modified Sharps model with adjustable sights and a grip that your hand wraps around like a lover's embrace."

"What the hell did you just say?" Wes asked through a disgusted sneer.

Without missing a beat, the salesman walked over to him and explained, "It's one of my own designs." He held it in both hands and turned it to several different angles so his customers could enjoy it from all sides. Along with the mechanical modifications, there was also Hayes's own stamp etched into the metal just behind the trigger guard. It was a large *H* with a smaller *Z* laid on top of it. "For an extra fee," he added, "I'll even specially craft it to fit your very own hand."

"Why would I want that?"

"Because it reduces friction in your grasp. You see, when aiming over long distances, even the slightest shift can put your shot several feet wide of its mark. With my tailor-made stocks, there won't be any shift at all. I'll tell you what," the salesman added. "For no extra charge, I'll even carve the stock down to fit against your shoulder like it grew there."

"Like it what?"

"Just try for yourself."

Wes brought the rifle to his shoulder, grumbling under his breath as he shifted his feet and made slight adjustments of the stock against his shoulder before finally sighting down the barrel. Judging by the angle of the rifle, he was aiming for one of the circle targets in the middle row in front of him. After a long pause, he pulled the trigger. The rifle bucked against his shoulder and sent its round through the air without so much as scraping the edge of any target.

"That one broke, too?" Wes's big companion chuckled.

"You're drunk, Mose," Wes said. "Now shut up." Handing back the rifle, he glared at the salesman and said, "Seems like these guns ain't worth the price of a bullet. That's about what I heard, anyway."

The salesman took the rifle and straightened up as if he'd been struck across the face. "I beg your pardon? What did you hear?"

"Just that you're nothin' but a huckster and the wares you got for sale belong in a scrap heap."

"Who told you that?"

"Man down at the store over on the corner."

Looking toward the nearest street, the salesman doffed his top hat to a window marked GRABLE'S FIRE-ARMS. "Miserable slander coming from a defeated competitor. After so many years of my weapons upstaging his, Mr. Grable has resorted to rumormongering to attract more business. I assure you," he added while motioning toward the banner stretched across the top of the wooden structure, "Zachariah Hayes crafts and sells only the finest weapons. If you would like a demonstration to allay your reservations . . ."

"All right, then, *Mr. Hayes*," Wes said, speaking the salesman's name as if it were a joke, "I believe I'll take you up on that. Show me what a fine weapon that is."

"Gladly." With that, Hayes took the rifle and settled it in his grip. He took ample time to place the stock against his shoulder, align his fingers just right, and even place his cheek against the side of the rifle in just the right spot.

Mose scratched his head and let out a grunting laugh. "Well, if you take all that time to take a shot, it had better be good."

"Nothing should be rushed, my friends," Hayes said as he reached along the barrel to reposition the sight.

"How was I supposed to know you had to do *that*?" Wes snarled.

Hayes would not be distracted. As he spoke, he did so while moving the barest minimum of muscles to form his words. "I will be happy to provide instruction . . . for a nominal fee, of course. Otherwise, you can simply read the documentation provided with every sale."

"Documentation, huh? Never had no documents when I bought a gun. All I needed was bullets and somethin' to shoot at."

"That's because you are buying common weapons, sir," Hayes said. "My wares are anything but."

Once he was situated, Hayes drew a deep breath, held on to it for a few seconds, and then let it go. When most of the air had been expelled from his lungs, he squeezed his trigger. The rifle barked once, the sound of which was followed by the metallic clang of a bullet striking one of the painted iron circles. He smiled broadly while lowering the rifle and nodded with satisfaction. The circle that was still shaking on its rail had a chipped section of paint at the one o'clock position midway between the center and its farthest edge.

"There, now!" Hayes declared. "Perfect working order."

Wes grimaced as if he'd just coughed up something sour. "Sights still seem a bit off."

"I am a gunsmith, sir. Not a sharpshooter."

"Pathetic shot, is more like it."

Nudging his partner with an elbow, Mose said, "Better shot than you."

"Anyone could make a shot when he takes all that time to fuss about," Wes groused. "We ain't gonna have that kind of time!"

"Well, then," Hayes sighed as he set the rifle down onto the rack and removed his top hat. "I suppose this puts us in something of a predicament."

"I guess it does," Wes grunted. "You enjoy that predicament and I'll go buy a rifle that I can use without reading a book to figure it out."

Hayes allowed the two men to take a few steps away from the front of the shooting gallery before saying, "I have a proposal."

Wes stopped and turned around. "You knocking some off the top of the price of that rifle is a proposition I'll like an awful lot."

"Better yet, why don't I show you how well my rifles perform with the help of a third party?"

"What'll that prove?"

"No offense, sir, but we all have bad days. Any number of factors can account for you missing that target or me hitting it. Whatever the reason, it is not the fault of my rifle and . . . more important . . . my rifles are the only ones in town that can be so easily modified to nullify any particular shortcoming."

Wes stepped up to scowl directly into Hayes's eyes.

His chest nearly bumped the salesman when he growled, "What shortcoming are you talking about?"

Taking half a step back, Hayes showed him a nervous smile. "Just allow me to show how I can modify this rifle for anyone's use. Surely you'll see the benefit of buying your firearms from a craftsman instead of just plucking one from a rack." Turning away from Wes, Hayes glanced around as if he didn't see Aldus standing nearby. Then, after a second look, the salesman pointed at him and said, "You, sir!"

Aldus recoiled slightly and then tapped a finger against his chest.

"Yes . . . you," Hayes announced. "Would you care to try one of these fine rifles?"

"I . . . suppose I could," Aldus replied.

"Come on over here!"

Mose rolled his eyes. "This ain't gonna prove anything other than you're a lousy shot, Wes. And I already knew that."

"Which is all the more reason to buy a specially crafted weapon," Hayes said. "The right rifle can make any man a marksman, no matter what he may lack in raw skill. That's the whole reason I—"

"I *ain't* lacking!" Wes said.

"Poor choice of words on my part," Hayes said quickly. "Would you care to see if someone other than me can hit their mark with this rifle?"

Wes glanced toward Grable's Firearms and shrugged. "Might as well."

"Much obliged." Now that Aldus was standing nearby, Hayes turned toward him and gave him a curt bow. "Pleased to meet you, sir. Would you happen to be an expert in firing a rifle?"

"I've done plenty of hunting," Aldus replied.

"Have you ever tried your luck at a shooting gallery?"

"Yes, sir."

Handing over the rifle, Hayes said, "Then try your luck at this one. Why not start with one of the bottles?"

Aldus put the rifle to his shoulder, sighted along its barrel, and fired. His bullet whipped through the air without shattering any glass. "Thought I was dead center," he grumbled.

Nodding, Wes chuckled, "I know how that goes."

"Try again," Hayes urged.

Once more, Aldus took aim and concentrated. This time, his shot nicked the top of his bottle just enough to set it to wobbling on its shelf as a fine mist of glass shards spattered onto the dirt behind the rack.

"Now, then," Hayes said as he took the rifle from him, "if you'd allow me to make some slight adjustments. It appears your shots were a bit high and to the right." His fingers adjusted the sights so minutely that no real movement could be seen in them. However, the salesman continued to ease the sights along a narrow track built into the barrel and then made some similar adjustments to the sights closest to the grip. He handed it back and said, "There, now! Give that a try."

Aldus held the rifle as if it were some new thing that he'd never seen before. "Do I do anything differently?"

"Not in the least. Just aim and fire as you did before."

First, Aldus squinted through the sights. Then he opened his eye as wide as it would go. Once he'd settled on some middle ground between the two, he squeezed the trigger and sent a round through the air that caused a bottle to explode into gleaming fragments.

"Well, I'll be!" Aldus proclaimed.

Wes bared his teeth and looked at the lowest rack as if he expected that bottle to somehow still be there. "That was a fix! You two are working together!"

"I noticed your shots were most likely high as well,"

Hayes said while levering in the next round. "Whether this man is a stranger or not, the fact remains that I adjusted the sights thusly. Why don't you see if there's a difference for yourself?"

When he took the rifle after Hayes had touched up the sights again, Wes seemed more than a little reluctant to take his shot. He went through the motions of positioning himself and settling the rifle against his shoulder more as though he was mimicking what he'd seen from the others. He started to fire, eased his finger back, and took a deep breath. Finally the rifle bucked against his shoulder and spat a round into the lower portion of one of the round targets. He seemed more surprised than anyone to hear the resounding metallic *clang*.

"You see?" Hayes beamed. "And that was with only minor adjustments. When you purchase a rifle of your own, I will adjust the sights and balance to your specifications. I even have plenty of other rifles for you to choose from. You may just find one with the added punch you requested, and if you don't, I can craft some ammunition to fit the bill."

"How much punch?" Wes asked.

"How much do you need?"

Wes and Mose looked back and forth at each other, neither one wanting to say whatever was going through his mind. Measuring his words carefully, Wes said, "I'll need something that's good from at least a hundred yards. Give or take."

"Looking to do some hunting?"

"You might say that."

"Well, I can modify this very rifle to suit you and," Hayes added, "I'll also be willing to press some ammunition that will be much better than the normal rounds you'd buy at most stores."

"Fine," Wes said as he set the rifle down. "Get this

adjusted and I'll come back around in a bit to give it a try."

"I guarantee you won't be disappointed," Hayes said.

Wes and Mose each looked Aldus up and down before turning their backs on the shooting gallery and walking away.

Aldus watched them go until both of the other men disappeared from his sight. Still looking in that direction, he asked, "You think they'll be upset when they find me working here later?"

"Won't take away from the quality of that rifle."

"I suppose you're right. Only problem is that he seemed to want a rifle a bit too much."

Hayes grinned widely and draped an arm around Aldus's shoulders. "A customer who's too eager? No such thing, my friend."

Chapter 4

The saloon was a clean little place situated on the edge of town within eyeshot of the shooting gallery next to Hayes's wagon. Consisting of canvas walls wrapped around a wooden frame, it drew most of its business from those who either couldn't wait to get into Cedar Rapids for their drink or needed one on their way out. Aldus and Hayes sat at their usual table next to a flap held open by a hook that fit into a ring stitched into the thick canvas. The table itself was half of a circular dining table. Two of its legs were originals and the others were boards that had been nailed on after being sawed to something close to the correct length.

"This one's on me," Hayes said as he eased a shot glass across the table.

Aldus took it and waved it beneath his nose. "As a bonus to my regular pay?"

"Indeed. That man was set to walk and pay our neighbor Mr. Grable a visit."

"Nonsense," Aldus said. "He wasn't gonna go anywhere. He needed a rifle and he meant to have one. Otherwise, he would've walked away long before I had a chance to step in."

"Well, that means he'll be coming back. And that

leads us right back to this." Hayes lifted his glass and took a drink.

Aldus did the same.

After allowing the firewater to work its magic, Hayes said, "We should be moving on soon."

"What? We hardly just arrived!"

"It's been almost three weeks, Aldus. I hear there's been some Indian scares a few days west of here, and that means folks will be looking to arm themselves. We must seize any opportunities that come our way."

"That sounds kinda grim, don't it?"

"We sell guns," Hayes replied. "You've been doing this long enough to know that we have to go where the need to buy is greatest. Just like anyone else selling their wares."

"I know. It's just . . ."

"Ahhh," Hayes said. "You just now got what you were waiting for at the post office. Is that it?"

"Something like that."

"So your little system is working out?"

"It's not just a little system," Aldus said. "You make it sound like I'm a child."

"Not my intention, I assure you."

Aldus had known Zachariah Hayes for several years, which was plenty long enough to know when he was trying to slip one past him. Although salesmen weren't generally very trustworthy, Hayes was an exception. He did enjoy playing the part of showman, but he wasn't a cheat. More important, he was a good friend. Aldus nodded slowly and set the whiskey aside so he could remove the letters from his back pocket.

"These were waiting for me," he said, "so I guess our little system worked just fine. I just tell her where we'll be and she sends them on to the post offices I listed."

"That's good to hear! Us moving along shouldn't be

much of a bother. All you need to do is send your lady friend word that we'll be headed to our next stop sooner rather than later and she can start mailing your letters there. You did make arrangements to receive letters there, right?"

"I did."

"Good, then. It's settled. Start breaking down the gallery and we'll leave in the morning."

Aldus grinned and watched the other man expectantly.

"What is it?" Hayes asked.

"You seem to be in an awful hurry to get moving. Wouldn't have anything to do with them two that were so eager to get their hands on a rifle, would it?"

Hayes dismissed that with a wave. "If I was skittish about dealing with men who wanted to arm themselves, I'd have no right being in this line of work. If they're not back by later tonight, they weren't coming back at all."

"There was something more to those men," Aldus warned. "Something that didn't set right."

"Well, if they come back and decide to start any trouble, we can deal with it or get the law to do so."

"You think they'll get riled up if they see that I work for you?"

Hayes shrugged. "They already suspected. Besides, it's not like we cheated anyone. Just a little bit of a show to catch their attention. That modified Sharps I showed him spoke for itself. As for what those men might do with the rifle after they buy it, that's not our concern."

"All the same, I'd like to keep a record of them two just in case some lawman needs our help."

"You looking to become a deputy now?" Hayes asked with a bemused grin.

"No. I'll just be ready in case someone needs any questions answered."

Hayes finished his whiskey, put his top hat back on his head, and patted it into place. "You can keep all the records you like, just so long as you do it after breaking down the gallery and stowing everything away for the night. We're moving out tomorrow, so make sure everything is tied down good and tight."

"I've done it plenty of times, Zeke. I know how it goes."

Although not one for putting on airs, the salesman was never fond of being called by that nickname. He'd long since given up on correcting Aldus, so he merely sighed as he walked away.

Aldus chuckled, knowing full well how he'd perturbed the other man. Shifting his weight in the chair, he felt the bundle of letters in his back pocket. More than anything else, he wanted to take them out and read them one at a time. For him, that would have been a slow process, and there was much work to be done. Hayes would be making one last push to make sales, especially with the interest he'd sparked in those two men. After that, the tedious process of dismantling the shooting gallery awaited.

No, Aldus decided. He couldn't sit and read those letters. Even reading just one would have been more torturous than pleasurable because he would simply either want to read it again or move on to the next one. Better to just wait until the day was through so he could indulge in peace.

As the day wore on, Hayes was able to drum up plenty of business. There were regular customers who bought from him whenever his wagon pulled into town. There were men stopping by to pick up guns that Hayes had been repairing. Some newcomers were drawn in by the colorful signs, and of course there was the evening's extravaganza where Hayes lowered the price for anyone to step up to the shooting gallery and test their skill.

That last part was the bane of Aldus's existence. Being Hayes's apprentice, he always had to keep the gallery stocked with targets. Clay pipes and bottles had to be replaced. The bull's-eyes on the iron circles had to be painted. The weighted ducks sometimes got jammed. And every so often, there were enough bad shots in a row to chip away at the wooden racks and shelves. In that event, Aldus had to run out there and nail them together again or replace them quickly enough so the paying shooters wouldn't lose interest and walk away.

When there weren't any shooters, Aldus collected spent bullet casings and cleaned the rifles. As if that wasn't enough to keep him occupied, the entire setup had to be prepared for deconstruction so the process wouldn't take until the wee hours of the night. Bit by bit, targets were removed and supports were dismantled so there would be just a little less for him to do once Hayes closed up business. It would have been a lot of work for a pair of men to do, but Aldus bore the weight of it upon sturdy shoulders. He was no stranger to grueling tasks and physical discomfort. Compared to getting his face pounded in a boxing ring for dozens of rounds a night, his apprenticeship was a piece of cake. Granted, it was cake that left a gritty texture on his teeth and the acrid taste of burned gunpowder on the back of his throat, but cake all the same.

As he worked, Aldus was aware of two things: the letters in his pocket and the knife in his boot. The latter was a wicked-looking weapon with an eight-inch blade and a thick guard covering his knuckles that was dented from years of impacting against men who came around looking for trouble. The knife had protected his winnings in his boxing days, and it would discourage the two men Aldus watched for on this night.

He was certain he'd see Wes and Mose strut up to the

wagon at the worst possible time. Probably when there were a good number of customers keeping him busy and Hayes was off by himself. Perhaps the men would circle around to the other side of the wagon and sneak in when Aldus wasn't looking. As with any traveling salesman, there was always a risk that he would be robbed for his profits or wares. It was part of Aldus's job to protect both.

But his watchful eyes found nothing unusual throughout the entire day. The wearier he felt, the more vigilant Aldus forced himself to be. Even as Hayes rolled up his sleeves and pitched in to help with the final dismantling of the shooting gallery, the only ones to show up were a few children who enjoyed watching the structure come down. When they were through and the wooden beams were loaded onto the wagon, Hayes walked around it to make sure everything was secured.

"This was a profitable day," the salesman declared. "We made enough for me to treat us to some steaks. What do you say, Aldus?"

"I say I'll take two of them and a third for a little later."

"You eat more than the horses, but you pull just as much weight. Let's get a move on before Kay closes up her kitchen for the night."

Kay Felts owned the small hotel where Aldus and Hayes rented rooms. She was a sweet woman and also a night owl, which meant it was never a problem to convince her to serve them a late dinner. Considering Aldus's appetite, she'd quickly realized that the bit of inconvenience of cooking for him at odd hours would be balanced by the sheer amount of food he could consume. They walked farther into town, past Greene's Opera House, and arrived at the Sundown Hotel. Kay was stitching a sampler in her parlor and gladly put it aside to cook up their steaks.

"I had some set aside," she told them. "I knew this would be a busy day."

"You're a saint," Hayes said.

They had their pick of the tables in the dining room and sat down at a small one on the periphery of the glow of a lantern hanging on a wall nearby. "So," Hayes said as he removed his coat and top hat, "how's the delightful Miss White?"

"Haven't had a chance to read her letters yet," Aldus replied.

"You always blush when I mention her."

"I ain't blushing," Aldus snapped. "But if I react at all it's because of the way you talk about her. It's like you take me for some doe-eyed kid."

"I'm thinking nothing of the sort," Hayes replied, even though his wry grin told another story. "It's just good to see you so happy. I suppose you'll be reading your letters soon?"

Aldus nodded. He'd first started getting her letters after a chance meeting with Bethany White some years ago. He'd known Bethany since they were children and had always had a soft spot in his heart for her. Bethany had a smile that could light up a room, and her sweet, curly hair was the softest thing he'd ever touched. Aldus had never been outgoing, and that was even more so when he was younger. Some folks referred to themselves as painfully shy, but for Aldus the pain was excruciating. Not scooping up Bethany White when he'd had the chance was one of his few real regrets, and mending those bridges, one letter at a time, had become his most important job.

All of that rushed through his mind whenever he thought about those letters, so Hayes was correct in his observation regarding Aldus's flushed appearance. At least the salesman had learned to stop offering to read the letters to him. Although Hayes meant well, Aldus would prefer to trudge through his difficulty alone than be led by the hand like an infant. He did, however, need help in writing his responses.

"It took a while for them to get here," Hayes said. "I hope everything is all right with her. Usually there's a bundle of them waiting for you when you arrive at one of the spots you told her you'd be."

"I'm sure she's fine. Her boys are getting older. They must be a handful."

"Most definitely. How old are they?"

"Five and eight," Aldus replied without pause.

"Good Lord Almighty," Hayes said. "They must be a handful, indeed. I'm surprised she has time to write you at all. Still . . . it does seem odd that it took so long for you to get them. Perhaps it has something to do with the post office. Maybe they were stuck behind a sack or something."

"Maybe."

"Well, just so long as you let her know where we're headed next."

"I did," Aldus told him. "Sent that letter off today."

"Good. By the time we get to Omaha, she should have another bunch of fine words sent off to you. Perhaps one of them will be scented with perfume?"

"It ain't like that," Aldus said.

"Why not? You've been writing back and forth for over a year. I thought I saw a spark when you told me about her at the very start."

There had been a spark. Aldus knew it was there, but Bethany had just lost her husband that spring and he didn't think it proper to make his feelings known when her loss was still so fresh. For him, the spark had never faded no matter how much time or distance got between them.

"You know ... she's not that far from Omaha. Perhaps we should divert our course to pay her a visit," Hayes said. "The first time we wound up in that sleepy little town was because we got lost after that storm. You remember?"

"Yeah."

"Maybe it's time we get lost again, eh?"

"There's no call for that," Aldus snapped. "I ain't a lovesick puppy dog and I ain't some kid that needs to be coddled."

"I thought neither of those things," Hayes replied. "I just thought it might be interesting to—"

"To what? Watch me make a fool out of myself by tripping over my tongue? Or do you mean to watch her wince when she sees me drag my sorry hide across the state just to pester her some more?"

"I highly doubt either of those things would happen."

"Well, I don't aim to find out, so just let the matter lie and keep to your own affairs."

It was rare that Hayes found himself at a loss for words. On this occasion, his silence lasted until their steaks arrived. The first part of their supper was eaten without a word passing between them. That was mostly due to the fact that neither of them had a spare moment when his mouth wasn't full. Eventually Aldus made a comment about his cut of beef and Hayes replied. One stilted sentence led into another and soon they were once more conversing about the day's events. Hayes was careful to avoid the subject of Aldus's letters. When he was finished, the salesman pushed away the small plate of apple cobbler he'd been given for dessert and stood up.

"I suppose I should excuse myself," Hayes said. "There are some repairs I need to finish if I'm to deliver Mr. Waylan's pistols before we leave."

"All right, then."

Hayes wanted to say more, but decided against it. Instead, he left Aldus to the rest of his meal and walked off to settle the bill. After a bit of small talk with Kay, he stepped outside to walk directly back to his wagon and finish his work on those pistols.

Aldus felt badly for leaving things that way. Hayes had always treated him well and given Aldus something to do besides take a beating for a living. He'd also become a good friend. Perhaps it had been a long day. Perhaps Hayes had struck a nerve when he spoke about those letters. More than likely, a bit of both was to blame for the stilted end of the meal.

Although Aldus wanted to apologize for being short with his friend, there was still a sliver of his second steak left and a plate of cobbler beside it that he was saving for last. Now that he was alone, he took the letters from his pocket and unfolded the oldest one so he could examine it. He'd made his way through most of the rest of what Bethany had written by the time he finished his dessert. While it would have been nice to get through the others, there was still plenty more to do before the night was through.

He folded the letters and pocketed them once more. After leaving the hotel, he made his way to the edge of town. When he saw the two shadowy figures lurking near Hayes's wagons, Aldus cursed himself for letting the salesman out of his sight.

Chapter 5

The first wagon was completely loaded. Long wooden beams extended from its back and were tied in place by several lengths of rope. It stood like a dark mass next to the second wagon, which was illuminated from the inside by a single lantern. While in a town for an extended amount of time, Hayes normally worked in the shops of blacksmiths whom he paid for the privilege. Tonight being his last night in Cedar Rapids for a while, he finished his last commissioned job huddled in the back of his second wagon. Upon hearing the sharp rapping of knuckles against the back of the wagon, he stuck his head out.

"Oh," he said as his smile quickly disappeared, to be replaced by a much more cautious one. "I thought you might be someone else."

"It's just me," Wes said as he stood with one hand resting on the grip of his holstered pistol. "Remember who I am?"

"Of course I do! Did you come back for that rifle?"

"Sure did."

"My time is rather limited this evening, seeing as how I intend to leave town tomorrow. If you'd like me to make those adjustments to the rifle, I can certainly oblige."

"That would be right kind of you."

"No trouble whatsoever." Hayes ducked back into the wagon and scrounged through some boxes. When he emerged again, he climbed down from the wagon with the Sharps rifle in hand. "I trust you've brought your payment."

"Yeah, I did."

"My normal policy is to receive the money up front before I make any modifications. Naturally it's more than adjusting the sights, but I should be able to accommodate you."

"On such short notice?" Wes asked. "That's right kind of you."

Hayes noticed the bigger man standing several paces behind Wes. Mose loomed like a ghost, his face and body blackened by thick shadows. The salesman's eyes didn't have to adjust very much before he could make out the distinct shape of a shotgun in Mose's hands. Smiling stiffly, Hayes said, "I made you a promise and I will deliver. Of course, if you'd rather wait until I come back to town, I'll be able to do much more extensive adjustments. I could even put together a new rifle completely, which I'm sure you'd find even more appealing."

"No. I'll take that rifle you showed me earlier. The one you fixed so I could hit them targets."

"There have been a lot of customers coming through," Hayes said. "I'll have to readjust the sights."

"That's fine," Wes said. "I'll wait."

Hayes nodded. He started to go back inside his wagon, but was stopped when Wes snapped his arm forward to grab his elbow. Maintaining his composure, Hayes said, "I'll need to get a few things inside."

"While you're in there, how about you fetch me some more of them fancy rifles?"

"Are you looking to make several purchases?"

"You could say that."

The salesman's demeanor changed drastically. He straightened up and steeled himself as he demanded to see the money that would be used for the purchases.

"You want to see my money?" Wes asked.

"That's right," Hayes replied.

"Just get the damn guns. I want the most valuable ones you got."

"Hand over the money and they're all yours."

"You must really be dense," Wes said. "You see my friend back there? He may just have a plain old shotgun, but it's more than enough to spread you open, and as for me, I don't need any adjustments made to my pistol to drop you where you stand, so be smart and gather up them rifles along with all of the profits you made while you were here."

"I don't keep so much cash on me!" Hayes declared.

Wes grinned and drew his pistol. "Then we'll go round it up," he said while thumbing back the hammer.

Hayes looked around at the darkened streets that led into town. Here on the periphery, the terrain was flat and open, but the buildings of Cedar Rapids were clustered nearby like a shadowy giant. "You truly intend to rob me right here in the open?"

"Yep."

"And where do you go from here? I mean—"

Stepping forward to jam his gun's barrel into Hayes's chest, Wes snarled, "Stop trying to waste time and do what I told you. Get into that wagon, collect them rifles, and then I'll have your profits. You make one wrong move along the way and I'll gun you down. You cut loose from me and try to run, my partner will blow you in half."

Hayes nodded slowly. "All right, then. Have it your way."

*   *   *

Mose stood back a ways from the wagon. The shotgun in his hands was mostly for show since it wasn't exactly the sort of weapon to pick a man off from a distance. He was confident he could draw his pistol if the need arose, so he kept the shotgun out where it could be seen. That way, he could discourage anyone from interrupting Wes and Hayes.

When he heard footsteps crunching against the dirt, he turned to see if anyone was foolish enough to walk right up and stick their nose where it didn't belong. The figure he saw was short and wide and rushed at him like a bull. Before he could adjust his aim to compensate for the lower target, Mose was hammered by a solid blow to his midsection. Aldus's shoulder hit with all of his momentum behind it, doubling Mose over and driving most of the breath from his lungs.

Aldus closed one hand around the middle of Mose's shotgun to keep it pointed away from him as he balled up his other fist and pounded it into the big man's face. The outlaw reeled back and might have fallen over if he hadn't maintained such a solid grip on his weapon.

Having seen Aldus creeping up behind Mose, Hayes had tried to buy as much time as possible for his partner to make his move. When the sound of the first impact rolled through the air, Wes turned to look over his shoulder. That's when Hayes brought the Sharps up to his shoulder.

"Stop right where you are," the salesman warned.

"Or what?" Wes asked. "You'll fire an empty gun at me?"

"You certain it's empty?"

"I'm pretty sure you wouldn't leave it around while it's loaded. And since you seemed mighty skittish from the start of our little talk here tonight, I'm sure you wouldn't have been prepared to hand me a loaded rifle whether I meant to pay for it or not."

Unable to argue with that logic, especially because Wes was absolutely correct in his assessment, Hayes lowered the rifle and then snapped it forward to jab the barrel into Wes's stomach. The outlaw's finger twitched on his trigger, causing him to fire a shot that blazed over Hayes's head to take a chunk out of the wagon behind him.

Aldus heard the shot, but there wasn't a thing he could do about it. Not only had Mose regained his balance, but the outlaw was angrier than a mad dog when he pulled the shotgun free from Aldus's grasp. Before Mose could take his shot, Aldus slashed his right hand out to rake a blade against the hand gripping the shotgun under its barrel. He'd had the knife the whole time but had kept it out of sight until it was needed. That way, he gave Mose a mighty big surprise when the time came.

The outlaw grunted in pain and dropped the shotgun like a hot rock as his fingers were sliced. He wasted no time at all before lunging at Aldus with a barrage of swinging fists. Keeping himself low and his arms tucked in close, Aldus avoided one swing after another. He bobbed his head and stepped to one side, patiently waiting for an opening. When he got one, he stepped in and drove his left fist into Mose's body. He tried to follow up with an uppercut, but Mose leaned away so the fist that was wrapped around the knife sailed less than an inch away from his chin.

As soon as he missed with that swing, Aldus knew he was in trouble. Sure enough, his arm was slapped away by Mose's thick paw of a hand with enough force to cause his entire upper body to twist around. Rather than follow up with a punch of his own, Mose swung his leg forward to drive it straight into Aldus's groin. When Aldus buckled, Mose clasped his fists together and swung them as if he were gripping an ax handle. The blow landed heavily between Aldus's shoulder blades, dropping him to one knee.

Ears still ringing from being in such close proximity to the pistol that had been fired, Hayes stepped aside and swung his rifle around to catch Wes on the wrist. The outlaw grunted in pain and his fingers twitched just enough to lose his grasp on the gun he'd been holding. Hayes took another swing with the rifle, but Wes wasn't going to stand still and be knocked out. He dropped straight down to let the rifle pass overhead while scooping up his pistol. When he had the gun back in hand and brought it up, he no longer had anyone to shoot.

Hayes had circled around his wagon and was now frantically digging into one of his vest pockets. He found the key he'd been looking for and immediately spun around to place it in one of the wagon's many side panels. The wagon was primarily used as his traveling store and contained many such panels, which could hold various items to offer his customers. Although Hayes did make his own ammunition, it never hurt to keep a good supply of standard rounds for his less discerning buyers. The panel he opened contained several boxes of rifle rounds, and he barely had enough time to collect a few of them before Wes came looking for him.

"Don't make me keep running after you," the outlaw warned. "It'll just get me madder."

Placing his shoulders against the back of the wagon, Hayes listened carefully while easing a few rounds into his rifle.

Every so often, he could hear a boot pressing against

the ground, but Hayes couldn't quite nail down which direction Wes was circling. Part of that was due to the swirling wind carrying noises from town along with it as well as the sounds of struggle as Aldus fought with the other outlaw. So Hayes continued loading the Sharps, praying he would get a chance to fire it before he felt the burn of hot lead.

This wasn't the first time Aldus had been hit below the belt. In his career as a boxer, he'd become all too familiar with the blunt, jarring impact that was inevitably followed by a rush of blinding pain flooding his stomach and lower regions before churning up into the back of his throat. For most men, taking such a hit was enough to put them down for a good while. For a man earning his livelihood in a ring, he couldn't let himself fall to such tactics whether they were legal or not.

Dropping to one knee had been a reflex meant to give him a moment to catch his breath. All Aldus needed to do was push through the first wave of nauseating agony so he could put the white-hot rage that followed to use. No matter how many times he'd been hit in the most tender of regions, it still hurt. What separated a professional fighter from anyone else was how he channeled such a thing into his next attack. As Mose prepared to finish him off, Aldus brought his fist all the way up from the ground and into Mose's chin.

The outlaw reeled back as blood sprayed from his mouth. It pained Aldus to get up, but he forced himself to stand upright and send his right fist out to follow up his left. He still held his knife in that hand, so he was careful to angle his hand to avoid gutting the outlaw like a fish. His reinforced knuckles pounded against Mose's ribs, which brought the outlaw down.

"Just like the McClendon fight," Aldus growled. "Chopped him down like an oak tree."

One big difference between this and the McClendon bout, however, was that Rory McClendon didn't have a shotgun waiting for him when he went down. As Mose dropped to all fours, he scrambled for the shotgun. Aldus tried to hit him again, but Mose absorbed the blow with a grunt before wheeling around to bring the shotgun to bear.

"Should've stuck me when you had the chance," Mose said.

"There's still time for that. Or we could ditch the weapons and have ourselves a fair fight."

"Fair fight?" Mose grunted. "Why would I want one a' those?"

Hayes had waited too long. He could feel it in his bones just as he could hear Aldus fighting in the distance. Since he couldn't hear much of anything helpful and the rifle in his hands was loaded, he dropped down to take a quick look beneath the wagon. There was nothing but the wheels on the right side. On the left he saw a pair of boots working their way toward the back end. Hayes brought the Sharps around and fired a quick shot beneath the wagon, catching Wes in the heel. He caught more boot than foot, but the impact snapped Wes's leg out from under him and sent him staggering amid a stream of curses.

Jumping to his feet, Hayes put another round into the rifle's chamber and jumped out to face the outlaw as he stumbled away from the wagon. It was a small miracle that Wes wasn't on the ground, but the effort to stay upright had taken all of his attention.

"Drop the pistol!" Hayes said.

Wes balanced on one leg for a second before tentatively setting his other foot down. Wincing as if expecting to feel pain from it, he realized the rifle's bullet hadn't taken more than a sliver of skin as it passed through his boot. Wes stood up and fixed his eyes on the man in front of him. "You ain't about to shoot me," he said.

"Are you going to put me to the test?"

"Maybe I will."

"You and your partner meant to rob me," Hayes said. "I'm well within my rights to defend myself."

"It ain't about rights. It's about having the sand to put a man into his grave. I'm not so sure you got that in you."

Hayes squeezed his trigger and nicked the upper edge of the outlaw's right arm. The bullet ripped through Wes's shirt like a claw and started a little trickle of blood that was soaked into the dirty cotton. "What about now?" Hayes asked. "You still want to test me? Perhaps next time my aim will be a little better."

Unable to decide whether or not Hayes had meant to deliver such a glancing blow, Wes let out an angry breath and let his pistol slip from his fingers.

"Wise decision," Hayes said. "Now . . ."

"Now nothin'," Wes grunted. "If you want to shoot me again, you'll have to put one into my back." With that, he turned away from Hayes and the wagon and started walking.

"Come back here!" Hayes shouted.

Wes dismissed him with a wave and kept walking.

Aldus heard the gunshots coming from the direction of the wagon, but he couldn't see much of anything when he risked a quick glance that way. Mose stood in front of him, also distracted by the commotion. When he caught the big man looking away from him, Aldus decided to try and rush forward to wrestle the shotgun away from him.

He made it about two steps before Mose snapped the shotgun back to target him directly.

"That's it, mister," the outlaw said. "I've had about enough of you."

"Go on and help your friend," Aldus told him. "I'm not about to stop you."

Mose was finished talking. His eyes narrowed and a cold look came across his face like shards of ice creeping across a pane of glass.

Aldus had nowhere to run. No gun to fire. Nothing left to say. When he heard the next shot crack through the air, he jumped.

"That's your only warning!" Hayes shouted.

To Aldus's surprise, he wasn't killed. He wasn't even wounded. Either that or his wounds were so grievous that he couldn't feel them yet.

Mose was still standing there. His eyes were just as cold, but he didn't look as certain as he had looked a moment ago. Every so often, his eyes darted past Aldus toward the wagon.

"Your friend is gone," Hayes announced.

The big outlaw scowled. "You killed him?"

"No," Hayes replied. "He skinned out of here and left you behind. I suggest you run along and try to find him."

"How do I know he ain't dead?"

"You don't. But if you don't lower that scattergun and let my partner go, you most certainly will be."

Seeing the conflict written upon Mose's face, Aldus said, "He won't kill you if you do what he says."

"I don't know that."

"Then keep that shotgun pointed at me until you think you're a safe distance away. Best be quick about it, though," Aldus added. "He could hit you in the eye from there without much of a problem."

Something caught Mose's eye. He grunted under his

breath and backed away. After a few paces, he lowered the shotgun and started running toward town.

Aldus stood his ground, hesitant to move a muscle until he was outside the shotgun's range. Before long, he saw the figure in the distance that had drawn the outlaw away. When Mose got close enough to his retreating partner, he started yelling at the other man as both of them bolted into the darkness. Aldus couldn't make out exactly what they were saying to each other, but he could tell the language was none too gentle.

"You all right?" Hayes called out.

Turning toward the salesman, Aldus started walking to the wagon. "Got knocked around a little, but it ain't nothing I can't handle."

"You're limping."

"I know."

Hayes moved forward with the rifle still at his shoulder. "Are there any more of them?"

"Don't think so."

Once Aldus was close enough, Hayes lowered the rifle and let out the breath he'd been holding. "So glad you decided to pay me a visit."

Wincing as he felt a lingering jab of pain in his nether regions, Aldus said, "I ain't so happy about it, but it all seemed to work out. What did they want?"

"You were right about them wanting a rifle awful badly. They also wanted to take as much of my inventory as they could carry as well as all of the profits we made."

"You don't have all that money with you, do you?"

"Of course not," Hayes replied. "It's locked away in my room just like always. Did you see where they went?"

"Back into town," Aldus said. "Probably holed up somewhere for the night already. You think we should chase after them?"

"Why would we do that? We're not lawmen. Speaking

of which, shouldn't someone be coming out to look in on all this shooting?"

"Why don't we go and look in on the sheriff instead?"

Hayes nodded. "Good idea. Go fetch yourself something from the wagon first. Wouldn't be wise to be unarmed when that kind of dangerous element is lurking about."

Despite the fact that there were two outlaws running loose who might very well decide to double back and finish what they started, Aldus was more unhappy about the walk over to the wagon and the arduous climb inside. Mose kicked like a mule, and though Aldus could fight his way through the pain, that didn't mean he wasn't affected by it. The pistol he carried on the infrequent occasions he went heeled was an older-model Schofield that he'd fixed up as part of his training and was comfortable in his grip. The gun belt was made from battered leather that looked as if it had been gnawed on by an angry dog and had the initials *JT* engraved on the holster. Aldus didn't know what *JT* stood for, but he knew the belt fit him like an old glove. Hayes had taken it as a trade for a box of ammunition along with the rusty Colt that had been inside it. The Colt was deemed too dangerous to fire, so Hayes had dismantled it for spare parts. After buckling the old Schofield around his waist, Aldus followed Hayes into town.

Cedar Rapids was bustling with activity centered mostly on Greene's Opera House. A performance of some kind must have let out not too long ago because folks in fancy clothes loitered about in front of the theater with their noses in the air and smiles on their faces. Aldus didn't regard them in any sort of bad way, but his face was twisted into an angry grimace from the bad turn his night had taken. Every so often, gunshots cracked through the air from other parts of town, explaining why the commotion at the wagons hadn't attracted much attention.

Their conversation with the sheriff was a short one. Hayes did most of the talking and described the attempted robbery in a fair amount of detail.

"Yeah," the lawman replied. "One of my deputies said there was some shooting out that way."

"And why didn't anyone come to check on us?" Hayes asked.

The lawman shrugged. "You run a shooting gallery, don't you? Isn't there always shooting out that way?"

Aldus generally didn't give lawmen the time of day. Part of that was because many of the fights he'd participated in during his boxing days weren't exactly aboveboard. Also, on the rare occasions when he did seek help from the law, the supposed keepers of the peace were about as helpful as this one. Aldus didn't even bother catching the sheriff's name as he stood outside the office to let his partner deal with him.

Afterward, Aldus and Hayes walked back down the street as the sounds of other people's merriment drifted around them from saloons and a few restaurants hosting the theater crowd.

"So that's it?" Aldus asked. "The law ain't gonna do a thing about us nearly getting robbed?"

"They told me they'd keep an eye out for those two men. The sheriff thinks he knows who it might have been and has already been looking for them."

"Yeah," Aldus grunted. "And doing a real good job of it."

"We handled ourselves well enough," Hayes said. "That's all that ever counts. I doubt those two desperadoes will want to tangle with us again. Even if they do, we'll be ready for them." The salesman stopped at a saloon named the Corsican and said, "I need a drink."

"And I need to get off my feet," Aldus grunted.

"Well, I believe there are chairs as well as libations inside this establishment, so I propose that we take full advantage."

"It's too late for all them big words."

Hayes put a hand on his partner's shoulder and steered him toward the batwing doors. "How are these words for you? I'm buying."

Chapter 6

Aldus was used to getting up before sunrise. In his fighting days, he would wake up when it was still dark so he could hone his craft by punching wooden beams until his knuckles bled. Then he would drag sacks of grain up and down an alley or empty lot. Even though his work wasn't quite so demanding any longer, his schedule had been ingrained too deeply for him to keep his eyes from popping open at the same time every day.

Hayes, on the other hand, was a different sort of animal. The salesman kept later hours, oftentimes gambling away his portion of their profits at a card table or spending it on expensive liquor. Oddly enough, he would buy the same bottle of liquor as a consolation for slow days as he would to celebrate the busy ones. Aldus wasn't particularly opposed to such indulgences. He simply didn't partake in them because he knew how hard it would be to rein himself in again.

When Hayes couldn't be found after Aldus had his breakfast, it wasn't much of a surprise.

Aldus spent his morning preparing the wagons for the trail, making sure everything was tied down and cinched in tight. He took stock of their inventory, counting all the rifles and pistols while ensuring that all of the panels on the side of the larger wagon were locked. By the time he was done with that, despite the eggs and bacon he'd had earlier, Aldus's stomach was growling.

He went to their familiar restaurant nearby and had a big bowl of hot oatmeal with honey drizzled on top. Resisting the urge to order a pork chop to go along with it, Aldus finished his coffee and walked back to the wagon. Hayes was still nowhere to be found. While it was possible the salesman was sleeping off a hard night, it wasn't like him to be so late on a day when they were going to be leaving town. Because of the trouble the night before, Aldus still had the Schofield at his side. He checked to be certain the gun was loaded and then reached down to pat the ankle where his knife was strapped. He started walking to Kay Felts's hotel, confident he was prepared for any trouble he might find along the way.

As soon as he rounded the corner that brought him to the correct street, Aldus saw the hotel. More important, he spotted the two people huddled on the porch in front of the hotel. Hayes was sitting on a stool and Kay herself was hovering over him, dabbing at his head with a rag.

"Where have you been?" Aldus asked once he'd gotten close enough to be heard.

"There was a bit of trouble," Hayes replied.

Kay fretted over him still. When she pulled the rag away from his head, Aldus could see the blood that had soaked into it. Aldus hurried onto the porch and leaned in to get a closer look. "What happened to you?" he asked.

"I was on my way down to breakfast when I thought I noticed one of those fellows from the other night standing in the street," Hayes explained.

Aldus looked out at the street and then cast his gaze across the way as if the outlaw might still be there. "Which one was it?"

"The big one. The one who knocked you around."

"You were attacked as well?" Kay asked.

Not wanting to explain to her, Aldus quickly said, "I'm fine. They're just a couple of idiots who thought they could take our money."

"That's terrible," she said. "Someone should tell the sheriff."

"So what happened to your head, Zeke?"

Hayes didn't flinch upon hearing that nickname. It seemed he'd already flinched more than enough while Kay dabbed the wet rag against the bloody portion of his scalp. "That big fellow was gone before I could notify anyone, so I went about my preparations for the day. I gathered up my things, took the strongbox under my arm, and headed outside."

"You just walked out there with that box under your arm?" Aldus asked. "You knew them other two would be after it!"

"I didn't just have it out for all to see! Besides, I was armed."

Normally Hayes wore a nickel-plated .45 that was one of the most visually striking pistols in his inventory. It packed a tremendous kick and was easy on the eye. Big seller. Now his finely tooled holster was empty.

"The box was wrapped up in my coat," Hayes said while waving toward the porch. "I stepped outside and walked down the street and was struck from out of nowhere."

"Was it that big fella?" Aldus asked.

"Couldn't tell you who it was exactly, but it had to be one of them. All I know is I felt a sharp pain, my ears were set to ringing, and before I knew it, I was on the ground." Placing a hand gingerly on his temple, Hayes added, "Still feels like my head is full of cotton."

"It is," Aldus grunted while taking rough hold of

Hayes and pushing aside Kay's hand. "You should have come and got me before walking out with that money."

"Why didn't you come for me this morning?"

"I did! I knocked on your door and you didn't answer. What was I supposed to do? Break it off its hinges?"

Hayes looked up to Kay, who nodded to him and said, "He was there, all right. Bright and early."

When Aldus smacked Hayes upside his head, the salesman twisted around and asked, "What was that for?"

"For having to look to her instead of taking my word for it."

"I suppose I had that coming," Hayes sighed.

Feeling guilty more because of the look he got from Kay than the swat he'd given to Hayes, Aldus pushed aside some of the other man's hair.

"I already said I had it coming," Hayes groused. "No need to make it worse."

"Just hold still," Aldus said as he leaned in closer. "Let me have a look. I've had plenty of these kinds of wounds myself and have seen plenty more."

The wound was ugly and wet with blood, but that was to be expected. Hayes had been hit toward the back of his head on the right side. "Doesn't look so bad," Aldus said.

Kay grimaced. "I don't know. It was bleeding an awful lot."

"Any knock to the head is gonna bleed a lot. What about this?" Aldus asked as he grabbed Hayes by the shoulder and rocked him back and forth.

The salesman planted his feet and used his arms to steady himself before reaching back to knock Aldus away. "What do you think you're doing?"

"Feel like you're gonna vomit?"

"No, but I feel like I would have been in better hands if those robbers were still here."

Coming around to stand in front of Hayes, Aldus squatted down to get to his level and held up three fingers. "How many fingers do you see?"

"Three, now get them away from me!"

Holding his hand as far back as he could, Aldus switched it to four fingers that were kept close together. "What about now?"

If Hayes had glared at his attacker the same way he now glared at Aldus, the outlaw might still have been rooted to his spot. "Four," he said in a terse voice.

"You'll be fine," Aldus said. "If you were hurt really bad, you would have heaved up yesterday's supper when I shook you that way and you wouldn't be able to see straight enough to count two of my fingers. Now answer me one question."

"What?"

"Why didn't you answer your door when I knocked?"

Hayes sighed and rubbed his eyes. "I was still asleep. It was a rough night."

"By that, you mean you drank too much."

"Yes. If you insist on pressing the matter, yes. I probably drank too much. Are you satisfied?"

"I'd be satisfied if you could pay me my share of the profits," Aldus said. When he saw the pained expression on the other man's face, he said, "Fine. I'll ease up a bit. You want to see a doctor for that head?"

Reaching up to tenderly touch his bloody scalp, Hayes looked at his fingers and said, "Looks like the bleeding's stopped. Do you recall enough from your fighting days to dress that wound?"

"I could stitch your face back together and set a broken nose if it came down to it," Aldus told him. "This shouldn't be much of a problem."

"Fine, then. Let's get to it."

Kay brought Aldus clean water and some thin material he could tear apart for a dressing. Since she'd already been tending to the wound before he'd arrived, there really wasn't much left for Aldus to do other than wipe away the last of the blood and wrap some makeshift bandages around his head. Although cuts in a man's scalp tended to bleed profusely, they didn't do so for long. Hayes was back on his feet in no time. A little wobbly for his first couple of steps, but doing better by the time he'd walked back to the sheriff's office. This time, Aldus didn't even bother going inside with him.

The salesman stepped outside in a few short minutes, wearing an expression that didn't inspire much hope.

"So, what did he tell you?" Aldus asked, even though he was reluctant to hear the answer.

Hayes held his top hat in hand and placed it on his head. Despite the pained wince that drifted across his face, he forced the hat down as far into place as it would go over the bandages. "He offered his condolences and assured me he and his men would be looking for those outlaws."

"And what about our money?"

"If it is found, he will keep it safe for us until we can claim it."

"I just bet he will," Aldus grunted.

"No need for that kind of talk," Hayes scolded. "The sheriff may not have exactly risen to the occasion here, but I highly doubt he's the sort that would deliberately cheat us. If he finds that money, I have no doubt he'll keep it safe until we come back to town."

"So that's it? We just tuck our tails between our legs and leave town?"

"Unless you want to organize a posse to scour the country looking for those two outlaws."

That was exactly what Aldus wanted to do, but even he couldn't entertain that thought for long. First of all, he was not a tracker or a lawman. Since the lawmen in Cedar Rapids didn't show any interest in taking this bull by its horns, there wasn't much of a chance that Aldus could convince them any better than Hayes could. Second, there was no telling where those outlaws had gone. They could be hiding somewhere in town or miles away in any direction. Third, even if he did catch up with them, Aldus wasn't a gunfighter. He'd been lucky to survive last night's fight and knew his chances were slim of walking away from a rematch.

"You're right," Hayes said as he started walking down the street. "It was my fault."

"I never meant it was your fault."

"Didn't you? Well, you should have."

Aldus shook his head. "That wasn't the first time someone tried to rob us. Wasn't even the first time someone got away with it."

"It's the first time they got away with so much of our money," Hayes said with an edge in his voice that was sharp enough to cut to the bone.

"I just wanna do something about it, is all."

"Unfortunately, my friend, there isn't a lot we can do." Hayes lifted his chin and pulled in a deep breath. Soon he was wearing a smile that was as tired as it was genuine. "All that's left for us to do is dust ourselves off and move along. We may yet reclaim our money when we come back here, and then it'll be like a found fortune. In the meantime, we roll up our sleeves and work harder to line our pockets once again."

"I hear what you're saying. . . . I can even see how you're right about a few things," Aldus grudgingly admitted.

"Just a few things?"

Not ready to let go of the dark scowl that had taken residence on his face, Aldus placed his hand on the holstered Schofield as if he was looking for any excuse to draw it. "I just don't like running away from a fight."

"Don't knock running away. If we'd done that sooner, we wouldn't have been in this predicament." Since his partner wasn't responding to the joke, Hayes himself chuckled at it. "We're not running," he said. The single nod he gave after those words made it seem as if he'd said them for his benefit more than anyone else's. "We're just getting on with our lives. We were set to pack up and move on today, and that's just what we'll do. Somehow those outlaws will pay for what they did. Until then, it doesn't do us one ounce of good to hinder ourselves any more than we already have been."

"They'll pay, huh?" Aldus asked with a raised eyebrow.

"Most assuredly."

"Are you just saying that to keep me quiet?"

The salesman shrugged. "I would think of it more as lifting your spirits, but we do have a schedule to keep."

"We do, don't we?" Aldus took a deep breath and lifted his chin the way Hayes had done a few moments ago. The air was crisp, cool, and smelled of burning wood. Someone was baking bread nearby, which always brightened his spirits. At least, it took some of the sting out of the day's events. "Tell me one thing, Zeke."

"No, Aldus. I'm not going to pay you out of my own pocket. We'll have to pool everything we have just to make it to the next town and make enough to put us flush again."

"That's not what I wanted to ask."

"Oh," Hayes replied. "Go ahead, then."

"Did you at least wound that gunman when you shot at him last night?"

Chapter 7

It was a bit early in the day for the showgirls to be kicking up their skirts on either of the stages at Tennison's. Apart from a few drunks who'd probably spent the entire night passed out in one of the saloon's corners, most of the customers in attendance were sitting at poker games that had been going on for several hours or even several days. With no music drifting through the air, the place felt somehow darker now than it did at midnight. The sunlight coming in through the front window was an unwelcome guest, and the tables it shone upon were purposely left empty.

Wes and Mose sat at one of the small square tables near the bar. While the bigger of the two scraped at a plate of runny eggs, Wes sifted through a small stack of money. "Where is that weasel?" Wes snarled.

"You mean Jimmy?" Mose asked through a mouthful of dry toast, which added crumbs to the strings of egg stuck in his beard.

"He was supposed to be here. I thought he was always here."

"Man can't stay in one room forever. Have some breakfast."

"I'll eat when we get this matter settled," Wes said.

Sneering at his partner's messy face, he added, "And I'll eat something other than the slop they serve in this place."

"Suit yerself."

After watching the front door for a few seconds, Wes asked, "You sure nobody saw what you did this morning?"

Mose nodded.

"Tell me again what happened."

This time, Mose at least swallowed the food he was chewing before saying, "I waited in front of that hotel where we followed them gun salesmen to the other night. When the one in the fancy suit came out, he was carrying a whole bunch of things with him. I waited for him to walk by and then I cracked his skull open with the butt of my pistol. As for anyone seeing me, I can't say for certain. I do know no lawmen saw me because there wasn't much of a commotion." Mose scooped up some eggs and studied his plate as though he were painting a scenic landscape in yellows and whites. "I went through the things he was carrying and found the lockbox. Didn't want to linger any more than I had to, so I took the lockbox and the guns he was carrying with him and left."

"And did you walk back out to the street or go through an alley?"

"I ain't stupid," Mose replied. "I cut across a couple different streets until I was sure there weren't nobody following me."

"What about the other one that was with the dandy?" Wes asked. "The big fellow that knocked you around last night."

Pointing the dirty end of his fork at him, Mose said, "I knocked him around plenty. Don't you worry about that."

"Did you see him or not?"

"No. What are you so worried about, anyways? There's enough in that lockbox to pay Jimmy's fee with some left over. You should be happy about how things are panning out."

"It just felt too easy."

"Would've been easier if we could've gotten more of them rifles," Mose said. "Sounds like we're gonna need plenty."

Wes shook his head. "No, we won't. I've taken a look at that rifle you brought back, and it's a beaut. I saw what he did when he adjusted them sights the first time, and I should be able to get them fixed up real good."

"What about the pistol?" Mose asked. His mouth hung open as if he was about to drool over the prospect he was contemplating more than he had drooled when his breakfast had first been set in front of him. "I'm still keeping that pistol, right?"

"Sure. It's only fair that we split the profits just like we'll split what's left over from that money we stole."

When Wes had first gone to the saloon, he'd been so focused on Jimmy that he'd overlooked the rooms on the second floor. That wasn't hard to do since there were only four of them near the back of the room partitioned by a waist-high wall that allowed the people up there to look down on the rest of the saloon. One of those four doors opened now and Jimmy stepped out to gaze down at the bar and tables. He spotted Wes and Mose immediately and then made his way to a narrow set of stairs that would take him to the portion of the saloon reserved for gamblers and their games.

"Don't mention another word about that money," Wes hissed.

Mose scraped at the last of his eggs. "I don't think Jimmy's gonna care where it come from just so long as we have it."

"It ain't that. If he knows we got more than what he needs, he'll boost his price to clean us out."

The bigger man shrugged, making it plenty clear that he was more interested in his breakfast than the upcoming negotiation.

Jimmy descended from the second floor, ignoring the outlaws completely as he made his way to the same table where he'd been sitting earlier. He wore a dark brown suit that was so rumpled it looked as if it had been wadded up in the bottom of a saddlebag and then trampled by a team of horses. Before he even had a chance to get comfortable in his chair, one of the serving girls rushed over to ask what he wanted. She was walking away to fill his order as Wes and Mose made their approach.

"You boys are bright-eyed and bushy-tailed," Jimmy said. "I see at least one of you tried the food."

Mose patted his belly. "Fixin' to have seconds."

"Brave man."

"You don't like the food, you should have stayed somewhere else," Wes offered as he sat down. "Plenty of other places in town."

"I can eat things that'd make a billy goat sick," Jimmy said. "I like this place for other reasons."

Wes glanced up toward the second floor just in time to see that other reason step out of the room Jimmy had left. She was wrapped in a red dress that barely covered her generous curves. Long, flowing hair swept over smooth, creamy shoulders, and the look in her eyes as she surveyed the saloon from her vantage point made it clear that she was once again open for business.

"I'm startin' to like this place myself," Wes said.

"You got my money?" Jimmy asked in a voice that was sharper than a rap of knuckles against the table.

Wes reached into his pocket and removed a roll of

cash held together by a length of twine. "It's all there if you wanna count it."

"I do."

Although Jimmy didn't have any qualms with unrolling the money and flipping through it, the two outlaws shifted in their seats and started watching the door as well as every man at the nearby tables.

"What's the matter?" Jimmy asked.

Wes quickly replied, "Nothing."

"Then why are you squirming so much?"

"Because that's a lot of money and . . ."

"And you think someone's gonna steal it?" Jimmy smirked at the irony he'd hinted at with that question. "There's reasons other than the women and the beer why I like this place. The law don't come around here much since it's just outside town limits. The owner has his own boys keeping the peace in here, and I've got an arrangement with them that makes it plenty safe for me to conduct my business however I want." His brow furrowed when he asked, "You don't have the law sniffing after you right now, do you?"

"No," Wes said. "Now, what about the rest of our deal?"

Without another word, Jimmy looked back down to the money. When he was finished counting, he weighed the money in his hand and tucked it away. In order to get to the pocket where the money was stored, he had to open his jacket and reveal the holster strapped around his waist. He kept the jacket open and drew a .44 Smith & Wesson that was as weathered as the man who carried it.

"What's that for?" Mose asked.

"Some men like to snatch their money back after I say my piece," Jimmy told him.

"That ain't us," Wes said. "You know me."

"Sure I do. Just like I knew some of the other men who thought they could get the drop on me. This gun stays and if either of you makes a move for yours, I'll send you out of here in a pine box. Same goes if I see someone else coming along to back your play."

Staring across the table, Wes fought the urge to show just how displeased he was. "All right," he said through gritted teeth, "you made your point. You got your money. Tell us what we need to know."

Although Jimmy relaxed somewhat, he didn't take his hand away from the .44. When he spoke, his voice took on a harsh, strained quality as if it was a painful effort for him to force it up from his lungs. "The train is arriving in Omaha in ten or eleven days. It'll stay put for three or four days and pull out at six a.m."

"How will we know what train it is?" Wes asked. "There's plenty of trains coming and going from there."

"It's number twenty-four. It's also gonna be the one that's guarded by at least ten men. There'll be a few on top of the cars as well, since they like to have a good vantage point when they leave. There'll be some inside and some standing between the cars."

Mose shook his head fiercely. "There ain't no way the two of us can go against that. Give that money back before you say another—"

"Shut up," Wes snapped. To Jimmy, he said, "He's right. And I could've seen this much on my own."

"What you don't know is that all those guards are mainly there to protect the largest load of money that will be brought in and stored in a vault in the car just in front of the caboose. That's a small fortune, but it ain't all that train is carrying. There's also smaller loads kept in sacks and crates that are already portioned out to pay some of the smaller payrolls along the way. At least half of them guards I mentioned will leave the station to pick up that big load, and they'll be escorted by three of the four men who'll ride ahead to make sure there ain't no robbers lying in wait along the train's route." Jimmy smiled, which made him look like a filthy, yet amused, corpse. "All two enterprising gunmen would have to do is wait for all them men to ride away, pick off a few guards from afar, and then make a quick sweep through that train to gather up as many of them smaller sacks as they can carry."

"You're sure they're in sacks?" Mose asked.

Jimmy frowned and looked at the big man as if he'd been addressed by a child who had somehow found his way to the table. "What's that matter?"

"It sure matters to the man that's gotta carry it off of that train!"

"Some of it's in sacks," Jimmy said. "I saw them being loaded myself."

"When was this?" Wes asked.

Looking over to him, Jimmy said, "I've seen that train get loaded three times in all. There's always a bunch of sacks brought to it soon after it arrives. They look like the bags that mail is carried in. There're also a few strongboxes, so be ready for that."

"How much money is in there?"

"I don' know for certain. I never took it upon myself to count it. What I do know is there's a whole lot of it since there's so many men guarding that train," Jimmy explained. "When those guards ride off to collect the main load, most of what's left behind are riflemen who stay inside the train as well as one or two watching it from a rooftop. Usually from on top of the station."

Wes nodded slowly as he pictured it as best he could. "So if I could spot them and then pick them off from a distance, all Mose would have to do is storm that train."

"That's all, huh?" Mose grunted.

"I'll come in to help. Don't you worry."

"I'm more worried about you with the rifle. You ain't that good a shot."

Wes glared at him, which quieted the bigger man down.

"You'll need something with power and accuracy," Jimmy said. "Not just some hunting rifle or whatever piece of scrap you stick in your saddle's boot."

"You have experience shooting at trains?" Wes quipped.

"No, but I got plenty of experience in hunting, and the first thing you gotta do when you're looking to bring an animal down is make sure you've got the right tool for the job. You'll have the element of surprise, but it won't last forever. You need to make your shots count, and they have to hit hard enough so one per man is all you need."

Mose studied the man across from him and said, "You really do sit and think all of this through."

"It's a talent," Jimmy replied. "I got an eye for detail."

"Why don't you come with us?" Wes asked.

It would have been impossible to tell which of the two other men was more surprised by that proposition.

"Why would I want to go with you?" Jimmy asked.

"Because if we had an extra man on this job, especially one who knows as much as you do about it all, we might be able to get our hands on the real money being loaded onto that train."

"You mean whatever is being put inside the safe?"

Wes nodded as if he was about to lick his lips.

"I work alone," Jimmy told him. "And I'm too fond of living to tangle with the very thing that all them men are there to guard. You want to take a run at it? That's up to you to decide. My job is to tell you what I know, and I get paid because I know an awful lot." Leaning forward, he locked eyes with each man in turn. "If you go after the safe instead of just snatching what you can carry and riding away as fast as you can, you're idiots. Now, since that's all I got to say on the matter, you can go."

Both outlaws stood up from the table and walked away. Once they were outside, Mose looked over to Wes and asked, "So . . . do you think that talk was worth the price we paid?"

Wes pulled in a deep breath of crisp air and savored it. "I think," he said as he exhaled, "that this job is gonna get real bloody real fast. After it, though, we are gonna be very rich men."

Chapter 8

Both of Hayes's wagons rumbled down a trail that was wide enough in spots for them to roll side by side. It was a well-worn trail over a grassy stretch of prairie that stretched out as far as the eye could see. At this time of year, it was a beautiful sight filled with rich brown and golden grasses that swayed with the slightest of winds. Trees still bore their leafy canopies but were just starting to show the colors of an encroaching autumn. The sky was a mix of light blue and gray, accented by thick clouds resembling so much raw cotton pulled into shreds.

Hayes drove the wagon containing the disassembled shooting gallery and all of the ammunition and gunsmithing tools stored in rows of locked cabinets. He was at the front of the small procession with Aldus trailing behind in the covered wagon.

As beautiful as his surroundings were, Aldus didn't take the time to drink them in. It wasn't that he couldn't appreciate such things, but he'd simply seen those sprawling grasslands so many times before. Hayes's business was run from his wagons, and those wagons followed a few small circuits that brought them to the same towns at various times of the year. Every so often they might stray from their beaten path, but they would quickly find their way back to a more familiar route. Part of the salesman's reasoning for this was his desire to have the broadest customer base possible. He could reach a certain number of folks by opening a store in one spot, and he might even earn a reputation that brought folks in from other towns. But if he came to them, he could see even more business. And if he came to them on a regular schedule and stayed in that town for a few weeks at a time, it was close to having a shop in several different towns. He did earn his reputation as a master of his craft, and that reputation spread well beyond the places he visited. Every town where Aldus set up his gallery, he saw new and old faces alike. There were custom jobs commissioned by lawmen or soldiers that Hayes would work on so they could be delivered the next time the wagons rolled back to town. And there was plenty of business to be had in selling ammunition or more common firearms.

But that was only a part of Hayes's reasoning. The other piece that kept him moving was a natural-born wanderlust. Zachariah Hayes simply didn't like staying in one spot long enough for the grass to grow beneath his feet. In fact, he'd been well off his normal route when he'd first crossed paths with Aldus Bricker.

Aldus had been fighting in New York City on the docks where the air smelled like a salty mix of river water and blood. Having come off a win that took thirty-two rounds to get, Aldus had been a heap of broken bones and busted cartilage. If he was to keep the purse he'd won as well as appease the promoter who treated his fighters like slaves in a pit, Aldus would have had to wade into another fight the very next day. He was no coward, but he knew he would be in no shape to beat an animal like Darian Waterman. That grizzled Canadian would have been a challenge on any day. In the shape he'd been in, Aldus could either forfeit or surely get his head caved in. He'd chosen the latter.

After eight torturous rounds and a loss ending when Aldus could only open one eye, he sat in a squalid saloon with a good view of the water. As Aldus nursed a warm beer, a man approached him with a proposition. Hayes had needed a guide through the less refined portions of the city and was willing to pay for the privilege. While quite an odd proposition for that particular moment, it was Hayes's second offer that sealed the deal. Quit the fight game now before he was killed in the ring.

"Wh-who are you?" Aldus asked through a mouth that was too swollen to fully articulate his words.

Hayes gave him a quick explanation of who he was and what he did for a living. Since he hadn't even owned a gun at the time and didn't know much about them other than which end was the most dangerous, none of that meant a lot to Aldus.

"Wha . . . do you want?"

"I have some deliveries to make here in New York City, special orders and such," Hayes explained. "I could use someone who knows his way around. But more than that, I could use someone to travel with me and protect my interests."

"Like a guard?"

"Exactly. There's various other duties as well. Basically I just need another set of hands to help me in my work. When you're not making sure that the profits aren't in danger, I can teach you how to do simple things like pack ammunition, clean firearms, and take inventory."

"I don't know a thing about . . . any of that," Aldus said through his swollen mouth.

"I'll teach you. It's actually fairly simple work, but it needs to be done. Having someone reliable do it for me will free me up to do a lot more specialized work. I used to have other assistants, but they didn't prove to be very reliable."

Lowering his head, Aldus took a few moments to wait for more of the cobwebs to clear from between his ears. When he looked up again, Hayes was still there. "Why come to me with this? I never done this kind of work before."

"Because I've been told you're a good fellow. A real straight shooter. And," Hayes had added cheerily, "you have a nasty look about you. That will go a long way when it comes to protecting my interests. Are you good with your hands?"

Aldus had held up his hands, which, at the time, had looked like hams that had been soaked in buckets of water for about a week and a half. "Not today but yeah."

"I'll pay you enough to act as my guide here in New York to make ends meet for a while. At least give you some time to heal. After that . . . we'll see."

It turned out that Hayes had been an old friend of Basil Polaski, the grizzled old man who ran the docks where the fights were held. That old-timer had not only given Aldus a place to stay but had been trying to convince him to quit fighting while he could still see through both eyes and remember his own name. While Aldus had been more than happy to take whatever odd jobs Polaski could offer, he just couldn't find one that stuck. Eventually someone would come along to take the job away from him or he would leave on his own. No matter how badly it hurt, there just wasn't a substitute for being in the ring.

During a fight, Aldus felt as if he was truly doing what he'd been put on earth to do. Doing anything else would have been a lie. At times when he was battered, bruised, and in constant pain, he wished he had it in him to quit.

Inevitably he would come up with some other reason to go on, some new improbable hope that he could make something out of the mess his career had become. The truth of the matter was that he didn't have a career. He had a dream, and that didn't put food on a man's table.

When he met Hayes, Aldus couldn't help liking him. While he was in town, the salesman had to visit a few shops in some neighborhoods that were very familiar to the boxer. Showing him around was an easy job that ended in a nice little bit of pay. The two had gotten on fairly well, and when Aldus bought Hayes a few glasses of whiskey, the salesman told him about his travels out West. Looking back on it, Aldus didn't know why he accepted the offer to join Hayes as an assistant, bodyguard, and sometimes apprentice. He'd been in New York City for several years and perhaps had acquired some touch of wanderlust himself. Or perhaps his head was still ringing and his body was aching so much that any other prospect seemed appealing. In the end, it had been Polaski's words that had gotten him to pack up his things and take a chance with a whole new life.

"There's fights held everywhere, Brick," Polaski had told him, calling him by the name he used in the ring. "You can always start one up wherever you land. It ain't every day that you get a chance to start fresh. Any place you land has gotta be better than this, right?"

Aldus shrugged.

Rubbing him on the head as if he were one of his fourteen grandkids, Polaski said, "You talked about that girl you used to know back home. Why don't you pay her a visit before you get yer head knocked off a' yer shoulders?"

And that had cinched it. The very possibility of kindling something with Bethany was more than enough for him to pack his things into a single carpetbag and join

Hayes as he went back into the wildlands west of the Mississippi River. If his head had been clear, Aldus probably wouldn't have gambled so much on such long odds. When he'd gotten his first letter back from Bethany, he never looked back.

The first time Aldus had ridden on this particular circuit, he couldn't wipe the smile from his face. He'd been a small boy when he'd last been through Iowa and Nebraska, and it felt mighty good to be back. The air was cleaner than he recalled, and he was picking up what Hayes had to teach much quicker than either of them had expected. Aldus didn't think he had a future as a gunsmith, but he could do his job well enough to allow Hayes to take on new circuits and expand his professional repertoire. Whenever some cowboy would get upset by his performance at the gallery or try to snatch his money back after holstering a new gun, Aldus fell back on his older set of skills. Truth be told, when he got a chance to take a few punches before knocking another man into next week, it felt as if he were being welcomed home by an old friend.

Aldus didn't like to think about that sort of thing when Bethany was still fresh in his thoughts. Somehow it made him feel as if he'd been caught in a compromising position. As he sat in the wagon's driver's seat now, his mind wandering back to earlier days, he propped a foot upon the buckboard and wrapped the reins around one beefy wrist. The trail ahead was straight as an arrow, and since he was following behind Hayes, he didn't need to see anything more than the wagon in front of him. After traveling this circuit so many times, the horses probably knew their way to the next town better than anyone.

Bethany's most recent batch of letters was in a satchel of his personal things. They were wedged in between his father's Bible and his mama's book of old poetry, which were the two things he used to try and hone his reading skills. He handled the letters as the precious things they were, unfolding the first one and rereading it.

As before, she was doing well. The kids were fine. She held him in her thoughts.

Aldus removed the next letter and immediately noticed something different. It struck him right away as he took in the familiar lettering and the lines of each individual word. Normally he drank in the sight of her words to him, but these were different and didn't flow as naturally as the letter before or any of the ones that had preceded it. When he tried to nail down exactly what was bothering him, Aldus couldn't quite put his finger on the reason for his concern. Since the meaning of the words themselves wasn't immediately apparent, he studied them carefully to try and piece some together.

She was doing well. The kids were well. She hoped he was well. The exact words she used varied somewhat, but not by much. When he was through reading that letter, he turned it around, thinking there had to be more. Normally Bethany had so much to say, even if it wasn't about anything important. This time she was just saying a few simple things in a very simple way.

He lowered the letter as a knot formed in his stomach. In his line of work, Aldus rarely had to let it be known how difficult reading was for him. When folks asked about it and he told them, they always looked at him differently. Oftentimes they regarded him as if he was stupid or couldn't understand what they said. More often than not, they regarded him with pity and looked at him as if he were a poor, wounded animal.

Could Bethany have figured out Aldus's trouble in reading her letters? The letters she received from him were written in his own words even if Hayes was the one who actually put them to paper for him. Could she have figured this out as well? Could Hayes have written something other than what Aldus had told him to write? For the moment, he decided not to believe any of those things. It was one abrupt letter. For all he knew, she could have been having a bad day when she'd written it. She could even have said as much in one of the sections he hadn't quite sorted out. So Aldus read it again. He didn't find anything that he hadn't found the first time through, so he went on to the next one.

The third letter was the shortest yet. It was so short and concise that Aldus thought for certain Bethany had somehow discovered his difficulty and was now addressing him as if he were feebleminded. He set the letters down and shifted all of his focus to the trail ahead.

They stopped for a short spell to water the horses at a creek. It was late in the afternoon and Aldus guessed they would arrive at their normal camping spot before dark. When Hayes walked by, he asked if that was, indeed, the case.

"Actually," Hayes replied, "we're going somewhere away from the normal circuit. It's a little town called Seedley. Ever heard of it?"

"Nope."

"Well, a colleague of mine referred me to that spot as a potentially lucrative location."

Even though Aldus had trouble with the written word, listening to Hayes spout off with all of his fancy phrases and terminology made him plenty familiar with the spoken ones. Just to be certain, however, he asked, "You mean we could stand to make a lot of money there?"

"That's exactly what I mean. That colleague works out of Cedar Rapids as well. He told me a few special orders came in from Seedley that he was too busy to fill and suggested a man with my abilities could stand to make a small fortune if I made quality gunsmithing services available without the need to go all the way to another town."

"What colleague?" Aldus asked.

"Jack Grable."

"Grable? As in Grable's Firearms in Cedar Rapids?" Hayes nodded.

Squinting as if he wasn't sure exactly who or what he was looking at, Aldus asked, "As in Grable's Firearms . . . our biggest competitor?"

"I'll grant you it's a spirited competition between us when I'm in town, but it's mostly a friendly one."

"What about when that colleague cut his prices so low that he took a loss just to make sure we didn't make a lick of profit last summer?"

Hayes winced when he recalled that incident. "I did say it was *mostly* friendly. I've pulled a few tricks of my own to tip the scales back in my favor, but that's all a part of the game. Besides, he only stands to gain by us making our profit anywhere other than Cedar Rapids."

"Won't we be taking away business from the men who might bring it there?"

"Yes, but he'll make up for that little bit we take away by getting the rest for himself."

Aldus glared at the salesman until he made the other man look away. "There's something you ain't telling me, Zeke."

"Grable will get Cedar Rapids to himself . . . until late summer."

"You mean we skip it for two whole circuits? Cedar Rapids is one of our best stops!" Aldus said. "I get a percentage of them profits, too, you know! That hurts us both!"

Hayes turned around and held his hands out in a placating gesture. "I know, I know. I should have consulted you first."

"You're damn right you should have consulted me! What made you go to Grable in the first place?"

"We have drinks whenever I'm in town. Every now and then . . . the occasional card game."

"*What?*"

"I knew you wouldn't approve," Hayes said. "You tend to look at our competitors like they're standing across from you in a boxing match. Business isn't like that. Not all the time, anyway. It tends to be more of a give-and-take instead of knock down and drag 'em out."

Aldus had learned plenty in his apprenticeship with Hayes, and one of his first lessons was that he didn't know the first thing about business. If he did, he might have been able to wrangle better deals for himself when he was in New York City. While he didn't always understand what was going on when it came to finances and such, he liked to think he'd picked up a thing or two about strategy. Putting himself in that frame of mind, he asked, "All right, then, what was the give-and-take in this deal?"

Sensing that Aldus had eased up a bit, Hayes relaxed as well. "I was having coffee with Jack before we left, and I talked to him about the robbery."

"When did you have a chance to do that?"

"While you were breaking down the rest of the gallery and getting the wagons ready to go," Hayes replied. "And don't give me that look, Aldus. Those are part of your regular duties."

Aldus sighed, choking back his impulse to chastise Hayes for exchanging pleasantries with the opposition while he did all the heavy lifting. "You're right. Go ahead."

"Anyway, we always have one last drink before I leave

town and he usually proposes some idea or other meant
to keep me out. It's something of a joke, but I'm sure he
would jump at any chance to get Cedar Rapids to himself. Anyway, he told me about a steady stream of customers that come from Seedley. Actually he didn't tell
me the name of the town until I agreed to hear him out
about the rest of his proposition."

"You mean the part that costs us money?" Aldus
growled.

"Well . . . yes. But," Hayes was quick to add, "we could
stand to rake in some fine profits by heading over there
right away. It seems the usual contingent arrives like
clockwork at certain times every couple of months, and
they were due to make the ride into Cedar Rapids in a
week or two. If we set up shop there for a while, we could
get some of that business and plenty more. After all, if
they need to visit a gunsmith on such a regular basis,
they undoubtedly have smaller jobs that need to be done
or purchases they'd like to make that don't warrant the
trip into another town."

"How can you be sure about that?"

There was a look in Hayes's eyes that came along
when he knew he was on to something good. Sometimes
it seemed as if the salesman could smell the money he
was about to make much as Aldus had been able to smell
fear in the men who stood across from him in the ring.
That look was in Hayes's eyes when he said, "There's a
real chance to make serious money in that town. Any
business venture boils down to meeting a need, and
Seedley is ripe for the picking."

Aldus let out a slow breath while removing his hat so
he could swipe a hand across the top of his head. It
wasn't a particularly hot day, but the sun was beating
down on him and it felt good to have a breeze rush past
to cool him off. "I suppose you're right, although I some-

times miss the days when the only need I had to meet was my need to remain standing while the other man fell down."

"You must see the wisdom in riding out to strike where the iron is hot. We could stand to make a whole lot of money in a short amount of time, which is exactly what we need right now."

"I still say you should have consulted me before agreeing to taking Cedar Rapids off the circuit."

"It's only for two circuits, but yes," Hayes said, "I should have consulted you. The only reason I didn't was that there wasn't enough time. Jack made his proposition out of friendship as well as business sense, but the latter was quickly overtaking the former. He wanted to keep us out of Cedar Rapids for an entire year, but I managed to talk him into a shorter amount of time. If I didn't agree the moment we reached a favorable compromise, he might have thought twice about it and backed out altogether."

"Or," Aldus said, "he started negotiating at a higher range and would have been more than willing to bargain if you would have acted like you were ready to walk away."

Hayes's smile was positively beaming. "I see I've made some genuine progress with you! You'll be a real businessman in no time. In the future, I'll be certain to consult with you in all matters that affect both of our profits. I'd hate to think this slip in judgment has dimmed your view of me."

"Well . . . there is something you could do to make it less dim."

"What might that be?"

"After we're done with Seedley, we're bound for Omaha."

"That's right," Hayes said with a cautious nod.

"Instead, we go to Corbin."

After taking a moment to think, Hayes asked, "That sounds familiar. Who's Corbin?"

"Corbin, Nebraska. It's about a day's ride southwest of Omaha."

Suddenly Hayes's face brightened. "That's right! Corbin is where Bethany lives. You want to pay a visit to your lady friend? By all means, you can spend some time there with my blessings!"

"No," Aldus said. "I don't just want to spend a little time there. I want to stay there for the duration of our visit to Omaha, and I don't want to be riding back and forth."

"No need for you to ride back and forth. I can tend to business on my own. I did it before you signed on to ride with me. I can do it again."

"That was before the shooting gallery became the cumbersome thing it is now. And if we stand to make as much money as you're talking about in Seedley, I'm not about to let it out of my sight. Part of that is mine, you know."

"I know." Hayes stepped up to place a hand on Aldus's shoulder. "You go on ahead and spend as much time as you like in Corbin. I can handle business in Omaha."

But Aldus shook his head. "You don't know you'll make enough of a profit to run a one-man operation. I want your guarantee that even if you don't make any money at all in this Seedley venture, we'll get a long stop in Corbin. Even if that means having to set up the gallery and run an entire stop in that town before we go to Omaha. I know Omaha is a ripe stop on the circuit, so we'll have to go there sooner or later. I just want to go to Corbin first and I want to stay there for a while."

"This seems like something more than a visit," Hayes

said as he furrowed his brow while looking at him intently.

Although he wasn't one for talking to just anyone about his affairs, Aldus knew that Hayes wasn't just anyone. Considering how much he knew about the letters that were written to Bethany since the very first batch, there wasn't much of a reason to keep Hayes in the dark now.

"There's . . . something wrong," Aldus said as he felt something akin to a weight being slowly lowered onto his shoulders.

"Something wrong with Bethany?" Hayes asked. In his voice was an urgency that made it seem as if he felt the weight almost as much as his partner. "Something wrong with the children? What is it?"

"I don't know. It's in her letters, though."

"Have you managed to read them any better?"

"No. It's just . . . I don't know," Aldus said in words that were becoming increasingly difficult to get out. "She's not herself. She's sad about something."

"Well, she is alone with those two boys after losing her husband. That's not an easy thing. How long has it been now?"

"Going on three years. But it's more than that. She's been sad before and she's told me about it. There have been scares with her boys when they both had bouts with fevers, and we nearly lost one of them last winter. I mean . . . she nearly lost Michael last winter. There's been trouble with money. She's been lonely. I've had my hard times as well, but we've always told each other about them."

"I know," Hayes said. "I've been right there with you."

Even though Aldus was all too aware of the fact that Hayes wrote the words that Aldus had given him, he was glad that his friend didn't rub it under his nose. It truly did feel as though Bethany was a friend to them both. However, she meant more to Aldus than he'd ever let on to the salesman, and it was difficult to keep that from being seen at this moment. Turning away from Hayes so he could start hitching the horses back to the wagons, Aldus said, "There's something wrong. It's something that's under her skin and I don't think she's telling me about it. I . . . I'd like you to read the letters."

Hayes's voice was quiet, almost reverent, when he said, "Those letters are meant for you, friend. I think she may even say things in them that she wouldn't want a stranger to read."

"But you're no stranger. Whether she knows it or not. Also, you're my friend and I need your help." Aldus averted his eyes as if he couldn't even look at the horse in front of him. "If she was saying something important to me . . . If I missed something like that when she was trying to let me know . . . I don't think I could live with myself."

"If that's what you want, I'll gladly read those letters. I'll even promise to skip over any sections that you might find . . . embarrassing."

Aldus turned around to look at the salesman. "What kind of things are you expecting to find?"

"Nothing unseemly, I assure you," Hayes said with a nervous chuckle. "I just know that you're not the sort who would be comfortable with letting anyone see . . . well . . ."

"Well what?"

Hayes took a breath and met the fighter's gaze. "I just wanted to assure you I'll only look for the sort of thing you want me to look for and nothing else. Anything more than that . . . no matter what it is . . . isn't my business. That's all I meant to say."

Slowly, Aldus nodded. "Fine. And we'll set up the gallery in Corbin?"

"I still don't see why you need—"

"I have my reasons," Aldus snapped. "After you went behind my back to make arrangements to skip Cedar Rapids in favor of some unproven town, you owe me that much."

Hayes took a step back. "Calling me out and making it impossible for me to refuse, eh?" He smiled good-naturedly as he added, "I truly will make a real businessman out of you."

Chapter 9

It was another two days of riding before Aldus would catch sight of Seedley. The little town was a bit south of their normal route, and they were forced to take a different path. Once they'd steered away from the wide, straight trail to which they were accustomed, the journey became a bit more difficult. The grass became thicker and the terrain became rougher. There were shallow creeks that needed to be forded, and the wagons were slowed to a crawl while Aldus rode ahead to pick the best spot for their crossing.

There were a few bluffs along the way that also hindered their normal rate of progress. The horses had to slow as they climbed the gradual incline. Afterward, they wound their way around a series of ditches and a dried riverbed that could have overturned one or both of the wagons if the drivers weren't careful in their approach. It would have been a much easier ride if the men were on horseback, but they couldn't exactly leave the wagons behind. When they made camp, Hayes sifted through Aldus's letters. He read them carefully while Aldus collected firewood and was still reading them when it was time to fix supper. Aldus suspected the other man was dragging his feet simply to avoid his share of the chores, but rather than make a fuss about it, he warmed up a mixture of beans and salted pork.

"So," Aldus said as he scooped some of his supper into his mouth from the old pie tin he used as a plate, "what did you make out from them letters?"

"She didn't say anything alarming as such," Hayes replied. He picked at his meal with a spoon the same way he would eat a bowl of soup at a fancy restaurant. "Much of the simple details were the way you described. As for the rest, I didn't find anything alarming."

"Maybe it's just because I can't read too good."

"No, there is something to your concerns. I just don't know if it's particularly alarming."

"If you got something to say, just say it," Aldus demanded.

"She does mention . . . someone else."

Aldus's face darkened. "Like who?"

"A friend of hers. Nate Talbott. Perhaps you've seen the name mentioned."

There were plenty of words that Aldus didn't recognize when he read something. The main difference with Bethany's letters was that he stuck to the task long enough to make out enough to get what he needed. Much as a person might watch someone's facial expressions as he spoke to him in another language, Aldus had developed a knack for making just enough sense out of the written word to get some sort of meaning from it. There came a point, however, when he had to give in to the fact that he was still missing a lot. It was a defeat that stung worse than the ones he'd been handed in the ring. Admitting that defeat to his friend and employer in the quiet of that campsite as night crept in around them was somehow worse than falling face-first in front of a roaring crowd.

"No," Aldus said. "I never seen that name."

"Well, she only mentioned it a couple of times. He's been coming around to visit and seemed to have made an impression on one of the boys. But there was something about the way she talked about him in the last letter that was markedly different from the first time Nate was mentioned."

"How did she talk about him?"

Hayes paused, measuring his next words carefully. "It didn't seem romantic. Not overly so, anyway."

That made Aldus wince.

"She mentioned him as a friend," Hayes continued. "In fact, she went out of her way to say that you might have a lot in common. Apparently this Nate fellow did some boxing as well. They seemed to have had a falling-out. It was just a small mention in the second letter. You may have overlooked it even if you could read every last word."

When Hayes pointed out his shortcoming, Aldus didn't feel as though it was an insult in any way. Even so, he didn't like hearing it from a man he respected so much.

"I know what you were talking about in the letters," Hayes continued. "There was a change in her. She does seem a bit forlorn and distanced once she mentioned that she had some sort of falling-out with Nate. After that, she is sad. To be honest, I may not have picked up on it at all. Just reading the letters, I would have thought she was distracted or possibly didn't have much to say. But when you mention it, I believe you're right. I think this Nate fellow is troubling her and the boys. It's just something she said in the last letter. Nothing specific, but there is something . . . off about her. If I may ask, how did you pick up on it?"

There were plenty of things that didn't set right with Aldus where those letters were concerned. Most of all, the last one seemed as if she was scratching it out with a hint of anger instead of crafting her words the way she normally did. Rather than explain any of that to Hayes, he said, "I know her well enough to know when something ain't right."

"Well . . . I believe you have a good point. Perhaps it is good that we spend some time in Corbin. Besides, her boys seem delightful."

"Yeah," Aldus said with a smile. "They do."

The next day, Hayes insisted on getting a move on since Seedley wasn't too much farther ahead of them. Once the horses were hitched to the wagons, the small procession got moving once again. Aldus would have felt better if he knew they were making a straight line toward Corbin, but a good portion of what Hayes had told him about Seedley had sunk in. It did seem like a good move to go there. If Jack Grable was pulling some sort of trick just to keep Hayes out of Cedar Rapids, then he would be very unpleasantly surprised indeed when Aldus returned to pay him a visit.

If not for the directions given by Jack Grable, Hayes and his wagons could very well have missed the town of Seedley altogether. Not only were the wagons on an unfamiliar trail, but the town was about a mile off that trail nestled in among some hills on the western edge of Iowa. It was the tail end of a gloomy day when they rolled into town. The sky was gray and the clouds had been threatening to douse them ever since the previous night. Instead of a good, hard rain, Aldus and Hayes were spat upon by little droplets that hit their cheeks and spattered upon their horses' backs.

By the time he spotted the town in the distance, Aldus was wet and chilled to the bone. His coat and hat had collected just enough of the little droplets to soak through his clothing. He'd allowed Hayes to get a bit farther ahead than normal, so he was able to see Seedley's paltry collection of homes surrounding a few buildings that were no more than two floors high. As far as he could see, the entire town wasn't much more than three streets and two intersections.

"Oh yeah," Aldus grumbled to himself. "This place is really gonna cover our losses from Cedar Rapids."

"What was that?" Hayes shouted back to him.

"Nothing!"

"It's not the size of the town that matters, you know. It's how well we do our jobs that will determine how much we walk away with."

Aldus couldn't decide which irked him more at that particular moment: Hayes's unwavering optimism despite being drenched, tired, and cold or the fact that he'd been able to read Aldus so accurately without even having to look at him.

One small comfort was that the trail that had made their progress thus far such an effort widened and became much smoother as it took them closer to the edge of town. Alongside the trail, there was a sign written in bold letters upon large wooden planks. The wagons were going slow enough for Aldus to make out a few very familiar words: *forbid* and *firearms*.

After waiting to hear from the man ahead of him, Aldus called out, "Hey, Zeke! You see that sign?"

"I did."

"You think we'll make a lot of sales in a town that don't allow guns?"

Hayes leaned over to look behind the wagon while holding his hat on with one hand. Instead of the more expensive top hat he used when working, the one he wore now was an older style with a wide brim intended to shade him from the sun and offer some bit of protection from the insistent drizzle. "That sign was just a warning about a town ordinance."

"Well, an ordinance against guns don't seem much better."

"The ordinance forbids the carrying of firearms that haven't been registered with the town law."

"So we'll have to check in with a sheriff before we get something to eat?" Aldus asked.

"Since we're riding in a wagon filled with firearms, I'd say that would be a prudent course of action."

"You think that's why those men have to leave town to get their guns repaired?" Aldus asked as a burst of thunder rolled overhead.

Hayes stuck his hand out to signal for both wagons to come to a stop. After pulling back on the reins, Aldus set the brake and climbed down from his seat. As he passed the horses, he gave one of them a few pats on the neck and the other a quick rub on his nose. That calmed them both down while the storm brewed in the skies. Walking around the lead wagon, Aldus glanced over his shoulder at the sign. There was nothing else written on it and not a living soul to be found in his field of vision. Even when he turned back around, the town itself was as still as an oil painting while the horses and even Hayes himself all shifted in their spots.

Scooting all the way to the edge of his seat, Hayes climbed down to stand beside Aldus. "What did you say back there?" he asked.

"I was wondering if that ordinance could be why those men have to leave town to get their guns fixed."

"Could be. What concerns me is that we make a good first impression when we present ourselves to the law. It would probably be best if I presented myself as the man in charge."

"You are the man in charge," Aldus said.

"Yes, well, it may be prudent for me to pass you off as less than what you are."

Aldus chuckled. "Wouldn't be the first time."

"I've been to a lot of small towns like this one," Hayes explained. "This was before I got a system down as polished as it is now. You know how you were able to read between the lines . . . so to speak . . . with Bethany's letters?"

"Yeah."

"Well, I can read between the lines here. This is not a place that will take that ordinance lightly," the salesman said as he leveled a finger at the sign they'd passed. "It looks like that notice has been repainted a time or two and the sign is in real good condition. Other towns . . . that sign would be shot full of holes just because the men doing it thought it was funny. But not here, which means there's likely someone enforcing the letter of that particular law and they do not take kindly to being disobeyed."

Aldus held up his hands. "I wasn't thinking we should disobey anything. I'd just like to get in out of the rain."

As if on cue, the spitting sprinkle of cold droplets became just a little heavier as another ripple of thunder worked its way through the thickening clouds.

"When I present myself to the sheriff," Hayes continued, "I'll have to explain myself fully and probably turn these wagons over for inspection. I don't want you to protest or put up any kind of fuss."

"When have I ever caused a problem?" Aldus asked.

"You haven't. It's just when someone is enforcing a rule like restricting firearms, it means either they're worried about trouble or they had some pretty serious trouble not too long ago. That's the kind of trouble involving life and death, which tends to make folks nervous. Lawmen . . . doubly so. That's why I don't even want to introduce you as an apprentice because then we'll just have to spend that much more time with you answering the same questions I probably will. All you do is clean up after me. Got it?"

Aldus scowled reflexively, much the same as he had in the days when he'd first started trying to make a name for himself as a boxer and Basil Polaski had introduced him as the man who cleaned the floors instead of one of the fighters. Even though he had been cleaning floors at the time, being regarded as so low on the totem pole made him feel as though he'd been lumped in with the dog.

Suddenly Hayes pointed stiffly at Aldus instead of the sign at the side of the trail. "See?" he said. "Right there. That look in your eyes is what I'm trying to avoid. You're about to speak up for yourself and tell me you do more than pick up shell casings."

"No, I wasn't," Aldus lied.

"Whether you were or weren't, it doesn't matter. You look like you resent how I described you, which looks suspicious. And when you look suspicious to men who are already nervous enough to enforce an ordinance like that one, it doesn't bode well for our chances here. I don't have to tell you that we both need this stopover to work as well as it possibly can."

"I already know that."

"So don't look like you want to knock my teeth in when I say those things to whoever I need to report to, all right?"

"Yeah," Aldus said. "Let's just get moving again so we can dry off."

Hayes patted Aldus on the shoulder and sent him on his way, but not before saying, "I do the talking when we get into town. Agreed?"

"I won't say a word."

"It's only for the best. Also, it would be a good idea to not have any guns on our person when we arrive."

Aldus was already heading back to the second wagon. As soon as he climbed into the driver's seat, he removed his Schofield from the old leather holster and set it under his seat before releasing the brake and flicking his reins. The wagon lurched forward to follow Hayes, who'd already driven back onto the trail leading into town. As they got closer to Seedley, the drizzle turned into a steady rain. The drops were still small but fell in a much quicker drumbeat against the top of Aldus's hat and the canvas cover of the wagon. He reached once more beneath his seat, rummaging around under there until he found a bottle that was about a quarter full of whiskey. Aldus pulled the cork out and tipped the bottle back to take a drink. The liquor was harsh and did a mighty fine job of warming his innards.

They drove down Main Street, which cut all the way through the entire town. Aldus didn't have any trouble reading the little sign marking the street because he'd seen that word on more street signs than he could count. At the town's second intersection, Hayes signaled for them to come to a stop. The building at the corner on the left was one of the taller ones in town and had the star of a lawman painted onto its front window. Aldus pulled his hat down over his eyes and stayed in his seat as Hayes climbed down to walk beneath an awning in front of the building.

"At least come in out of the rain," Hayes said.

Aldus waved for him to move on. "Just go ahead. It'll probably be easier if I stay outside, anyways."

"You sure about that?"

"Someone should watch the wagons."

That was enough to convince Hayes, so he knocked on the door before opening it. Aldus could hear the beginnings of an overly enthusiastic greeting followed by an introduction before the salesman stepped inside and shut the door behind him.

A clap of thunder rolled through the air, and the rain started pouring down even worse. Gritting his teeth while reaching for the whiskey bottle, Aldus cursed himself for his choice to stay outside. Just as he thought about going into the lawman's office, the door swung open and a tall, lean figure filled the entrance. He was dressed in black pants and a white shirt with a badge pinned to the breast pocket. Stern eyes stared straight at Aldus, and the mouth partially hidden beneath a long, thick mustache was formed into a straight line.

"You'd be the fella riding along with Mr. Hayes?" the lawman asked.

Adhering to his previous orders to stay as quiet as possible, Aldus nodded.

"You'd best come inside so I can—"

Another clap of thunder exploded nearby. Almost immediately, Aldus realized it wasn't thunder at all but a gunshot. He twisted around to get a look in the direction from which the gun had been fired, only to find a man crossing Main Street while pivoting around to fire at the first intersection Aldus and Hayes had passed on their way to the lawman's office. He fired the pistol in his hand before another gunshot ripped through the air. Aldus could see a plume of smoke coming from in front of one of the shops on that side of the street. The silhouette of another gunman was outlined by the flickering light coming from behind that store's front window. That man fired again and the fellow in the street grunted in pain as he dropped.

"What in blazes?" the lawman shouted as he and two others raced from the office.

Hayes emerged from there as well, trying to clear a path for the others while also getting a look at what was going on.

The man now lying in the street fired once more before he was cut down by two more shots fired from the shadows. All of the lawmen were returning fire by now, and their bullets quickly shattered the front window, but the gunman had already run away from the store, emptying his pistol by firing wildly behind him as he fled. When Aldus heard more shots fired from the opposite end of the street, he turned just in time to see another figure standing directly across from the lawmen's office. Since the lawmen were all tearing after the first shooter, the one closest to the office had a perfect angle to shoot them all in the back.

Aldus jumped down from the wagon on the side closest to the lawmen's office just as a pair of shots punched through his wagon's canvas cover and drilled a set of holes through the seat he'd abandoned.

"There's another one across the street!" Aldus shouted.

Hayes was the only one who heard him since all of the lawmen who had emerged from the office were either checking on the man lying in the street or firing at the one that had bolted. "What?" the salesman asked.

"Across the street!"

"Just keep your head down!"

When he heard footsteps slapping against the rain-soaked ground to circle around the wagon, Aldus grunted, "Aw, hell," and rushed to meet the gunman.

Chapter 10

The only thing running through Aldus's mind was that he didn't want to be caught flat-footed if the shooter came around to take another shot at him. Also, since these men were obviously killers, he didn't want them getting away if there was anything he could do about it. Aldus wasn't thinking about any plans of attack or his own chances for winning a fight. He just knew there was nowhere to hide and his chances for survival were mighty slim if he stood his ground.

When Aldus reached the back end of the wagon, he came face-to-face with someone who was several inches shorter than him. He couldn't tell much more than that because the man wore a bandanna tied around the lower portion of his face. His eyes widened in surprise when he saw a stranger coming straight for him, and when more shooting erupted from the lawmen down the street, he turned tail and ran away. The smell of burned gunpowder was fresh in Aldus's nostrils, and the blood was burning hot in his veins as he hurried to close the distance between himself and the shorter man.

The gunman swore under his breath and put some extra steam into his strides. Aldus knew his limitations and he also outweighed the gunman by at least sixty pounds. For those reasons, he was certain it wouldn't be long before the gunman got away or at least gained enough ground to feel confident enough to turn around and fire at him. Since he was in this deep, Aldus wasn't about to give up. His hand went to the old holster at his side, only to find it empty.

Now it was Aldus's turn to curse as he recalled that his Schofield was still stashed away and dry as a bone beneath the driver's seat of his wagon. That only left one more card to play if he was going to put an end to this. Aldus dropped to one knee and pulled the knife from the scabbard in his boot. The familiar weapon filled his hand, but drawing it had granted the man in front of him a few precious seconds to pull even farther ahead.

Behind them, gunshots cracked through the air and voices shouted various demands and threats. Aldus thought he even heard Hayes screaming something, but he put all that aside as he ran to catch up to the gunman he'd spotted. Just as Aldus had feared, the gunman stopped, spun around, and raised his pistol to line up a shot. Aldus dived for the boardwalk in front of a small storefront with no window and a shingle hanging to the side of its front door. A shot hissed through the air above him, which hit that shingle to set it swinging. Aldus thought about rolling into the street before he was hit, but decided against it when he heard the flat *clank* of a pistol's hammer slapping against either a bad round or an empty shell. Without waiting for the gunman to take another shot, Aldus scrambled to his feet and charged forward once again.

The other man's eyes betrayed the panic that was pulsing through him as Aldus rushed at him with one meaty fist wrapped around the handle of his knife. Still fumbling with his pistol, he swung it to hit Aldus as he closed in on him.

The side of the gun thumped against Aldus's shoulder, skidded along his neck, and caught him in the side of the face. The blunt impact might have been enough to stun most men, but Aldus had had worse from much stronger opponents. He clamped his left hand around the gunman's throat and shoved him off balance while taking a swing at him with the hand that clutched his knife. Aldus's instinct was to strike with the metal guard across his knuckles instead of the blade. If the gunman hadn't twisted around to avoid the blow, he would have caught the full brunt of the impact square on the jaw. The loose clothing he wore also helped him squirm away from the fighter and only catch a glancing shot across his cheek and chin.

The gunman brought his pistol up to pound it against Aldus's ribs, which did nothing to slow him down. Aldus heard the workings of the hammer as it was thumbed back, followed by a deafening roar. Apparently there had only been one faulty round in the cylinder because this one burned through Aldus's side like a hot talon.

Aldus reflexively let the gunman go and reeled away. He fully expected to be hit again as he doubled over while pressing his left arm against the side that had been shot. Instead, the gunman staggered away to recover after having been cracked in the face. He made his way to the alley between the building with the shingle over its door and its closest neighbor. As he fell into a smoother step, he dropped his pistol into the holster at his side and drew another one that had been hanging at his other hip.

Pressing his side to the door beneath the shingle, Aldus checked his side for blood. There was a fair amount on his hand, but not enough to cause him concern. Of course, he had to bleed quite profusely before he was concerned about it, but a few cautious stretches and turns at the waist convinced him that the shot had merely grazed him across his ribs. It stung like nobody's business, but it wasn't enough to put him down. His fighter's instinct kicked in, causing Aldus to hold his ground as the gunman came to a stop near the alley several paces in front of him.

For a second, both men locked eyes.

In the distance, there were still shots being fired, but they were scattered and far apart.

Men were shouting and one was even screaming.

Other voices were nearby, but they spoke in hushed tones from all sides. More than likely, they were locals watching events unfold from the safety of their homes or businesses.

But Aldus didn't bother with that any more than he'd concerned himself with the crowd's taunts and cheers when he was in the thick of a bout on the docks of New York City.

Like those bloody fights when his knuckles were torn open and blood poured from his mouth, nose, and cheeks, Aldus saw only the man in front of him. He'd been told that his face took on a ferocity that was chilling in its own regard. Some said that ferocity alone had been enough to turn the tide of a fight. Even now, the man in front of him froze for a moment when he got a look at Aldus's rain-drenched face.

If Aldus had a gun, he could have taken his shot. His holster was empty, however.

If he was closer, Aldus could have taken a swing that would have put the other man flat onto his back.

The gunman had regained some semblance of his courage, straightened his arm, and fired a quick shot that knocked a chunk out of the post to Aldus's right. He then pivoted toward the alley to make good on his escape.

Aldus took one step forward, flipped the knife in his

hand to grab it by the blade, and cocked it back near his ear. A second before the gunman made it into the alley, Aldus snapped his hand forward and sent the knife sailing through the air.

It wasn't a pretty sight when the knife tuned end over end. With the knuckle guard weighing the handle down, the weapon wasn't anywhere close to balanced for throwing. But it was a knife that Aldus had carried with him since he'd first left his Nebraska home and made his way out to the eastern coast. It had been with him every day in New York City and saved his life on countless occasions. It had also won him more beers than he could recall by winning bets after performing feats similar to this one. Just like those long tosses into boards or walls, this one landed solidly into the gunman's calf a heartbeat before the man disappeared down the alley.

Although he might have been feeling jubilant after scoring that hit, Aldus wasn't about to chase an armed, wounded man. Instead, he turned in the opposite direction to run around the building's other side. That alley was wide and mostly empty apart from a few broken crates and several piles of trash. As he reached the end, Aldus slowed his steps so they weren't loud enough to announce his arrival from a mile away. Working his way along the backside of the building, he could hear the gunman grunting and cursing in the next alley over.

Every breath Aldus took was measured and shallow.

He kept one shoulder close to the building and tried not to lift his feet more than what was absolutely necessary to keep moving.

The wound in his side was hurting a little worse. The pain he felt now burrowed in deeper to spread throughout the muscles within his torso.

As far as he could tell, the gunman had almost reached the end of his alley. His progress was marked by a stuttering series of steps marked by the heavy impact of one foot followed by the long, dragging scrape of the wounded one.

Thump ... scrape.

Thump ... scrape.

Thump ... scrape.

The gunman was getting closer, quickening his steps as he built to a steadier rhythm.

Thump ... scrape.

Thump scrape.

Thumpscrape.

Thumpscrape.

The moment Aldus saw the barrel of the other man's gun protrude from the alley, he reached out to grab the wrist directly behind it. As soon as his hand locked shut in a firm grip, he pulled the gunman from the alley like removing an arrow from a wound. The other man staggered forward awkwardly as his finger tightened around his trigger.

Aldus's ears were still suffering from the last couple of shots, and this one washed away every sound in his world apart from a piercing ring. The gunman said something as he was dragged through the sloppy mud, his words lost as lightning crashed silently overhead. Aldus gritted his teeth, committing himself to finishing what he'd started by clenching his fist even tighter and twisting until the pistol slipped from the gunman's hand to fall onto the top of Aldus's foot.

Having swung the gunman away from the alley, Aldus now pulled him in closer while pounding his right fist straight into his nose. The impact was solid enough for Aldus to hear the muted crunch against his knuckles despite the ringing in his ears. When the gunman toppled over, Aldus let him drop.

Aldus's heart thumped in his chest. His breath roared

through his head. After lifting his head to the falling rain, sounds started to roll in as if from several miles away. Ignoring the approaching footsteps and shouting voices, he squatted down to take hold of the knife protruding from the unconscious gunman's leg. Aldus unceremoniously yanked the blade free, wiped it on his soaking shirt, and slid it back into its scabbard.

Rough hands grabbed him from behind and gun barrels were jammed into his back. The only thing that went through Aldus's mind was that he would finally be getting out of the rain.

Chapter 11

It took several minutes for Aldus's ears to clear. Even after he could hear again, he kept his head down and his expression blank. Most of the voices around him were yelling about half a dozen different things, so he thought it would do him some good to take just a bit more time to catch his breath.

After dropping that gunman in the alley, Aldus had been arrested and dragged back to the office of the lawmen Hayes had been so keen on visiting. The main portion of the office was the largest of three rooms on the building's first floor. The other two rooms were easy enough to see since their doors were open. The closer was a room filled with a few gun cabinets, some chairs, and a desk, while the farther contained a row of jail cells. For the time being, Aldus sat on a chair in the middle of the largest room as Hayes and the others paced around him like a bunch of circling vultures. At least they'd been civil enough to give him a few rags to press against the shallow wound in his side.

"It is completely ridiculous for you to arrest this man!" Hayes loudly proclaimed. "If anything, he should be commended!"

"We're still trying to figure out what's going on," said

the tall lawman in charge. He was the same one who had stepped out of the office before the first shot was fired. His thick black hair was shot through with a liberal amount of gray, a pattern that was also reflected in the whiskers sprouting below his nose. He stayed in front of the largest desk, remaining within Aldus's line of sight while only pacing one or two steps in any given direction at a time.

The other men were younger and could barely contain themselves as they darted back and forth behind and in front of Aldus. Hayes stayed near the front of the room. Whenever he tried to approach Aldus, the tall man with the salt-and-pepper hair reached out with a long arm to keep him back.

Aldus's knife had been taken from him and now lay on the largest desk. Outside, the rain pelted the windows and roof like a herd of wild animals scratching to come in from the cold. He must have reacted to something he heard because the tall lawman directly in front of him stepped forward to knock the side of his boot against one of the legs of Aldus's chair.

"You hear me, don't you?" the lawman asked in a growl that sounded like something from a Texas bull.

"I do," Aldus said.

Hayes had been trying to speak to Aldus ever since his arrest, and he rushed over to the chair before one of the younger men could hold him back. "Why are you treating *us* like the criminals?" the salesman asked. "I demand to be treated like the upstanding citizen I am!"

"Just keep yer demands under your hat for now," the tall man said. "The man who was gunned down in the street was one of my deputies, and there's a bloody mess in my jail. Until I straighten out what happened here, the two of you can sit tight and answer a few questions."

The younger man who'd tried to restrain Hayes grabbed a chair and set it down facing Aldus.

Before taking a seat, Hayes said, "You have no cause to place us under arrest."

Oddly enough, the tall lawman smiled. "You got that right. I suppose that was just my way to get you two wrangled in one spot so we could have ourselves a conversation."

"You could have just asked," Hayes pointed out.

"Sure, I could've asked. Arresting you was quicker. As soon as our conversation is over, barring any sudden outbursts from either of you, I'll turn you loose. How's that grab ya?"

Hayes nodded and reluctantly lowered himself onto his chair. "I suppose that's fine, since we've nothing to hide."

"Just what I like to hear." Turning his attention to Aldus, he said, "I'm Sam Borden, marshal of this town. I've already met Mr. Hayes over there. Who might you be?"

"Aldus Bricker."

Borden's eyes narrowed and he angled his head slightly. "Bricker? Did you used to box in New York City a few years back?"

"Yes, sir."

"I caught one of your fights. You went up against some big fella."

"Near as I can recall," Aldus said, "they were all pretty big."

But the marshal was lost in thought for the moment. When he found his way back, he snapped his fingers and said, "Dennis Thorpe! That was the other fella's name."

Aldus nodded. "Peg leg Thorpe. Big Englishman with no hair and a killer left hook. Just about took my head off."

"Peg leg?" Borden asked. "I don't remember him having only one leg."

"They used to call him Peg leg because he used to

knock men down so easy they all seemed to only have one leg to stand on."

"Sounds about right," the marshal said through a wide grin. "I was out by way of New York City visiting my brother. He bet on you on account of you being called the Brick. Told me it would be foolish to bet against someone with a name like that. I told him all them fighters had colorful names and I put my money on the one who looked the part."

"Put your money on the Englishman, did you?" Aldus asked.

"Every cent. Thought I had it won, too. That is, until you snuck in that sneaky jab in the ninth round."

"It was five sneaky jabs. They just all added up. Everyone likes to see the haymakers, but it's the jabs that win most fights. I opened a cut over his ear and kept tapping it until Thorpe got wobbly. One more tap, a little harder than the ones before, put him down for the count."

"I lost a bundle on you," Borden said while wagging a finger at Aldus. "But it was still a sight to see. Well worth the price I wound up paying that night. You're full of surprises, Brick."

Aldus knew where this was headed, and he wasn't anxious for it to get there.

The rest of the men had settled down by now. They were younger fellows, ranging in age from somewhere in the early twenties to one man who Aldus guessed was close to forty or so. The oldest of that bunch was clean shaven and seemed to be the calmest of the lot. Of course, that was excluding Marshal Borden himself. The lawman in charge of all the others seemed to have ice running through his veins.

"Mr. Hayes over there tells me you're his assistant," Borden said.

Aldus sat up straight and immediately regretted it.

Pain lanced through his side to stab at his gut and put a cringe on his face. It wasn't crippling but had caught him by surprise.

Hayes stood up. "He's hurt. Can't you see that?"

Nodding toward Aldus's chair, Borden said, "Take a look at that, Mark."

The man who Aldus guessed was in his forties stepped forward. His face was pockmarked and had several deep lines etched into its surface, making him look even older as he got closer. Although he didn't reach for the gun at his hip, both of the other deputies in the room held theirs at the ready in the event Aldus got any crazy notions in his aching head.

"Unbutton your shirt and hold your arms up," Mark said.

Aldus peeled open his shirt and stretched his right hand back behind his head. When he breathed in, he did so slowly and not too deeply, falling back on habits acquired after too many rib fractures. Glancing down at Mark, Aldus asked, "You know what you're doing?"

Without taking his eyes away from the bloody tear in Aldus's side, Mark told him, "I was a field medic in the army. I've stitched together plenty of bullet wounds. As far as wounds go," he added while prodding at Aldus with the tip of one finger, "this one isn't so bad. You can use some stitches, though."

"Can it wait?" Marshal Borden asked.

"The bleeding's stopped, but I wouldn't want to wait too long."

"Fine. Collect what you need to do the job. We shouldn't be much longer." Looking over to the rest of his men, he said, "Why don't you offer our guests something to drink?"

The rain outside grew louder as Mark opened the front door and hurried from the office. When it was closed again, Aldus couldn't help feeling cooped up and restless inside that room with all those eyes pointed in his direction.

"So we're guests now?" Hayes asked.

"Like I told you before. Arresting you was just a formality. You're still obliged to tell me what I want to know, though, so don't get too comfortable on that high horse of yours."

"I didn't . . . I mean . . . ," Hayes stammered. Finally he settled on saying, "We're not here to pose any problems, Marshal."

"Good. First let's start with why you are here."

"I told you when I first arrived," Hayes said. "I repair, build, and sell firearms as well as ammunition. I was told to say hello to Cal Overland when I got settled."

"Who sent you?" Borden asked.

"A good man by the name of Jack Grable. He's a merchant like myself in Cedar Rapids."

"I know who he is."

Smiling as though the matter were already resolved, Hayes said, "Well, then! It truly is a small world."

None of the other men in the room, Aldus included, shared Hayes's enthusiasm. Impressed least of all was Marshal Borden. "What brought you to Seedley?" he asked. "I'm guessing it was more than to give Cal your regards."

"I do plenty of work in Cedar Rapids myself," Hayes explained. "Mr. Grable and I both noticed that there's been a steady stream of demand for our particular brand of work from men representing this very town."

"By work, you mean building guns?"

"Building, repairing, supplying. You name it. Any need that has to be met in the field of quality firearms that can't be met by a simple blacksmith. Gunsmithing is a craft all its own, as I'm sure you're aware."

"So this Grable fella asked you to drag your wagons and your associate all the way into town?"

"Look," Aldus growled. "I know you had a bad time of it here with this shooting and all, but we don't have to be raked over the coals just because we happened to show up at the same time."

The marshal nodded. "It does seem like a mighty big coincidence. And since you two were in the thick of it, I need to see if there's anything else you can tell me about what happened."

"You were there just like we were," Aldus said. "Although . . . you did miss that one fella who I tore after."

"Now, now," Hayes warned tersely. "No need for hostilities."

Aldus shifted uncomfortably in his seat. The wound in his side was nagging at him like a row of fire ants biting into tender flesh.

Looking at the marshal, Hayes said, "We're at your service."

"Good," Borden replied. "Since your hired hand there seems to have a burr under his saddle, perhaps he could tell me why he took it upon himself to chase down that other man."

"Because he took a shot at me," Aldus said.

"How'd you know he'd be there?"

"I didn't. I just saw him after he fired."

"You saw him when none of my men could see him?" Borden asked.

"That's right."

"Pardon me," Hayes said. "But it seems that my friend here is being questioned when he should be thanked. After all, he did take it upon himself to put his life in jeopardy when he could very well have sought shelter and let that dangerous criminal get away. If he didn't take the action he did, you wouldn't have anyone in your jail right now."

"You got a real good point there, Mr. Hayes," Borden said. "I'm just making sure this wasn't some kind of setup instead of the long string of coincidences that it appears to be. You see, a man in my line of work doesn't generally like coincidences."

Hayes had always been a curious man. Many times, his incessant questioning of everything around him had taken him and Aldus in some unusual and sometimes profitable directions. His interest was piqued now, and his tangled, messy eyebrows rose when he asked, "Is that so? How many coincidences do you mean?"

But the marshal wasn't going to indulge Hayes's curiosity in the slightest. He shut it down with a quick "Not your concern" and shifted his eyes back to Aldus. "Most men don't exactly run toward gunfire, so perhaps you could see why I might have a concern or two about you."

"He was shooting at us," Aldus said. "Shooting at you, too. I didn't have a lot of places to hide and figured I'd just get shot if I stood still."

"You could have hidden behind that wagon," Borden pointed out. "Or even under it, for that matter."

"I thought I could do something better than hide." Aldus straightened his posture, and when he felt the pain from his wound, it was reflected in the fire in his eyes. "Maybe you should ask your questions to the man in the cell back there."

The marshal's eyes remained locked on Aldus. Then they shifted over to Hayes as if he was sizing up each man, straight down to his soul. Nodding toward the doorway at the back of the room, he said, "Paul, give us a moment."

One of the deputies, a portly fellow with a beard that

covered the entire lower portion of his face, walked into the room with the jail cells and shut the door behind him.

"Don't you worry none," Borden said to Hayes and Aldus. "I'll be asking plenty of questions to my guest back there. And if what he tells me doesn't match up with what you did, we'll have ourselves another go-around."

"That man tried to kill us," Hayes said. "Surely you can't expect him to be honest under questioning."

"Let me get to the bottom of when he's honest or not. Before I cut you loose, what can you tell me about the men who came to see you in Cedar Rapids?"

"I don't believe I got any names," Hayes replied. "To be perfectly frank, it was my associate Mr. Grable who dealt with most of them."

"What can you tell me about Grable, then?"

"What does this have to do with anything?"

"It's got to do with the fact that I've had almost a dozen men turn up dead here in Seedley and it wasn't by natural causes," Borden explained. "Some were shot. One was stabbed. The rest were strung up just outside town."

"Sounds like the work of a lynch mob," Hayes said.

"I figured as much on my own," the marshal told him. "Since some of the men were under my protection, it also seems like the work of someone who's getting word from inside this office. What might you know about that?"

It was rare that Hayes was at a loss for words. When it happened this time, his mouth hung open, some of the color drained from his face and he looked over to Aldus for support.

"What are you telling this to us for?" Aldus asked.

"Because I wanted to see if you knew anything about

it," Borden explained. "And don't feel too privileged. Just about everyone in town who's paying attention to the bodies being found already knows most of what I just told you. But one thing they don't know is that some of the guns used in these killings were bought and paid for in Cedar Rapids."

"How can you be sure of that?"

"Because I got it straight from the source. I can arrange for you to get a look at the man who told me, and when I do, all I need is for you to verify that you've seen him before."

"What if I can't?" Hayes asked.

"Then I go about my job and you go about yours. I haven't seen him around lately, so you'll have to wait until I can scrounge him up."

"So we're free to ply our trade here in Seedley?"

The lawman nodded. "It'll give you something to do, since I'm gonna ask that you don't leave town for a few days. You saw the sign posted regarding the firearms registration ordinance?"

"I did. That's why I came in to introduce myself in the first place."

"That ordinance was started to give me something to work with where these troubling matters are concerned. To that end, I'll need to know what you're bringing into Seedley."

"I keep very good records," Hayes said proudly.

"I'm sure you do." The marshal stood up as his front door came open and Mark hurried in out of the rain. "I'll let you get stitched up, Mr. Bricker. It's a real pleasure to meet you." He extended a hand and when Aldus shook it, the marshal added, "I'm real appreciative of what you did where bringing in that shooter is concerned."

"You can repay me by sending some business our way," Aldus replied.

"I'm hoping you won't have any shortage of customers while you're in town." The lawman excused himself to step into the room containing the jail cells.

Even though getting his wound stitched together wasn't exactly a pleasant process, Aldus would much rather have been in his seat than the prisoner's.

Chapter 12

The rest of the day, while not as eventful as their arrival, was exceedingly busy for Aldus. After he was allowed to leave the marshal's office, he and Hayes had to scout for a good location to park their wagons. Rain was falling in steady sheets, but that didn't prevent them from riding back down Main Street to essentially retrace their steps from when they'd entered Seedley. The other end of town was overgrown with tall weeds, leaving them with limited choices to set up their gallery. Deciding on a mostly clear field about two hundred yards southeast of town, they lined their wagons up and parked them.

Hayes ducked into the covered wagon carrying most of his supplies so he could find the ledger with the inventory list requested by Marshal Borden while Aldus unhitched the horses and took them back into town. There was a stable on Rose Street, which was the first one to cross Main. All of the horses were tired, wet, and very happy to be inside once arrangements for them were made. Aldus paid for two days in advance before stepping out into rain that showed no sign of letting up.

So far, Aldus had spotted two general stores and one feed store in town. What caught his interest, however, was the hotel and saloon that were built almost directly across from each other on Main Street. He meant to go to the hotel first to secure a place for them to stay, but walking for so long in the pouring rain had drenched Aldus to the bone. Not only were his stitches a source of discomfort, but every one of his joints felt like rusty parts in an aging machine. The saloon was closer than the hotel, but even if it had been on the other side of town, he'd have gone there first.

The place was called the Prospector. It was longer than it was wide, which wasn't saying much since its single floor was about the same size as the stable Aldus had just visited. The bar was cobbled from spare lumber, most of which looked to have been old doors. Instead of a mirror or a painting behind the bar, there was only an old pickax and a few dented tin pans. More than likely, there was a story behind those items, but Aldus didn't want to hear it when he stepped up and slapped his hand upon one of the salvaged doors to catch the attention of the barkeep.

"What can I get for you, friend?" the barkeep asked.

Aldus let out a tired laugh. "Friend? That sure beats the reception I got from the lawmen around here."

The barkeep stood just under average height with long, stringy hair growing down to a set of bony shoulders. His smile was genuine enough, however, to offset his somewhat ghoulish looks. "Marshal Borden's probably just jealous that you got more of his work done today than he did."

"You saw what happened out on the street?"

"We sure did," the barkeep replied. "Damn shame about what happened to Lefty."

"Who's Lefty?"

The barkeep's expression darkened considerably as he said, "William Leftinson. He's the deputy who was gunned down."

Aldus lowered his head. "He was a deputy?"

"Yep. Fine man, too."

"Sorry about what happened."

Although still saddened by the news, the barkeep put on a good front and placed a glass in front of Aldus. "You sure did take off running after that other one. None of us even saw that fella until you flushed him out!" The others the barkeep referred to were an assortment of men scattered at the bar and a few of the five small tables in the saloon. Most of them were positioned as close as they could get to a potbellied stove against the back wall. They all nodded in agreement to what the barkeep had said. A few even raised their drinks in a silent toast.

"I just got angry, is all," Aldus said. "Come to think of it, there was angry and a liberal dose of stupid to go along with it."

"Whichever it was, it was a sight to see. Let me set you up with a drink. How about a whiskey to warm you up? You look like you been dragged through a river."

"And you look like my new favorite man in town."

"Don't get too happy, friend. After that first drink, you'll pay just like everyone else."

"Wouldn't have it any other way. I'm Aldus Bricker."

"Folks around here call me Swede. What brings you to town?"

"I work for a gunsmith who just got to Seedley. We travel all throughout these parts, but never got around to coming here until today."

"Picked a bad day to get here," Swede said. "Gunsmith, you say?"

"That's right. We sell firearms, repair them, you name it." Just then, the front door opened to allow a sopping-wet figure hurry inside. "Speak of the devil," Aldus said. "Here's my partner now."

"Any friend of Aldus is a friend of mine!" Swede declared. "He gets a free drink as well. Step up and enjoy."

Despite the water trickling down his face, Hayes smiled as he asked, "Another boxing enthusiast?"

"Just someone who looks out his window," Aldus replied. "You on your way to see the marshal?"

The salesman stood beside Aldus at the bar. He held his coat closed over a thick ledger, which he revealed when he removed the book and set it down. "After being treated like common criminals when we were clearly caught in that cross fire, I'm in no hurry to appease that man."

"Hear, hear!" Aldus said.

As soon as he got his drink, Hayes mirrored that sentiment before downing the whiskey.

As soon as he set down his empty glass, Aldus held it out for Swede to fill it. "How'd you know where to find me?" he asked Hayes.

"I didn't," Hayes told him. "I just couldn't find where you hid that bottle you keep in the other wagon and came over here to warm up. Did you get us a place to stay?"

"There's a hotel across the street," Aldus replied. "Looks as good as any other."

"Did you get the rooms?"

"Nope. Figured I'd come in here first."

"Just as well," Hayes said. After a pause, he added, "So . . . it seems Jack Grable's friend isn't very popular around here with the law."

"Who?"

"Cal Overland," Hayes said in an impatient tone. "The man Jack Grable told me to mention to get that gun business that flows from this town. If he's somehow wrapped up in that shooting, then dropping his name to that marshal when I first arrived was about the worst thing I could've done."

"If it was so bad, I don't think that marshal is the sort of man who'd hesitate to put you behind bars. He was just tryin' to scare us."

"You sure about that?"

"Yeah," Aldus said. "I've been on both ends of that evil eye he was givin' to both of us. Them lawmen were sizing us up and trying to see if we'd crack."

"Another thing you learned as a fighter?"

"You'd be surprised how much you can learn when you're thrown to the wolves. That marshal talked to me like some of the men from them docks in New York. They bark and snarl at you just to see if you're all talk. If you stand your ground and don't flinch, they'll either respect you or back down. Sometimes, if you're lucky, they'll do both."

Hayes lowered his voice, but was unable to hide his glee when he said, "It seems to me that you accomplished both in that office. Very impressive."

"What's gonna be impressive is if you can muster up enough sales to pay for our hotel rooms and a few meals."

"Why do you say that?" Hayes asked as the glimmer in his eye was snuffed out quicker than a candle in a windstorm.

"Because it seems there's some trouble in this town that's gotten bad enough for lawmen to be shot down in the street. Tell me you don't think that'll make people skittish to approach us."

"It might," Hayes sighed. "Or it might make them want to arm themselves for protection. For the moment, I'd rather put that unpleasantness aside."

"Sorry to spoil it," Aldus said.

"We should still be able to make some money with the shooting gallery. That's always a popular attraction."

"Sure. For a day or two. It's not enough to make up for what we lost."

"Maybe we should still visit Cal Overland," Hayes said. "There's always a chance that this matter is just some unfortunate event that has nothing to do with what brought us here. Mr. Overland sounds like an influential man around here. There's no reason to assume he's wrapped up in anything suspicious."

"A steady flow of men coming from a flea speck of a town looking for guns?" Aldus mused. "Nothing suspicious about that."

"Eh, just finish your drink."

It rained for the rest of the day and well into the night. That was fine with Aldus since it meant nothing much could be done to set up the shooting gallery. Even though he'd gone through those motions several dozen times, it was still a grueling and tedious process that never failed to put a kink in his back and a whole lot of splinters into his hands. Since he didn't have to worry about that tonight, all that remained was to run across the street and rent two rooms in the Main Rose Hotel. Aldus didn't have much trouble reading the name of the place on the sign out front because they were the same words on the street signs nearby. For once, someone else's laziness actually made something a little easier.

Despite the simple name, the Main Rose had clean rooms that included a bath if more than one night was purchased. Aldus took his bath as soon as he'd brought his things into his room. The tub was in a room at the back of the place with a window that offered a prime view of the outhouse. The warm water felt so good that Aldus didn't even mind it when the occasional guest would walk through to go outside and relieve himself.

His wound stung as soon as it hit the soapy water. Aldus gritted his teeth and wrangled the pain down like an unruly animal that had to be shown its place. Back in his fighting days, he'd learned to embrace pain to a certain degree. He didn't relish it like some of the other men. Those fighters were the crazy ones, wild-eyed and full of rage. Men like that were dangerous in the first few rounds because they fully expected to get hurt and didn't flinch no matter how many good punches smashed into them. The way to beat them was to weather the storm at the beginning of the fight, keep chopping away at them, and wait for the damage to pile up. At a certain point, it didn't matter how tough a man was. If he couldn't take a breath or lift his hands, he couldn't defend himself. And if those men couldn't defend themselves, it wouldn't be long before they were out cold. Of course, those were the same fighters who saw their career as a string of personal vendettas. They didn't take to losing very well and might very well seek out the one who'd dropped them the night before.

Aldus thought about mad dogs like that every time he felt a sharp pain jab all the way through his body. He winced and let his mind wander as the pain soaked through him now. Unlike those fighters with the wild eyes, Aldus had learned to live with his discomforts. If it wasn't feared or avoided, pain could serve a lot of purposes. It could keep him going, clear the weariness from his body, and sharpen his focus. Pain could push a man where simple desire could not. And if a man lived with his pain for long enough, it would fade for a while. The sharp pain Aldus felt from his stitches faded now, allowing him to loosen his grip on the edge of the tub and settle back down into the water.

Aldus's mind drifted in another direction as his muscles soaked up all the heat from the water. The soap he'd been given had a sour, bitter smell that stuck in his nose but was a lot better than the dirty sweat that had caked onto him beneath his wet shirt. He closed his eyes, imagining what he might say to Bethany when he finally saw her face, as someone stepped onto the boards just outside the door that led outside.

Hinges squeaked as the door was pushed open and the pungent smell from the outhouse drifted through the room. Focusing on the smell of the soapy water, Aldus waited for whoever it was to make their way through the room. After taking a few steps, the person stopped. Since the tub was barely large enough for Aldus to sit in with his legs tucked close to his body, the whole thing shook when it was kicked.

Aldus opened his eyes to find a man looming over him. He was dressed in a long coat that was dripping from the rain. The hat he wore was the same that could have been found on any number of cowboys, but even more distinctive was the burlap sack covering his face. There were two crude squares cut out and a pair of dark green eyes glared defiantly through them at the world as if they despised it and everything in it.

"You'd be Aldus Bricker?" the man asked.

"I am."

The other man lunged with one hand extended, which Aldus reflexively batted aside. If he hadn't already been contained within the tub, Aldus could have done more. As it was, he managed to climb partway up while taking a swipe at the masked man with a right cross. The punch connected, snapping the man's head to one side. When he turned back to Aldus, the dark green eyes behind the mask burned with a familiar fire. He was one of the crazy ones.

Aldus tried to get up, but his bare feet skidded against the slick bottom of the tub and he dropped down to splash into the water. The other man leaned over to try and get a grip on him, growling like a dog as he stepped around to the end of the tub where Aldus's head had been resting. Rather than take another swing at him, Aldus grabbed the sloppy remains of his soap and reached up to slap it against the masked man's face. Although most of the water was absorbed by the burlap, some of it made it into the eyeholes because the man let out a grunt and straightened up.

Taking that moment to get his feet beneath him, Aldus stood up and stepped halfway out of the tub. With one foot still in the water, he grabbed the masked man's coat and twisted around to try and leverage him over the side and into the tub. But the masked man wasn't about to go down so easily. Just like those mad-dog fighters, he ignored the sting of his knee pounding against the tub as he stretched out his left hand to keep himself from falling in. From there, he pushed off and landed awkwardly with both feet on the floor at the foot of the tub.

Rather than be dragged along with him, Aldus let go of the masked man. He'd spotted the gun belt under the man's coat, so he circled around to get a hold of him before he could draw.

The masked man was having none of it. He swiped a left jab across Aldus's face to keep him away. Aldus shook it off as he snapped a sharp punch into the man's stomach. If not for the tub getting in his way, Aldus would have laid the masked man out with another punch. Instead, the man was able to back away and draw the gun from his holster.

"Get out and leave us be!" the masked man said.

Aldus quickly realized the man wasn't talking to him. There were two others looking in from the next room.

Both of them nodded and raised their hands while backing away.

Shifting his focus at Aldus, the masked man pointed the pistol at him and thumbed back the hammer. His eyes, reddened by the soap, now reflected what was surely a wicked-looking smile hidden beneath the burlap.

"Who are you?" Aldus asked.

"That don't matter. I know who you are, though."

"What do you want?"

The masked man stalked forward, keeping the gun at chest level. When he was close enough, he balled up his left fist and drove it straight into Aldus's nose. It would have been a lie if Aldus had told anyone that a punch in the nose didn't hurt. Then again, after having his nose broken a few times, it hurt a bit less than it did for most folks. That, coupled with the fact that he'd spent a good portion of his years in New York City being tenderized like a cut of beef, meant he was able to glare right back at the masked man after the punch had landed.

Perhaps rattled by the way that Aldus's knees hadn't buckled, the masked man pulled his fist back and punched him again. This was a wild blow that landed more on Aldus's cheek than his jaw. When he felt blood trickle against his tongue, Aldus spat it into the other man's face.

The pistol was brought up and its barrel pressed against Aldus's forehead. "What did you tell to the marshal?" the masked man asked.

"He asked me about what took place outside his office, so I told him."

"What happened to the man you chased?"

"He's locked up in a cage."

"He been charged?"

"How should I know?" Aldus asked. "If you're so curious, why don't you go have a talk with the marshal yourself?"

Aldus expected to be hit after that and he wasn't disappointed. The punch was delivered to his body and thumped against muscles that were tensed to form a solid wall.

"You're gonna go back to the marshal," the masked man said, "and you're gonna tell him the man you chased was innocent."

"He shot at me and my partner. Plenty of folks saw it."

"He was startled by the shooting in the street and was defending himself."

"My word doesn't hold any water with the marshal," Aldus explained. "I was barely able to get out of there without being tossed into a cell myself."

"Then you shouldn't have any problem convincing him you made a mistake the first time you talked to him. Just tell him the man you chased didn't do no harm to nobody."

Aldus nodded. "All right. I'll tell him."

The masked man started to step away, but quickly jammed the pistol barrel even harder against Aldus's head. "You'll do exactly what I tell you! Otherwise, I'll come back and blow your brains onto the closest wall I can find. And the same goes for that dandy friend of yours. You step out of line and you both die. Got it?"

"Yeah."

The masked man stared at him for a few more seconds, probably waiting to see a hint of fear in the man before him. The gun, the way he stood, the crude mask, they were all meant to inspire fear. But Aldus had stood in front of scarier men than this one, even considering the gun.

Although the first two people to look into the bathroom had been frightened away, there were plenty more stirring within the hotel. The masked man lowered his gun, placed a hand flat on Aldus's chest, and shoved him

backward. Aldus swore as his wet, soapy feet skidded
against the floor and slipped out from under him. The
masked man found that to be mighty amusing and made
sure Aldus could hear him laughing as he pulled open
the back door and walked outside.

"Are . . . you all right?" asked the little old man who'd
been bringing hot water every so often to keep the bath
warm.

"I'll be fine."

"You're bleeding."

Aldus touched a few spots on his face and then raised
his arm to test his stitches. They seemed to be holding,
but he was definitely bleeding from his side as well as his
nose. He climbed to his feet, feeling more wounded in
his pride after being knocked down than anything else.
There were questions he wanted to ask and precautions
he needed to take. But first, he had to put on some pants.

Chapter 13

It had been a long time since Aldus had made a habit of wearing a holster when he wasn't on the trail. Carrying a gun while driving a wagon was expected and oftentimes necessary. There were snakes, robbers, coyotes, or any number of other threats that could sneak up on a man when he was miles away from the civilized world. Aldus had no qualms with wearing his gun then, but he never saw much use in wearing it in town. He worked for a gunsmith, after all. If there was trouble, he could just grab a pistol from the inventory and some shells from one of the cabinets on the side of Hayes's wagon. There was no need to wear a holster.

That had changed.

As soon as he put some clothes on, Aldus had gone to his room to fetch his holster. The Schofield hung at his side as he walked back to the lobby to find the old man he'd approached earlier about fixing a bath. Upon seeing him, the spindly old fellow with hair that looked more like cobwebs that had been stuck to his wrinkled scalp laughed nervously and said, "Good to see you're decent again."

"Who was that?"

"You mean the man with the sack on his head?"

Aldus walked forward with his fists clenched. Even though he didn't lift a hand to threaten the smaller man, the old fellow cringed as if he'd already been hit. "Of course I mean the one with the sack on his head," Aldus snarled. "Who was he?"

"I don't know! I couldn't see. You know ... on account of ... the sack."

"Did you fetch the law?"

The old-timer shook his head. "N-no."

"Why not? When some masked intruder storms in waving a gun at one of your guests, shouldn't you find the marshal?"

"I ... I ..."

"Don't you have a weapon around here?" Aldus asked as he kicked the front desk, which was less than two feet away from the stool where the old man was sitting. "What about a shotgun? Hell, even a club would have done some good since you or anyone else had all the time in the world to get behind the man who was knocking me around while his back was to a door!"

"Sir!" someone shouted from nearby.

Aldus turned around to find the tall man who'd taken his money for the rooms standing near the front desk. He had a scattergun in his hands and was currently staring at Aldus over its barrel.

"There, now," Aldus said. "I see someone's got a weapon. Too bad he don't know who to point it at!"

"My name's Danny Mclean and I own this establishment," the man with the shotgun said. "I understand you're upset, but threatening people won't make things any better."

"I haven't even begun to threaten yet." Once he took a breath, Aldus looked around to see if anyone else had a gun pointed at him. Instead, he saw two other folks huddled nearby. They, along with the old man directly in front of him, had stark terror in their eyes. Aldus stepped back and held his hands out to show they were empty.

"I'm sorry about what happened," Mclean continued. "Let's avoid any further trouble."

"Sounds fine by me," Aldus said.

"Step away from him."

Aldus nodded and moved all the way back to the opposite wall. When the old man pulled himself up off his stool, Aldus looked at him and said, "Sorry about that. I was just worked up after ... well ... you know."

"Yes, I do know," the old man replied. "I'm sorry I didn't step in on your behalf. I should have—"

"He shouldn't have done anything of the sort," Mclean interrupted. "He's not the law."

"All right, then," Aldus said as he looked at the tall, spindly fellow with the shotgun. "You're the one who's armed. Where were you when I was being attacked in your establishment?"

"Can we talk in a civilized manner?"

"Yeah."

Mclean lowered the shotgun slowly. Every muscle in his arms was tensed, however, in case the weapon needed to be lifted again. Aldus stayed still, making certain not to give the other man a reason to defend himself. Once the shotgun was down, Mclean walked over to a tall, narrow door that looked as if it had been shaped especially to fit him. There was a sign on the door that Aldus couldn't read.

"Would you like to come into my office for a moment?" Mclean asked.

Suddenly feeling embarrassed by his outburst, Aldus stepped into a small room with bookshelves on two walls. There was a little rolltop desk in the far corner and a small circular table beside it with a silver teapot and three cups on saucers.

"Please, have a seat," Mclean said. Once Aldus had lowered himself onto one of the chairs, Mclean shut the door and walked over to the little round table. "Would you like some tea? I find it does wonders to calm the nerves."

"Sure. I'll take some sugar in it, too."

"Excellent. You didn't sign the register, so I don't believe I caught your name."

"Aldus Bricker. We met when I paid for the rooms."

"Ah yes." Having poured two cups of tea and stirred sugar into them both, Mclean handed one cup over to Aldus before sitting down.

The tea was lukewarm and could have used another scoop of sugar, but it did help quiet the excited jangling in Aldus's ears. After taking another sip, he said, "We're being real civilized, so do you think you can tell me who that gunman was who stormed into your place? And don't tell me you don't know on account of the mask."

"There have been some ... unsettling events transpire in this town, but I assure you they usually don't spill over to include innocent gentlemen such as yourself."

"Usually only the guilty men are dragged from their baths and beaten?"

"Not in so many words," Mclean replied with a nervous chuckle. "But usually the incidents only involve known troublemakers."

"What incidents?"

Mclean sipped his tea. "There have been altercations at the marshal's office. Men were taken out of his custody after being caught ... forcing themselves upon women. It was two local young men and they were put on trial only to be released with a fine. Another young girl went missing. This one was in another town, but those same two young men were found to be the cause of it. There was another trial scheduled ..."

"Let me guess," Aldus said. "Them boys never made it to trial."

"That's right. They were taken from the marshal's own cell."

"And lynched."

Mclean nodded slowly, averting his eyes as if he was ashamed those words even had to be spoken in his establishment. "So you know about them?"

"I've heard enough about vigilantes to know how they work," Aldus said. "Truth be told, there's been plenty of times when I could understand what they were doing. Sometimes the law just don't seem to get it right."

"No, it doesn't. There have been other incidents over the years. Most of the time, Marshal Borden does his job well enough. Other times, he's not able to prevent bloodshed. As I mentioned, most of the incidents happen outside town. More often than not, they happen to men who . . . quite honestly . . . have it coming. The marshal enforces the letter of the law, but those vigilantes have kept Seedley safe."

"Why tell me all of this?" Aldus asked. "Not that I don't appreciate hearing it, by the way."

"I thought I should tell you before you go around town trying to find the same answers elsewhere. As you've seen, these men do not want to be known and they do not take kindly to it when folks poke into their affairs."

"What happened here was as much my affair as it was his."

"I agree," Mclean was quick to say. "But I wanted to warn you that there is more to be concerned about than this one fellow. Most of the others aren't so brash. It very well could be that they will see this instance as one man stepping out of line and are dealing with him as we speak."

Aldus studied the man in front of him and said, "You really take comfort from that?"

"Of course, you're right. There's no comfort to be had in hearing that. I suppose what I really wanted to tell you ..." Mclean shifted in his seat as if he'd suddenly grown too big for his own skin. He wasn't quite able to meet Aldus's eyes, and his lips moved as if he was taking a dry run at saying the words he meant to spit out.

Thinking about the times when he'd been asked to throw a fight, Aldus said, "You want me to do what that man in the mask asked me to do."

"I actually didn't hear everything," Mclean said.

"But, whatever he said, you want me to do it."

"It could make things go a lot smoother. Did he ask you to do anything dangerous?"

"No."

"Then you might want to consider it. These men," Mclean said urgently. "They are well armed and will go to great lengths to get their way."

"Sounds like something the marshal ought to handle."

"It is, and Marshal Borden has taken many steps to try and get a grip on the situation. But when it comes to regular people, people like you and me, it's better and safer to not make any waves."

Aldus stood up. "Is that all you wanted to tell me?"

Standing up and setting his tea down, Mclean said, "I wanted you to know what you're dealing with. There are several of these men. They're armed and have already proven to be formidable."

"Sounds to me like they're runnin' this town."

Mclean seemed genuinely offended by that. "We are not being run by those men! They step in and have solved several potentially terrible problems in a way that's discouraged more blood from being spilled."

"Make up your mind, sir," Aldus said. "You can't be against them and for them at the same time."

"I suppose they've done more harm than good."

"Suppose, huh?" Aldus handed over his teacup. "Not from where I'm standing. Anything else you want to tell me?"

Once again averting his eyes, Mclean shook his head. "No."

"I hope you'll at least refund a portion of my room to make up for the bath."

At the front desk, Mclean got some of the money Aldus had paid and handed it over. "Do you still wish to stay at the Main Rose?"

"From what you told me, it probably wouldn't make a difference if we moved to another hotel. At least this place has comfortable beds."

Although Mclean smiled and nodded, he couldn't hide the disappointment in his eyes.

The rain had eased up a bit but was still dripping from the clouds that kept Aldus from seeing any stars in the sky as he stepped outside. He went straight across to the Prospector Saloon. At this time of night, the place was more alive than the rest of the town had felt all day long. It wasn't filled to capacity, but the men inside told their jokes in loud voices and the women laughed loudly at every last one of them. Aldus had learned to ignore loud voices since most of the ones he'd heard in New York City rarely said anything worth hearing. One voice caught his attention, however, directing him to a poker game being played at a table closest to the bar.

"All right, gentlemen!" Hayes declared. "How about we make things interesting? Antes are double and jacks or better to open."

He sat at a table with four other men, two of whom had working girls on their laps. Hayes didn't have a companion yet, but he seemed a few drinks away from remedying that situation. Aldus approached and motioned for him to step away.

"This here is my friend Aldus Bricker!" Hayes announced. "He used to be a fighter in New York City. You'll be able to hear all of his gruesome stories of survival in the ring when you pay us a visit at my shooting gallery, which will be constructed as soon as the weather permits."

Aldus responded to the couple of drunken cheers he got with a lazy wave. Leaning in close to the salesman, he whispered, "Step outside so I can have a word?"

"I'm in the middle of a game."

"It's important."

"What's more important than this game?" Hayes asked.

"Being in the sights of a bunch of vigilantes."

Hayes's eyes snapped back and forth to assess the other players. Judging by their faces and thanks to the efforts of the girls, they hadn't heard enough of that to become alarmed. "I fold," Hayes said while standing up. "But I won't be long, so save my seat."

A few of the players grunted that they'd heard him as Hayes staggered in a very familiar way from the table. Once they were outside, the salesman shed his drunken demeanor as if he were flipping a switch. "What did you say about vigilantes?"

"Are you still pretending to be drunk when playing cards?" Aldus scoffed. "Doesn't that act ever get old?"

"Not when it helps me slip past their guard. Now, what's this about vigilantes?"

"I was having a bath when a fella wearing a sack over his head stormed in to toss me around a bit."

"Good Lord. Are you all right?"

"My stitches are aching, but I'm fine," Aldus said. "I would have knocked him into next week if he hadn't pulled a gun on me."

"Why would anyone do that?"

"He told me to march over to the marshal's office and tell him I chased down the wrong man."

"You mean the one who was shooting at you?" Hayes asked. "The one who's locked up?"

"I'm guessing so."

Hayes glanced in the direction of the marshal's office, but there wasn't much to see down the darkened street. His mind moved like an intricate machine as he sifted through countless angles and possibilities. Finally he said, "That man in jail must be a friend of the man who barged in on you."

"Really?" Aldus chided. "I hadn't thought of that! Now I see why you run the show, with you being so smart and all."

"All right, so maybe I did have a few drinks to sell my little act. How do you know they're vigilantes?"

Aldus quickly spelled out what Danny Mclean had told him in his office at the Main Rose. When he was done, Hayes was completely sobered up.

Running a hand over his head, Hayes said, "That explains why men from this town would want so many guns. They're supplying a group of vigilantes. I should have guessed as much."

"How could you have guessed that?"

"Maybe not that exact thing, but I should have seen something was wrong. And I should never have insisted on coming here." Suddenly Hayes needed to walk forward so he could lean against one of the hitch rails in front of the saloon.

Standing beside him, Aldus nodded to a man and woman passing by on their way down the street. To his unsteady friend, he said, "There was no way you could have known about any of this. Besides, I agreed to it, too. I ain't just some dog that follows you around everywhere. We both look out for our interests."

"I know, but I'm the one who's been in this business the longest, and if there's one thing I know, it's that you should always be wary when you're selling guns. I usually do keep my eyes open, but after the robbery and losing all of our profits, I guess I just let my guard down."

"It doesn't do us any good to assign blame," Aldus said. "What we need is to figure out what comes next."

"As appealing as it may sound to just load up the wagons and put this town behind us, I think that would be a mistake."

Aldus's eyes narrowed. "I wasn't thinking of running away."

"It's not running," Hayes insisted. "It's just getting away from a mess before it becomes an even bigger mess. Besides, our odds of making it out of here without the marshal or one of his deputies spotting us are fairly slim. I've seen one of them walking up and down Main Street at various times while I was at the saloon. Marshal Borden has a pretty tight grip on this town."

"Not tight enough to keep that masked fella from slipping into the hotel. Have you taken that ledger over to the marshal yet?"

"I walked down there not too long ago, but there was just a deputy available and he told me to come back in the morning."

"Then that's what we'll do," Aldus said. "And while we're there, I'll tell the marshal about the man who paid me a visit."

"Do you intend to do what he wanted?" Hayes asked.

Speaking through gritted teeth, Aldus replied, "I ain't about to jump just because someone shouts at me."

"He had a gun," Hayes reminded him. "If what that man at the hotel said was correct, there's a lot of these men about and they all have guns. This isn't the first time I've ever crossed paths with vigilantes, Aldus. They're dangerous men. In fact, the only thing separating them from a bloodthirsty outlaw is the speech they give before they kill a man. Many of them are even tolerated by the law to some degree."

"I don't think Marshal Borden tolerates these men to any degree. I do think there's more that he could tell us, though."

"We don't need to hear much," Hayes said. "All we have to do is find a way to get out of this town clean and without anyone coming after us."

"If we want to be able to leave quickly, we might wanna reconsider setting up the gallery."

"I suppose you're right."

"Then we have our talk with the marshal tomorrow morning," Aldus said. "Skinning out of town in the dead of night looks suspicious and is cowardly besides."

"Do me a favor," Hayes said earnestly. "Just don't go off half-cocked. When you're dealing with the law, things can go astray very quickly. Vigilantes wear masks for a reason. We don't even know which one of these locals could be one of them."

Aldus nodded and patted the salesman on the shoulder. "Can you do me a favor?"

"Name it."

"Go back in there and try to win us some traveling money."

Chapter 14

Since he didn't need to set up the shooting gallery after all, Aldus thought it would be nice to sleep a bit later than normal. Unfortunately his eyes were on their own schedule and they snapped open at the same time they always did. Aldus tried to overrule them by rolling over in his bed and trying to get a few more minutes of sleep, but it was no use. His blood was flowing and his stomach was growling. The day had started without him.

He pulled on his clothes and took a look outside. At least the rain had stopped, but judging by the large puddles on the street and the rivulets running down his window, it hadn't stopped very long ago. Aldus slipped into his boots and almost left his room without buckling the gun belt around his waist. Wearing the gun was a reminder of the events that had happened since they'd arrived in town. And just in case those things slipped his mind again, there was always the ache in his face and side to bring them right back.

Not having to assemble the gallery was peculiar enough. Finding Hayes sitting at breakfast as if he'd been there for hours made Aldus wonder if he was having a strange dream. Hayes was known to get up when he had to, but he was usually more inclined to spend late nights in saloons gambling and drinking in what he referred to as drumming up business and spreading the word of his arrival among the locals. Today, the salesman sat at one of the few tables in the hotel's dining room with a plate of eggs and a cup of coffee in front of him.

"Care to join me, Aldus?" he asked.

"You seem chipper," Aldus said. "What's wrong?"

"Just anxious to see today through. Have you eaten yet?"

"No, but I'll have some oatmeal."

Aldus ate quickly as Hayes flipped through the ledger he'd brought with him to make sure everything was accurate and up to date. When they finished, both men headed straight down Main Street to the marshal's office. Two of the deputies stood outside the door. One held a shotgun and the other carried a Winchester rifle. Both glared at Aldus and Hayes, their grips tightening around their weapons when the two men tried to approach the door they guarded.

"What's your business?" the shotgunner asked.

Hayes held up the ledger. "The marshal asked me to bring this by so I could register my weapons."

"Stay here while I check if he wants to see you." The deputy stepped inside, leaving the man with the Winchester on the porch. Before things could get too uncomfortable, the deputy with the shotgun opened the door and said, "Come on in."

Marshal Borden sat behind his desk wearing a smile that shone through the thick whiskers on his upper lip. "About time you two showed up. I was about to send some of my boys to collect you."

Putting on a grin to match the marshal's, Hayes said, "I got a little sidetracked, Marshal. My apologies. I'm sure you know how that goes sometimes. The important thing is that I brought you that list of guns I promised." He set the ledger upon the lawman's desk.

Aldus, on the other hand, wasn't feeling so amicable. "You could have sent someone to my hotel last night," he said. "Then you might have caught the man who came to attack me."

The marshal's face shifted back to the more familiar scowl he'd had the day before. "What did you say?"

"You heard me. Someone stormed into the Main Rose last night, dragged me out of my bath, and threatened me with a gun. For a town that has more deputies than streets, I would have expected things to be a whole lot safer."

"I didn't hear anything about this," Borden said. "Why didn't someone tell me?"

"I'm telling you right now. Besides, it wouldn't have done any good since the man came and went without anyone but me lifting a finger to stop him. Why is it that I see deputies walking your streets in front of the saloon, but they seem to miss an armed man with a burlap sack over his head?"

"This was last night?" Borden asked.

"That's right."

"And he wore a burlap sack?"

"Yeah," Aldus said. "I got a real good look when he was sticking a gun in my face."

The marshal opened one of his drawers and removed something. "Was the sack anything like this one?" he asked while slapping an empty sack onto the desk.

Aldus reached out to pick up the mask and have a look. It was burlap and there were two square holes cut for the wearer's eyes. "Just like this," he said. When he held it even closer, Aldus even found blood spattered onto the burlap in the approximate spot where he'd spat into his attacker's face. "In fact, this could be the very one."

"And what about this?" Borden asked as he removed another item from his desk. This time, he placed a pistol in front of Aldus. "You recall that from when you were attacked?"

Despite the fact that he'd worked with Hayes for a while, Aldus wasn't as good at spotting firearms as his employer. At the time when the man had pointed a gun at him, he'd been more concerned with staying on his feet so he could defend himself. Between that and the blood rushing through his head, all he'd seen for certain was that the gun was a .45 Peacemaker. Aldus nodded and said, "That looks like it. I couldn't say for certain if that's the same one that was pointed at me, though."

"I'd bet everything I made this year that it was," Borden said. "Especially since the man who wore that there sack over his head is stewing in one of my cells right now."

"You caught him?" Hayes asked.

The marshal was already flipping through the salesman's register when he nodded. "Found him late last night, thanks to me having enough deputies to patrol my streets at all hours. Mark spotted this one skulking about and we went out to snag him."

"Congratulations!" Hayes exclaimed.

"Can I get a look at him?" Aldus asked.

Looking up from the ledger, Borden asked, "You don't believe we got him?"

"That man nearly killed me," Aldus said. "If he's behind bars, I want to get a look at him."

For a few moments, Borden merely stared up at him. Then he shrugged and nodded toward one of his men. "Go ahead and show him the prisoner. Couldn't hurt to have one more witness identify him."

Aldus followed the deputy into the next room, which was cut in half by a row of bars built into the floor and ceiling. The space behind the bars was halved again into two separate cells. One of them contained the man whom Aldus had knocked out when he'd first arrived in town. He lay on a cot in the corner of his cage, looked up at Aldus, and spat a tired profanity at him.

The man in the second cell was sitting on his cot with his back against the wall and his legs stretched out in front of him. He had cloudy blue eyes and a face that looked as if it had been trampled by a stampede of wild horses. A knot of thick bloated flesh on his forehead was stretched almost to the point of bursting. Unlike the dark purple bruises covering most of his face, the lump above his eye was bloodred. He couldn't hold Aldus's stare for more than a second or two before he shifted on the cot to put his back toward the front of the cell.

Walking into the main room, Aldus asked, "You sure that's him?"

"Course I am," Borden said. "My deputy caught him red-handed."

"Doing what?"

"Someone took a shot at Mark. He's the one who stitched you up. I helped drag him in myself and he was wearing that burlap sack while carrying that gun."

Looking down at the sack and gun that were still on the marshal's desk, Aldus said, "He just seems different."

"They all seem different when they're behind bars. Kind of like a dog once it's been tamed."

"I'd hate to see the wrong man get blamed for something."

Borden put the ledger down, stood up, and placed his hands on his desk. "Why don't you leave the speculating to those whose job is to decide who's guilty and who's innocent? Besides, there are men who deserve to be behind bars other than the ones who come after you."

"I've heard," Aldus replied. "It seems there are plenty of masked men running around this town."

"You have, have you?"

Stepping closer to the desk as if he were breaking up a fight, Hayes said, "Come, now, gentlemen. It's been a rough day or two and I'm sure we're all on edge. We're all just trying to do the right thing, after all."

"The marshal says that man in there is the one who came after me," Aldus said. "Shouldn't he be interested if I say he might not be the one? I was the one who should be able to tell you better than anyone else."

"The man was wearing a mask," Borden pointed out.

"He also fought like a wild man. That one in there is more like a whipped mule."

"Like I told you. Men tend to lose their fire when they land in a cage. Besides, he confessed."

"He did?" Hayes asked. Turning to Aldus, he added, "Well, there you go! That changes things."

Aldus looked around at all the lawmen in the room who were, at the moment, watching him carefully. Ignoring their cautious glares, he looked toward the jail cells and then back down to the mask and gun lying on the desk in front of him. "I hit him a few times when we tussled," Aldus said as the fight played itself through in his mind. "But it wasn't enough to make him look the way he does now."

"He was wearing a mask," the marshal said in an angry growl. "There's no telling what he looked like under there. You're a professional fighter. You could have easily hit him hard enough to get one of his eyes to swell shut."

"That man's eyes are blue. When he came at me at the

hotel, I could see both eyes beneath the mask and they were green."

Suddenly the marshal's demeanor lightened and he lowered himself back down onto his chair. "Come, now, Brick. You can't stand there and tell me you remember every last punch you give a man during a fistfight or what color his eyes were when they were partly covered by a mask. I've talked to other fighters and they say it all runs together after a while. I've been in my share of scrapes and even I could tell you that much is true."

"And what about them bruises?" Aldus asked.

"More marks from your scuffle at the hotel," Borden quickly replied.

"They're fresher than that."

"Can you honestly tell me you know that?"

"Yeah. I can. If there's one thing I know about, it's wounds a man gets after getting his face pounded. I've seen more shades of bruises than colors a poet's seen in a sunset, and them that are on his face weren't made very long ago. Did you or your men rough him up?"

Having flipped to the end of the ledger, Marshal Borden closed the book and stood up again. This time, he balled up a fist and slammed it down on top of the leather-bound volume. "If me or my men had to do more than ask politely to get an armed man into a jail cell, that's no business of yours! And if you want to stand there and accuse me of beating an innocent man, then you and I will have another fight on our hands."

"There's no need for that," Hayes said. "I'm certain my friend here is just trying to share his expertise with you because it may be of some use in your investigation."

"Investigation's over," Borden said without taking his eyes off Aldus. "He confessed to the crime and I got no reason not to believe him. There's a dozen ways someone could be mistaken, especially when they're talking about something that happened as quick as you said you were attacked. Even if he wasn't the man who took a swing at you, he still fired on one of my men.

"Besides," Borden added, "innocent men don't generally wear masks. From that remark you made earlier, it seems you've heard a thing or two about the vigilantes around here. They all wear those same sacks over their heads because they're cowards who don't want their faces to be seen. Even if the man in that cell isn't the one who took a swing at you, he's still wanted for plenty of other things. First among them is murder. The very same murder that you witnessed when you first rode into town."

"He confessed to that, too?" Hayes asked.

"He did. Gunned down my deputy like a dog in the street with this very gun," Borden said while placing a hand on the Peacemaker. "So you see, Brick, there's more on my plate than you getting pulled from a bathtub. In fact, now's a real good time for the two of you to tell me all about those men who rode into Cedar Rapids to buy guns and ammunition."

"Are you gonna mess our faces up, too, if we don't tell you what you need to hear?" Aldus asked.

"The reason I ask is the ordinances I've put into place to try and ease some of the violence around here. I started out trying to prevent guns from being carried in Seedley at all, but that caused more ruckus than it was worth. So I took to registering everyone's guns so people would know someone is at least keeping track of what's out there, and if they didn't register them, I had a legal right to take the guns away from them, which is what I was trying to do with the first ordinance. Whenever there was a problem with these vigilantes," Borden continued, "my men and I had the legal right to round up all the guns we could."

"You should be rounding up men," Aldus said. "Not just guns."

"We didn't have many men to go after," the marshal said. "There were a few names, but nothing came of it. I can't toss men into a jail cell just because I heard their name, and trying to keep the guns out of folks' hands was the next best thing."

"From what I hear, these men are buying weapons on a fairly regular basis," Hayes said.

"Ain't much of a surprise," Paul said. He was the deputy with the large build and thick beard. "Every time those vigilantes show themselves, there's more of them."

Marshal Borden looked down at the burlap sack on his desk as if the very sight of it disgusted him. "So that brings me to my first question. Who did you come to sell guns to?"

"We were told to speak to Cal Overland," Hayes said. "That's the only name I know."

"You seem to keep pretty good records," Borden said while tapping the ledger. "Any chance you might have written down another name or two?"

"Why?" Aldus asked. "Isn't the one we gave you good enough?"

"Cal Overland owns a good portion of land in this county," the marshal told him. "Including a sizable portion of the land Seedley is built upon. Lots of folks know his name."

Aldus let his eyes wander back toward the room with the cells before he looked around at the deputies and finally settled once again on Borden. "What about the man I brought down when your deputy was shot?"

"What about him?" the marshal asked.

"Do you know his name?"

After a few silent moments, Borden replied, "His name's Frank Healey."

"Is he important around here? Important enough to send someone to force me to say whatever I had to in order to get you to turn him loose?"

Slowly, the marshal nodded. "He's the son of Niles Healey. The Healeys own a mess of property as well. Between them and the Overlands, they have most of this part of the state wrapped up. Did one of them approach you?"

"The man who attacked me at the hotel," Aldus said. "He wanted me to tell you I made a mistake in chasing him down."

"But ... there were other witnesses who saw him shoot at you."

"I told you, this man was a wild one. He wasn't exactly the kind to think clearly before tearing someone's head off. The point is that he was sent to try and get that one in there off the hook."

"Just in time for that other man you recently arrested to be put on another hook," Hayes said.

The marshal looked over to the salesman and asked, "What's that supposed to mean?"

Hayes drew a deep breath to steel himself before saying, "It means that he didn't shoot your deputy."

Every one of the lawmen leaned in as if they didn't want to miss a single word. The youngest of them asked, "How could you know that?"

"He said he shot him with that gun, right?" Hayes asked as he pointed to the pistol on the marshal's desk.

Borden nodded. "He swore to it."

"That," Hayes declared as he swept a hand over the Peacemaker, "is a forty-five Colt. The shot that brought your man down in the street when we arrived didn't come from a forty-five. It was fired from a forty-four. In fact, I'd even wager it was a forty-four Remington."

"You'd wager?"

"Actually, I'd stake my life on it."

When he saw the looks that the lawmen were giving one another, Aldus stepped in on his friend's behalf. "If there's one thing he knows about, it's guns. Just hear him out. I'm sure he can back up what he said more than enough to convince you all."

"All right," Borden said. "Convince us."

Normally Hayes would have jumped on an opportunity to play to a captive audience. In fact, when Aldus had first watched him work a crowd, he was worried that he'd agreed to assist a huckster instead of a true craftsman. From the fancy clothes he wore to the way he projected his voice, Hayes oftentimes more closely resembled an actor than a gunsmith. But, as Hayes himself had reminded Aldus, showmanship was a large part of selling anything.

When he was given his chance to speak now, however, Hayes needed a moment to collect himself before saying, "I heard the difference."

"You . . . heard it?" Borden asked.

"That's right."

"And what did you hear?"

"I heard a shot from a forty-four-caliber Remington."

Angling his head as if he were examining a strange insect, the marshal asked, "And why didn't you share this bit of information before?"

"Because," Hayes replied, "you didn't ask."

"You can honestly tell what sort of gun was fired just by the sound it makes?"

"Why do you say it like that?" When he looked around at the lawmen, Hayes couldn't find one face that seemed convinced. "Would it seem preposterous if a tracker told you he could tell how big an animal is or what breed it was just by looking at the ground?"

"I suppose not," Borden said grudgingly.

"I have been working with firearms since I was a small boy. I build them. I take them apart. I modify them. I decorate them. I create them. I make every kind of bullet you could imagine and pack the powder that fires them. If you'd like me to prove my skill, I will be most happy to do so."

Borden stared at Hayes intently. He no longer seemed amused.

"Mr. Hayes is an expert in firearms," Aldus said. "If he told you the killer fired a forty-four Remington, then that's what he fired. I can also tell you he had green eyes."

"You're just being smart with me now," Borden growled.

"The man who attacked me in the hotel had green eyes," Aldus explained. "Perhaps it's a stretch to think he's the same person who killed your deputy, but I don't think it's a very big one. At the very least, it should prove you've got the wrong man in that jail cell."

"You two men are just full of these little facts that you've held on to until the last possible second," the marshal sighed.

"I wasn't sure if I could trust you," Aldus told him. "For all I knew, it could have been one of your boys or a friend of yours who attacked me."

"Why would a lawman want to be a vigilante?" Paul asked.

"I don't know why men do half the things they do. All I know is that it pays to be careful, and that's what I was doing. But since Zeke has laid all his cards on the table, so did I."

Looking back and forth between Aldus and Hayes, Borden asked, "Is there anything else you want to tell us?"

"Just that if there's anything we can do to help you in your efforts, we will be happy to assist," Hayes said.

Aldus rolled his eyes, mildly surprised that his partner hadn't topped off the statement with a grand, theatrical bow.

Marshal Borden smiled like a cat with feathers stuck between its teeth. "Seeing as how I've been waiting a long time to have more than a few suspicions to go on before storming up to the homestead of some of this county's most powerful men, I might just take you up on that. First, there's one thing I need to check."

"Excellent. We'll just leave you to it."

"Hold on, now, Mr. Hayes," the marshal said. Those words were barely out of his mouth before both deputies stepped in to block the front door. "I can do my checking right now, if you don't mind waiting."

"No," Hayes said as he looked at the two deputies who wouldn't have moved if there was a fire in the room unless they'd gotten word from Borden. "We don't mind at all."

"Speak for yerself," Aldus grunted.

The marshal took a book from his desk that was similar in size to Hayes's ledger. He flipped through it until he found the pages he wanted and then started running his finger down several columns of words. Before long, he said, "You mentioned a forty-four Remington?"

"That's right," Hayes replied.

"That's the gun that was fired when Lefty was killed?"

"Yes, sir."

"And you'd testify to that in court?"

"I would."

"I just so happen to have a forty-four Remington marked down as belonging to Jesse Overland," Borden announced. "Cal Overland's son."

"There you go," Hayes said with a smile. "You have someone to question. Let me know how it turns out."

"Oh, you'll know how it turns out," Borden said as he stood up and put on his hat. "Because you're going with us out to the Overland spread."

Aldus felt as if someone had snuck in a quick jab to his chin. "We're what?"

"Everybody knows that Overland has plenty of men on his payroll," Borden said. "Scouts, messengers, hired hands, whatever he wants to call them. If he's one of these vigilantes, it's possible any of them could be one of them killers."

"Right," Aldus said. "And it's your job to bring killers to justice. Not ours."

"Mr. Hayes was set to meet with them about buying guns, right?"

"Not him specifically," Hayes said. "But . . ."

"But your friend in Cedar Rapids told you to pay Cal Overland a visit when you got to Seedley," Borden said. "That's what you said before. Was that a lie?"

"No," Hayes sighed.

"Then you just drive your wagon on to that homestead and pay him a visit. While you're there, see what you can see. I've been there a few times myself," the marshal explained. "I know him and Niles Healey both have men riding their property lines. With you driving that wagon of yours up to his front door, you're bound to draw some of Cal's boys in to greet you. That'll create an opening so me and my boys can come in and see what we can see."

"If you've been there before, why not just go there again?" Aldus asked. "It's not like that would seem very strange."

"In case you haven't noticed, things have been coming to a boil around here," the marshal told him. "Them vigilantes have taken it upon themselves to kill one of my deputies, and Frank Healey is in my jail. Me riding right up to that property where I know I'll be outnumbered three to one ain't such a good idea."

"Why would any of them shoot your deputy, anyways?" Aldus wondered.

Coming around his desk, Borden placed a hand on both Hayes's and Aldus's shoulders and steered them toward the door. "How about we go and find out?"

Chapter 15

Aldus sat in the driver's seat of the covered wagon with Hayes beside him. They'd left town as soon as the horses were hitched, and the lawmen supposedly left soon after. Aldus hadn't seen hide nor hair of Marshal Borden or his deputies since leaving their office, and the only living things sharing the trail with them as far as he could tell were a few squirrels and some rabbits.

"He's probably not even coming," Aldus grumbled.

Hayes had been working on a Henry rifle for a customer who'd wanted it modified into something that could be even more accurate than the standard models. Aldus wasn't sure about the technical aspects, but Hayes had been tinkering with that rifle for almost a week. Now he loaded it and gave it another once-over. "I hope they don't show up," he said. "Because that means we can conduct the business we came for and be on our way."

"Don't tell me you're still looking to set up shop in this town!"

"Of course not, but the whole world doesn't need to know that. As soon as we find an opportunity, we can excuse ourselves and put this cursed place behind us."

"I vote we do that right now."

"That marshal is already on the warpath," Hayes said as if he was afraid the lawmen could somehow overhear him. "We don't need to draw any of that fire."

"For all we know, we're riding right into a fire! Didn't you ever think that one of them deputies could be connected to those vigilantes?"

"I highly doubt it."

"Why?" Aldus snapped. "Because a man wearing a badge couldn't possibly break the law?"

"No. Because any real gunman, no matter which side of the law he's on, wouldn't carry a forty-four Remington when he had a perfectly good Colt. The Remington is inferior in balance to the Peacemaker, and anyone who lived by their gun hand would know that."

"Maybe they're just not as knowledgeable as you on the matter," Aldus pointed out. "You ever think of that?"

"Of course I did," Hayes replied as he checked the Henry rifle yet again. "There aren't many people who are as knowledgeable on the matter of firearms. But we can't second-guess a lawman unless we have good reason. And from everything I saw, it seems very clear that Marshal Borden has no love for anyone belonging to that gang of vigilantes."

Aldus let out a tired grunt of a laugh. "I only saw one man in a mask and another with a bandanna over his face. That doesn't exactly add up to a gang."

"Maybe not, but one of those men stormed into your hotel without anyone standing in his way to threaten you. The other killed a man right in front of us. I don't need to see much more than that to convince me that something needs to be done around here. It may be a lawman's job to bring killers to justice, but it's our duty as citizens to help if we can."

Aldus let out a long, haggard sigh.

"What's wrong now?" Hayes asked.

"I hate it when I actually fall for one of your speeches."

"And I hate it that some of your fighting spirit has rubbed off on me. I guess that means we're both in a pickle, eh?"

"It sure does."

The Overland spread was four miles south of Seedley on a narrow trail that could just be seen through all the tall grass growing on either side of it. As the grass started to thin out, Aldus could see a fence line up ahead. There was no gate, so they continued along the path toward a large house in the distance. Although there were some crops planted here and there, it was obvious that Cal Overland was no farmer. A bit closer to the middle of the property was a pasture where about twenty head of cattle grazed on whatever they could find.

"Better put that rifle down," Aldus said.

"You're wearing that Schofield. I can carry a rifle."

"No! I mean you should put it down. Right now. Look!"

Following Aldus's line of sight, Hayes quickly spotted the trio of riders crossing through the field to his left. In the distance to the right of the wagon, two more riders could be seen. The pair of riders held position about a hundred yards out while the trio rode to stand in the middle of the road in front of the wagon. Aldus pulled back on his reins, stopping well short of forcing the riders off the trail.

Having set his rifle down behind his feet, Hayes waved to the riders and shouted, "Hello there!"

"Howdy," one of the riders said. "You men lost?"

"No, sir. We're here to see Mr. Overland."

"Well, this is his property. Is he expecting you?"

"I don't believe so. That is, unless Jack Grable managed to send word that we'd be arriving."

The riders all looked to be in their twenties and sat in their saddles with a young man's confidence that nothing on earth could knock them down. The man who'd been doing the talking wore a simple brown vest over a blue shirt and chaps over faded jeans. The other two seemed more than comfortable in their saddles and were dressed in a similar fashion. The lead rider looked back to the man closest to him and asked, "Mr. Overland mention anything about expectin' anyone?"

"Nope," the other rider said.

"What about Jack Grable? He mention that name before?"

The other rider shook his head before spitting tobacco juice onto the ground.

"Well, I was told to mention that Jack Grable recommended I come to see Cal Overland once I got to Seedley. My name is Zachariah Hayes. I sell firearms of all kinds, repair them, even modify them to perform better than you could imagine. I understand Mr. Overland has made several trips to Cedar Rapids for guns, and I thought I might be able to save him a trip."

All three riders merely looked back at them. After one spat some more tobacco juice, the young man at the head of the group shrugged and said, "I suppose you can come to the house. Can't guarantee that Mr. Overland will talk with you."

"That's fine. All I ask for is a chance," Hayes said.

"Follow us, then."

The three riders split up so the talker was still in the lead and the other two were behind and slightly to either side of the wagon. Aldus snapped his reins to follow his escort, fighting back the impulse to pull the leather straps to one side and go back the way they'd come.

As they ambled toward the house, Aldus spotted a barn on one side of it and a smaller outbuilding on the other that could have been a smokehouse or something used for storage. The pair of riders who'd been keeping their distance thus far hung back, making sure to keep pace with the wagon. About fifty yards from the house, the trail widened into a flat patch of land that was big enough to encompass the house, the barn, and the outbuilding before narrowing back into a trail past the spread.

"Wait here," the lead rider said.

Aldus set the brake and nodded. Leaning over to Hayes, he whispered, "Still think this was a good idea?"

"I believe I said it was our duty to help," the salesman replied. "Not that it was necessarily a good idea."

"Great. That's just . . . great."

The rider who'd been their guide went all the way to the house, where he was greeted by a man who seemed almost too big to fit through the door. He had wide shoulders and girth that looked to be more muscle than fat. Standing on the porch, he listened to what the rider had to say while staring out at Aldus and Hayes as if he were close enough to see the whites of their eyes. Before long, the big man strode forward. He moved fast for a man of his size before coming to a halt just close enough to the wagon to be heard.

"I'm Cal Overland," he said. "What brings you here?"

Hayes stood up in the wagon's seat and gave a slight bow. "Good day to you, sir. I've heard many good things about you."

"I'm told you sell guns."

"That's right. I've recently arrived in Seedley and thought I'd come out here to give you first chance at some of the finest firearms available in this or any other state."

"I've already got plenty of guns."

Aldus didn't have to look far to verify that. Apart

from the five riders who'd come out to greet them, another four had drifted in from all sides. Two emerged from the house and another two came from the barn. When Aldus glanced back to the field they'd crossed to get to the house, however, he could no longer see the pair who had been keeping pace with them ever since the wagon had crossed the fence line.

"I'm sure you do, sir," Hayes continued. "And some of those guns surely need to be repaired while others could stand to be replaced. When you get a look at my inventory, you may even find one or two that you simply won't be able to resist."

"All right, then," Overland said. "Since you came all this way, let's get a look at what you brought. Jesse, go have a look inside their wagon."

One of the men who'd come from the house behind Cal Overland hurried down from the front porch and strode past him. "Sure thing, Pa," he grunted as he hurried toward the wagon.

Aldus was feeling uncomfortable after losing track of the two riders in the distance. That feeling grew worse when he could no longer find the men who had come from the barn. He didn't feel any better once he got a closer look at Jesse Overland.

Although shorter than average height, Jesse had a wide, barrel chest and thick arms. His face sported several bruises, which could have been put there by a few strong punches. The damage to his face wasn't bad enough, however, to hide his dark green eyes. As Jesse moved past the wagon to circle around to the back, he grinned up at Aldus.

"That's him," Aldus whispered to Hayes. "The one who stormed in on me at the hotel."

"Are you sure?" Hayes asked.

"As sure as I can be."

Aldus could hear Jesse rummaging around in the back of the wagon. When he took another look around, he could see one man kneeling up in the loft of the barn and two more hurrying out through the wide double doors toward the back of the house.

"He's right, Pa," Jesse called out. "There's a whole lot of guns back here."

"What kind?" Cal asked.

"All kinds, looks like. Also some tools."

"Those are the instruments I use to ply my trade," Hayes said in a voice that was lacking some of its former confidence. "As I mentioned before, I'd be happy to make myself available for any services you require."

Cal's brow furrowed as he placed his hands on his hips. Eventually he said, "Why not? I'll take them guns you brought."

"Really? What can I interest you in? Rifles? Pistols? A little of both?"

"I'll take all of them. Jesse, start unloading that wagon."

Aldus reached for his pistol while climbing down from his seat. Before his boots touched the ground, several rifles were prepared to be fired. When he spun around, however, he saw fewer gunmen than before. One of the men who had been standing to the left of the house was now missing. Several others had appeared scattered in various spots around the wagon. Some of them looked familiar to Aldus, while others were just men pointing guns at him.

"Go on, big man," Jesse snarled. "Take one more step so you can be cut down."

"Sounds about right," Aldus said. "Especially from a man who has to wear a sack over his head for him to feel tough."

Although Jesse flinched at that, he quickly recovered.

"It don't matter what you know, boy. You won't make it off this property, anyhow."

"Boy?" Aldus growled. "Did you just call me boy?"

Cal's voice rolled through the air like a clap of thunder. "Jesse! Stop talking and start unloading those guns! Someone help him."

As two of the remaining gunmen started approaching the wagon, a tall figure strode forward as if he'd been dropped from the sky to land halfway between the house and barn. "What do you need to steal guns for?" the man asked. "You've got more than enough money to buy them."

Cal shifted on his feet and turned to face the new arrival. "That you, Marshal?"

"It sure is, Cal." Marshal Borden stood his ground about twenty paces from Cal Overland. "You don't even need guns," he said. "I saw the armory you have stored in your barn."

"I guess you would have seen them pretty soon, anyway," Cal said. "Seeing as how you don't have the sense God gave a mule to step aside when you were asked. When my boys roll through Seedley, you'll get a real good look at them guns."

"I wasn't asked to step down," Borden said. "I was threatened by a gang of vigilantes. The same vigilantes who killed my deputy."

"You were told blood would stain your streets if you didn't step down as marshal," Cal said through a cruel gaze that was colder than a slab of ice. "Whatever happened after that is on your head."

"It's funny," Borden said. "I was thinking it would be tougher to get you to fess up to being behind those men in the masks."

"And I thought you'd never try hard enough to figure it out for yourself. You forced my hand, though," Cal said. "And you've got Frank Healey's boy locked up in your jail. Did you even bother questioning the man I handed over to you? He should have confessed to anything you liked. You could have strung him up for the death of your deputy and you would've looked like a hero."

"That man was beat to a pulp. Anyone could see that. Killers don't just start talking when they're caught. Besides, that man who confessed wasn't no killer. He held his gun like he barely knew which end fired a bullet. Recently I got plenty more evidence to let me know he was a fraud."

Aldus listened to the exchange as he stood in front of Jesse. The younger Overland stepped away from the wagon to square his shoulders to him as an ugly, anticipatory smile crept onto his face.

"So you came up here on a hunch?" Cal asked. "That takes some sand, I'll give you that."

"Men were sent to try and weasel Frank Healey out of jail," Borden said. "I figured it wouldn't be long before them vigilantes would take a more direct approach. Considering my suspicions from before and the things that came to light now, this seemed like the best time to make my play. Seems it was worth the ride all the way out here."

"I've got ten gun hands on this property," Cal declared. "That's not including my son and me."

The marshal nodded. "My deputies saw some of your men as we rode in. Didn't have much trouble bringing down the two with the rifles on horseback. Them other two posted near the barn were a little tougher ... but not much. I'd say we're about even now. I might even have an advantage with the high ground." As Borden hooked a thumb over his shoulder, the man kneeling in the barn's loft tossed back a casual wave. It was Mark, the deputy who had stitched Aldus's side. Setting his sights firmly on Cal Overland, the marshal said, "So you've got two choices. You can hand yourself over and order your men to do the same or you can stand and fight like a man instead of shooting at me like a bunch of cowards in masks. Either way . . . this vigilante business ends right here and right now."

"Vigilantes?" Cal bellowed. "That's all you see after you got a look at the guns I got stored in my barn? I've been stockpiling weapons for months right under your nose! I may have started off taking the law into my own hands, but there ain't no reason to stop there. Not when there's so much money to be made by instating my own law."

"Are you really crazy enough to try and pull away from the Union?"

"The federals can keep running things how they like. No need to take such drastic action. Me and Niles Healey will just run all the roads coming through Iowa into Nebraska and Missouri. Once we get our militia armed and bringing more order to the towns around here than any lawman could, we'll be able to do as we please. Hell, I haven't even straightened out all the possibilities open to us once we kick out the idiots like you and take control."

"You'll be wiped out as soon as the army gets wind of it," Borden said as he shook his head.

Cal grinned and puffed out his chest. "See, that's just it. Nobody's gonna get wind of anything until me and my boys have run roughshod over three states. Once things get too hot, we pack up, head somewhere else for a while, and start again."

"Why would you do this?"

"Because the opportunity is there," Cal replied. "Taking risks that other men wouldn't is how I got to own half

of Seedley. Me and Niles weren't happy with the way
things were being handled in town, so we rode in to handle them ourselves. Since that became so easy, we both
figured we could grab even more if we set our minds to
it. The real beauty of it is that the Overlands and Healeys
have enough money to pave the way for just about anything we like. As of a few weeks ago, I've got the guns
and men to open a lot of doors. The only ones who sus-
pect much of anything are you and yours. Fortunately
you're all in one place . . . and all of you will be buried in
that field out yonder."

"This is insane!" Borden said. "You can't really think
you'll get away with this."

Cal shrugged again. "We have so far. It was even easier than I thought it would be. Didn't cost us much to buy
the loyalty of one of your deputies. When he found his
conscience and went to tell you about what happened, it
was a simple matter to take him down. To be honest, me
and Niles have only started putting our ideas together.
All we know for certain is that we're the ones who need
to run Seedley and we've got more than enough fire-
power to clean you and your deputies out. After that . . .
we'll come up with something. You don't need to worry
about any of that, though. Your time is done, Marshal!
You may have had good intentions, but it's time to step
down."

"Don't do this!" Borden said. "Men will die here today unless you come to your senses."

"More men will die if we live under laws that allow
killers to go free or wile away their time in a cell. You'll
see, Marshal. It'll be a lot better my way. Oh, wait," Cal
added. "You won't see. But the others will and I'm sure
they'll remember you fondly."

Aldus listened to the exchange as if he were distanced
from it all. A big part of him scarcely believed it was hap-

Chapter 16

Aldus didn't know who fired the first shot. His eyes were fixed on Jesse because that was the only man he could do anything about. As soon as one of the men in the stand-off pulled his trigger, gunshots ripped through the air in sporadic bursts. Aldus reached for his Schofield as hot lead whipped past him to dig into the side of the wagon. He cleared leather, only to take quick aim from the hip and pull his trigger. Even at such close range, Aldus's shot went wild, allowing Jesse to step aside and bump his shoulder against the rear corner of the wagon.

Men were shouting to one another nearby. Some were hollering in pain or desperation. Others were cursing and yelling like the ones Aldus had read about in the Bible who spoke in tongues. All of those words blended into more noise, which Aldus pushed aside so he could focus on the task at hand.

Jesse glared at him with his burning green eyes. The hatred in them was so distinctive that he might as well have not worn a mask at all when he'd stormed into the Main Rose Hotel. Aldus had no idea why this man hated him so much, and he didn't bother wasting time in trying to figure it out. Some men hated just to hate. Others just liked to hurt folks, and that kind of joy was a brutal, ugly

sight with which Aldus was all too familiar. Since the
only cover to be found was the wagon itself and getting
to it meant either rushing Jesse or putting his back to
him, Aldus took the only other option left to him and
dived to the right.

Jesse's gun spat a plume of fiery smoke. Its bullet
nicked Aldus's left sleeve, snagging his jacket and clip-
ping his elbow just enough to knock that arm back. Aldus was still on his way down and the bullet's passage
caused him to turn awkwardly as he fell. He slammed
against the dirt on his back, his next breath spewing out
in a gasp. At that moment, the rest of the world came
rushing in again as if he only just now realized it was
there. He was running on pure instinct now and he fired
the Schofield while his feet scrambled to find purchase
upon the dusty ground.

That shot punched straight through the canvas cover
of the wagon and ricocheted against something inside.
Jesse fired at him as well but obviously hadn't expected
Aldus to dive because his round hissed several feet
above him. Now that he'd come to a rest, Aldus steadied
himself with both legs splayed and his shoulders flat
against the earth. He did as Hayes had taught him by
extending his gun arm straight, sighting along its barrel,
and letting out a breath while squeezing his trigger.

The moment the Schofield went off, Aldus knew it
would hit his mark. Sure enough, Jesse was knocked
backward when he was drilled through the center of his
chest. The expression on his face was a mix of surprise
and disbelief as his finger tightened around his trigger.
Jesse's gun sent a round into the dirt before it flew from
his hand.

"Aldus! For God's sake, get back here!"

Aldus couldn't move. He was lying on his back with
chaos raging around him and shots flying in every direc-

tion and couldn't move. He'd just shot another man. If Jesse wasn't dead already, he would be soon, and that was all he could think about.

When footsteps scrambled toward him, Aldus reflexively twisted his body around to point the Schofield at whoever was coming. Even though he recognized Hayes, his nerves were wound so tight that he still almost pulled his trigger.

Hayes grabbed Aldus's forearm without a care for the gun clutched in that hand and started pulling. "You've got to get to your feet," he said. "All hell's broken loose!"

"I . . . I just . . ."

"Just nothing! *Get up!*"

Aldus had heard those words shouted at him several times throughout the years. Although his circumstances were something other than trying not to pass out after being walloped in the face, the demand struck a similar nerve, which got every muscle in his body striving to work in unison. He didn't need Hayes's help any longer, but having it only made him scramble to his feet quicker. Before he knew it, Aldus was huddled behind the wagon where he and Hayes had cover from at least some of the shooting.

"What's this all about?" Aldus asked. "What was Overland talking about? Is he trying to take over Seedley? Did he mention something about a militia?"

Hayes shook his head as if he couldn't stop. "I don't know what that was about. Obviously it's a feud or something similar that's been brewing since long before we got here." A gun was fired that was closer than the rest, sending a bullet all the way through the wagon to send wood chips fluttering down onto the salesman's head. "We don't need to figure out what's going on or why," he said. "We just need to get out of here with our skins intact."

Both of them were hunkered down behind the wheel and lower part of the wagon. Keeping his back pressed against the wooden planks, Aldus scooted over so he could take a quick look at the homestead. A few men were still in the open, either rooted to their spots in fear or just trapped where they stood and firing at anything that moved. The rest had sought shelter behind whatever was available. Barrels, water troughs, the house, the barn, all of it was being used for cover, which meant all of it was getting chewed up by hot lead.

Reloading the Schofield with fresh rounds from his gun belt, Aldus said, "This could have gone a lot worse."

"Really?" Hayes scoffed. "How do you figure?"

"The marshal and his men could not have shown up."

A stray round burned through the wagon's cover before sparking against something farther away. Wincing at the sharp sound that was in such close proximity, Hayes smirked and said, "Or we could be hiding behind the wagon containing my ammunition stores. What now?"

"I'd say our odds are better if Marshal Borden comes out of this on top, so let's do whatever we can to make sure that happens."

"I'm not a killer. I don't know if I can ..."

"We defend ourselves," Aldus said. "That doesn't mean we have to kill every man in our sights. Let's just draw some fire away from the law so they can do their jobs."

Hayes drew a deep breath, which went a long way in steadying the hands wrapped around his rifle. "I'm the better shot. Do what you can to keep them from ..." He swallowed hard as if choking on the words he'd been about to say. He settled with "Just keep them away from me." After that, he dropped down to all fours and crawled under the wagon. Once he'd found his spot, he stretched out on his belly and steadied the rifle against his shoulder.

Almost immediately Aldus spotted someone turning toward the wagon. It was one of Overland's boys. He could pick him out by the wild look in his eyes. Also, the fact that he'd been firing at one of Borden's deputies a few seconds ago helped erase any doubt when Aldus pointed his Schofield at him. The gunman fired at the wagon just as Aldus fired at him. Having had his sights set on Hayes, the gunman was startled when someone else returned fire.

Aldus wasn't ready to send another man to his grave, so his shots were purposely a few inches wide to the right. The gunman was caught in the open, and since Aldus was firing in one direction, he ran in the other. A few seconds later, Mark took aim from his perch in the barn's loft and gunned him down with two well-placed rifle shots.

It was difficult for Aldus to see the other man fall, but he knew that the same man wouldn't have lost a moment's sleep over killing both him and Hayes. Aldus didn't have time to dwell on the details since there was still plenty of shooting to be done.

The first shot Hayes took hit a barrel next to the house. He fired again, sending the man who'd been cowering behind that barrel running for more suitable cover. Unbeknownst to the fleeing gunman, Marshal Borden himself was standing around the corner with his back to the house along with his deputy Paul. As soon as the gunman saw both of them, he tossed his gun and threw his hands high above his head.

"Very nice!" Aldus said.

Hayes worked the lever of the rifle and replied, "Got lucky with that one. Get ready." With that, he fired over a small cluster of Overland's gunmen who were gathered near the side of the house opposite of Marshal Borden. Hayes followed up with another shot that was close enough to scatter them.

The men who had been gathered there didn't appreciate being driven from their spot and showed it by firing at the wagon. Aldus took quick aim, knowing the men were outside the pistol's most effective range. Just to be sure, he pulled his aim to the left and continued pulling his trigger. One of the three gunmen raced around the back of the house while the second and third charged toward the wagon. When Hayes's rifle barked again, one of the men coming toward him toppled over and grabbed his leg while screaming in pain.

"Sorry!" Hayes shouted. His apology was swallowed up by the next round he fired, which caused the second charging gunman to change direction so he could get behind a nearby tree.

The gunshots erupting behind the house rose to a crescendo, followed by shouting back and forth between two groups of men. In a short amount of time, the shooting died down and the marshal reappeared on the side of the house to throw a wave toward the wagon. He then looked toward the barn before pointing to the open plot of land in front of the house, where several men lay wounded or completely still. Mark was no longer in the barn's loft. Soon Aldus saw the deputy run outside. He kept his head low and his steps quick as he hurried to check on one of the men lying exposed on open ground.

In all the commotion, Aldus had stopped seeing most of the shooters as separate people and instead looked at them only when they seemed like an immediate threat. Most of that was due to the panic nipping at his heels. When Cal Overland stepped away from one of the pillars supporting the overhang in front of his house, Aldus took notice of him right away.

Cal had a gun in each hand but only brought up the right one to fire. Where Aldus and Hayes had been panicked, worried, or frightened, Cal seemed completely in his element. He took aim with utter confidence after having stood by for the last several seconds while the rest of the men fired at one another. In that moment, Aldus knew that Cal meant to kill Mark simply because he was the closest available target. When Aldus fired at him, Cal didn't bat an eye.

When Hayes fired his rifle, on the other hand, Cal took notice. The round whipped past Cal's head and took a notch from the pillar behind him. Spotting Hayes immediately, Cal shifted his aim. Aldus fired again, pulling his trigger until his hammer slapped against the back of one empty casing after another. Hayes fired as well, hitting spots in the ground directly in front of Cal meant to stop him in his tracks. The owner of the homestead shouted a string of foul language at the wagon until Marshal Borden and Paul stepped out to face him.

"It's over!" Borden hollered. "Three of your men are dead and one of them is hightailing it across a field. The rest are knocked out or tied up. You're finished. Toss them guns before we have to put you down."

Cal was too worked up to form a coherent sentence. His teeth gnashed together and he breathed in heavy grunts that swelled his chest to the point of busting open before deflating like a set of bellows. When he finally gathered enough air to speak, he shouted, "Someone shoot these men!"

There were no takers.

In fact, the only movement Aldus could see was a few petrified faces looking out through two of the house's windows.

"Zeke, get out from under there," Aldus whispered.

Hayes either had his sights set right where he wanted them or was unable to move.

"It's not our fight," Aldus said. "Get out from there before you catch a bullet."

As Hayes slowly scooted back to come out from beneath the wagon, Cal Overland strutted toward the marshal.

"I've got more men than the ones you see here, Marshal," Cal said. "You take me into your jail and they'll just escort me right back out again."

"We aim to visit the Healey spread as soon as we're done here," Borden said, "and we both know that he won't put up as much of a fight as you."

"This fight ain't over."

"You got nobody to stand there with you, Cal. It's over. You got one last chance to come out of this alive. If you think that's a bluff, then go ahead and try me."

Cal looked up at one of the faces in a second-floor window. She was a petrified woman who'd been watching them from the moment Marshal Borden announced his presence. The moment Cal turned away from the house, she screamed.

Overland pointed his gun at Marshal Borden.

Both lawmen in front of him fired.

Two rounds struck Cal in the chest. His last twitch clamped a finger around his trigger, sending a round into the dirt. Overland dropped.

Aldus could scarcely believe what he was seeing. The sheer chaos that had overtaken the Overland homestead had been overwhelming. Despite all the times he'd been shot at over the last several days, it was still difficult to watch Cal Overland be cut down like so much wheat. Once the older man stopped moving, the entire scene rushed in on Aldus at once.

Bodies were strewn on the ground.

Some men moaned in pain.

Others were crawling in random directions.

In the middle of it all, Marshal Borden stood, an object as unmovable as the house itself.

"Anyone else feel like trying their luck?" the lawman bellowed.

Behind the second-floor window, the woman who'd screamed was eerily silent. Her hand was clamped over her mouth to make certain she stayed that way. Others looked out from different windows. Some had fear in their eyes. Some had nothing but hate.

"I'm gonna tend to my men," Borden announced. "And then I'm bringing in them that can walk to my jail. Anyone tries to get in my way . . . I'll shoot them where they stand!"

Nobody said a word or made a move.

Slowly, Borden nodded and gave some orders to Paul. The big man hurried to start rounding up the surviving gunmen. It was only then that Aldus saw the man Mark had been tending to was Dan, the marshal's youngest deputy. Before long, Mark lowered his head and closed Dan's eyes.

"You men did real good," Marshal Borden said. His voice came as a shock because Aldus had been so mesmerized by the events unfolding in front of him that he hadn't seen the lawman's approach. Borden offered a hand to Hayes and helped him come out from beneath the wagon.

"You didn't tell us we'd be in the middle of . . . all this," Hayes said.

The marshal shrugged. "I didn't know it would come to this. All I wanted was to see if I could make certain Cal was one of the vigilantes. I knew things were coming to a boil, but—"

"Can we go?" Aldus asked.

Although he clearly didn't like being interrupted, Borden said, "Yeah. I'm not about to stop you. I appreciate your help."

"And we would have appreciated not being drawn into this."

"It's like I already told you—"

"Don't give me that," Aldus snapped. "You had to have known this might happen. You knew what kind of man Cal Overland was. We didn't. You knew how vicious these vigilantes truly were. We only heard a few stories."

"And you knew there were men stockpiling guns in this town," Borden said. "That's why you came here, right? To sell them more?"

Hayes was shaken by that. After taking a breath to steady himself, he said, "That's why I wanted to help out now. We're done here, Marshal. I don't know the history between your town and these vigilantes. I don't care what the Overlands or Healeys had to do with any of you. I don't even care about the nonsense that Mr. Overland was spouting about a militia. None of that matters anymore. I'm through with it."

Borden extended his hand. "Fair enough. You truly did well in covering us and I'm sorry about how things turned out. Truth be told, I wasn't even sure if I could trust you or not. You proved me wrong. Thanks for all you done."

Hayes shook the lawman's hand. Reluctantly Aldus did the same.

"What about that Healey fellow?" Aldus asked.

"He'll most likely surrender as soon as he realizes he don't have any of Overland's boys backing him up anymore," Borden said. "The toughest man he had with him was his boy Frank, and he's already locked up. At the most, there's maybe two or three armed men out that way. We can handle them well enough."

Before he had a chance to stop himself, Aldus said, "You sure about that?"

A tired grin drifted onto Borden's face. "Yeah, Brick. I'm sure. Just so you know, I can pay you a posse fee for what you did here today. It's the least I can do."

"Keep your money," Hayes said. When Aldus looked over at him, the salesman kept his eyes locked on Borden.

"All right, then," the lawman said. "Best of luck to you. I can take it from here."

Aldus and Hayes climbed into their wagon and left the Overland property. It wasn't until they were almost back in town that either man did anything other than keep the horses moving and watch for any hint of another attack. Hayes pulled to a stop on Main Street near the stable, and Aldus turned to look at him and say, "I'll collect the rest of the horses and hitch them to the other wagon."

"Need any help?"

"No. I done it plenty of times to know my way."

"Good," Hayes said.

"Zeke?"

"What?"

"We . . . could have used that posse fee."

"I know," Hayes said. "But we'll manage without it. I just want to be away from here without anything to remind me of this place. Anything at all."

Aldus couldn't argue with that.

Chapter 17

They rode for the rest of that day without saying much. Since Aldus and Hayes both had to drive their own wagon, they wouldn't normally have been very talkative, but even when they stopped, their words were few and far between. Mostly, Aldus was just tired. It hadn't taken long for them to join back up with the trail they normally took across Iowa, and the monotony of rolling in a familiar direction allowed his mind to take a rest. He didn't have to think about much of anything, especially the fiasco that the diversion into Seedley had become.

All there was to hear was the grinding of wheels against the ground, and all there was to see was the steady swaying of his horses' tails.

They had enough provisions to make camp, fill their stomachs, and get some sleep under quiet, familiar stars. When they awoke without any other people in sight, both of them found themselves in higher spirits.

Rather than dig even further into their provisions as they moved on, Hayes kept his rifle handy so he could take a shot at whatever game the wagons flushed out from the trees or bushes alongside the trail. After missing his first several quail, Hayes reloaded the rifle amid a string of grumbled curses.

"What's the matter with you?" Aldus shouted from the wagon behind him. "You're one of the best shots I know."

"It's been a long time since I've been hunting. That's all."

"It hasn't been that long since you showed off at the shooting gallery. How's this any different?"

"This is . . . well, it's . . . obviously . . ."

"I get it," Aldus said. "You've gotten soft. You're used to all the targets standing still."

"I did plenty well back at the Overland place, thank you very much!"

"Indeed you did. So let's see that straight shooting now!"

Hayes put the rifle to his shoulder and waited for a target to present itself. The wagons were moving at a slow, steady pace and the horses had a nice trail to follow. Also, it was the path they always took to Omaha and the animals could probably get there without the slightest bit of guidance. As the wheels rumbled toward a stand of trees, three birds exploded from the highest branches to take flight. Hayes picked one of them off with a single shot.

"That's more like it!" Aldus said.

"It's quite easy. I just pictured your head on those feathered shoulders."

"Whatever puts something other than beans into our stew tonight."

They drew to a stop long enough for Aldus to climb down from his wagon and collect the freshly killed game. As he walked past the lead wagon with bird in hand, Aldus heard Hayes say, "I've been thinking."

"Uh-oh. Nothing good's ever come of that."

"Perhaps going to see your friend in Corbin truly is a good idea."

"Yeah," Aldus said. "I've been thinking about that, too. Considering how badly we need money, it would probably be a better idea to go to Omaha as planned. Bigger market there, and all."

Hayes placed the Henry rifle on the seat next to him. "We can make a few rides into Omaha, but we could stand to broaden our horizons. How far from Omaha is Corbin, anyway?"

"Between ten and twenty miles."

"Is that it?" Hayes exclaimed. "Why haven't we been there yet?"

"Just never got around to it, I suppose."

"Don't give me that. The way you talk about her . . . the things you write . . ."

"What things?" Aldus said. "I've never said anything inappropriate!"

Hayes sighed dramatically. "I never said anything about you being inappropriate. What I meant was that you obviously have feelings for this woman."

"Oh, it's so obvious, is it?" Aldus grumbled. When he didn't get a reply right away, he added, "Is it really that obvious?"

"Only to someone who can read those letters."

If that had come from anyone else, Aldus might have taken such a comment as a slight. Since he knew with absolute certainty that Hayes wouldn't throw his reading problem in his face, Aldus said, "She's already keeping company with someone."

"We already know that isn't going so well."

"If it's not going well now, it will only go better later."

"And you know this because you have so much experience with women?" Hayes scoffed.

This time, whether he thought Hayes meant it as an insult or not, Aldus was compelled to defend himself. "I've had experience," he said gruffly.

"You know, for a man with your ferocious background, you can have quite the yellow streak sometimes."

"All right, now you're close to getting a walloping."

"I've been the one to write those letters for you," Hayes continued, "and I never had to write the words you truly wanted to say. You danced around them in so many ways, but you never said them outright."

"What was I supposed to say?"

"Do I really need to tell you?"

Aldus sighed. "She's seemed so happy. She's got two young ones. She's settled right where she is."

"So what?"

"How can you dismiss such things?"

"I'm not dismissing them," Hayes told him. "I just don't think they should stop her or you from pursuing what you both so obviously would . . . aw, forget it. I'm too tired for so many words."

"Now, there's a first," Aldus chuckled.

"Just don't—"

Aldus let out an exaggerated sigh. "I knew the silence wouldn't last very long."

Hayes leaned down from his seat to stare directly at his partner. "Just don't do anything you'll regret. And before you assure me that you're treading carefully to keep from doing anything stupid, let me remind you that the biggest regrets a man can have are the things he *didn't* do. Understand?"

"Yeah. I may have a thick skull, but I understand."

"Good. Now, let's put an end to all this lollygagging and get a move on."

Aldus gave him a halfhearted salute and carried the dead bird back to the other wagon, where it was hung from the side by a short length of rope wrapped around its feet.

They passed the rest of the day's ride with conversation that was sparse but pleasant. Hayes knocked another bird from the sky as well as some squirrels from a few trees. When they made camp that night, Aldus got straight to work cleaning the small game so it could be cooked over the fire Hayes was building.

"I'm a better hunter than I thought!" Hayes said as he broke the branches he'd collected and built them into a proper campfire. "You were right. Once I thought of it as one big shooting gallery, it became a whole lot easier!"

"You want another piece of advice?"

"Sure."

"Next time," Aldus told him, "aim for something bigger. Didn't you see them deer about five miles back?"

"Of course I did. I'm not blind."

"They had to be in range of that rifle of yours."

Glancing back at the rifle that was propped against the side of his wagon, Hayes beamed as if he were watching his youngest child take its first steps. "Within range and then some."

"So, what stopped you? You enjoy putting me to work with a bunch of little jobs or do you just love squirrel meat?"

Hayes opened his mouth to speak but stopped himself short. Wincing, he closed his mouth again. Finally he said, "I suppose I was taking your shooting gallery a little too literally. After all, it's no fun to just shoot the big targets."

Part of Aldus wanted to be angry when he heard that. They were hungry, relying on a steady aim and the good graces of nature itself for sustenance, while Hayes was just keeping score in his head. At the moment, however, that angry part of him was pretty small. The rest of him wanted to laugh, which was exactly what he did. Once he got started, it felt too good to stop. It wasn't long before Hayes himself joined in and they relished the moment until tears came to their eyes.

Some time later, the fire was roaring and the fattest squirrels were being cooked on spits. It was a beautiful autumn night. The stars were arranged like gems embedded in a wall of coal. Although smoke from the fire occasionally stung Aldus's eyes, its scent was more than enough to keep the smile on his face. It was slow to fade as he cast his eyes upward and held them there.

Hayes sat at the edge of the fire, pouring some of the coffee he'd just made into a tin cup. After swirling the dark brew around and cooling it with a breath or two, he sipped it and nodded in silent appreciation. Eventually he noticed what Aldus was doing and looked upward in the same general direction. Squinting at the sky, he asked, "What's got you so pleased?"

"Just enjoying the night," Aldus replied. "Feels good to be so far away from all that nonsense."

Not wanting to mention Marshal Borden, vigilantes, Seedley, or anything else that might tie a knot in his stomach, Hayes replied, "It sure does. You're looking at something, though. I can tell. You've got that same stare as a man who stands in front of a rack of pistols and tries to act as if one hasn't caught his eye. It's very distinctive."

"Can't a man just let his mind wander?"

"Sure," Hayes replied as he took another sip. "Just making conversation."

"I'm . . . looking at Orion."

Hayes looked up again. "You're a stargazer? I never would've guessed! Always wanted to figure out all of those constellations and whatnot. I can find the North Star, but that's about it."

"Where's the North Star?"

"North."

Aldus rolled his eyes and shook his head. "Guess I walked right into that one."

"You sure did."

"My mother used to know just about every star over her head. She tried teaching me at night when I couldn't sleep. There were plenty of nights when I would pretend to not be tired just so we could sit out on our porch. She'd point up and name them all. Cassiopeia. The Big Dipper. There was a snake, I believe."

"Really? Where?"

"Don't know," Aldus said with a shrug. "The only one that stuck with me was Orion. She used to say it's because I had a fighting spirit."

Hayes let out a low whistle. "Your mother had quite the foresight."

"I believe she was referring to a man fighting to get where he wanted in this world. If she knew I'd ever stepped into a real bout to get pummeled for scraps, she'd wallop me worse than any man I ever stood across from on them docks."

"Sounds like a good mother," Hayes said.

"She was. Hardest hit I ever took was when I found out she'd passed on." Aldus took a moment before sniffing once and looking back up again. "Whenever Orion's in the sky, I can always find him. Don't know why, exactly. He just sort of jumps out at me."

"The North Star is the only one I can ever find, and that's just because the handle of the Big Dipper points to it. Or . . . is it the Little Dipper? Whichever it is, I suppose I can spot that one as well. You know, it's not always a bad thing to be able to see just one thing clearer than the rest. Helps give you a direction."

"Either that," Aldus grumbled, "or it keeps a man from realizing he's mostly blind."

"All depends on how you come at it, I guess. There were a lot of different ways I could have gone with my business, but I only ever saw the road that led me to pack everything I owned into two wagons and make the rounds. If I'd been more susceptible to reason, I never would have gotten the fine life I have now."

"Susceptible to reason," Aldus chuckled. "I like the sound of that."

Pointing a finger at the other man, Hayes said, "This world is hard enough as it is. When you're given some direction, take it."

"I'm just talking about seeing one set of stars in the sky."

"Then follow them, my friend. And don't look back."

Chapter 18

Nebraska

As far as Aldus could figure, they'd crossed the state line sometime just before noon on the third day after putting Seedley behind them. Having ridden that circuit so many times, he could feel when he left Iowa as surely as if there were a large bump on the road marking that line on a map. His stomach clenched much as it used to when he was preparing for a fight. And not one of the easy ones, either. Today he felt the kind of apprehension he got when the crowd was roaring for blood, his opponent had the look of a starving animal, and the only thing on Aldus's side was his own two fists.

Back then, all he'd had to do to overcome those reservations was think about how badly he needed to win that purse. Today, he reminded himself of the peculiar tone to the last few letters he'd received from Bethany. Setting his jaw into a firm line, he gave his reins an extra flick and followed Hayes down the southern fork in the trail that took them away from their regular route into Omaha.

As they made their way down that trail, Aldus thought back to all the times he'd almost ridden there only to decide against it at the last minute. In fact, he'd never even mentioned in any one of his letters to Bethany that one of Hayes's circuits took them into Omaha. At the time, it had seemed like the best decision. Now he wasn't exactly sure what it seemed.

Late afternoon melted into early evening before he caught the first glimpse of smoke on the horizon drifting up from the chimneys of Corbin. Having grown up with Bethany in the northern part of the state, Aldus had never been to that town before. She'd described it as a quiet little place with plenty of other children filling the schoolhouse during the week and the church pews on Sundays. For a man who was accustomed to life in a wagon or on the docks of New York City, such a thing struck him as peculiar. Once the horses pulled him close enough to smell supper being cooked in some of the homes on the edge of town and hear the laughter of a few of those children, his nervousness began to fade.

"So, where can we find Bethany's place?" Hayes asked from the wagon ahead of him.

"Let's worry about that after we find a place to park the wagons. There should be an open field to the west of town."

"How do you know? I thought you've never been here."

"I haven't. Bethany wrote about a carnival that came to town last year. Unless another one's decided to show up, it should have a good spot for the gallery."

"Did she ever mention the town being run by a group of bloodthirsty vigilantes?"

"Nope."

"Good," Hayes said with a grin. "Then we're already better off than we were at our last stop." With that, he snapped his reins and continued onward.

The trail led them to Second Street, which appeared

to take them all the way through Corbin. It ran east and west, cutting through the two larger streets that were positioned to run north and south. Those two were Garver and Douglas. Since he knew there was a livery near the western end of Third and two hotels in the middle of town, Aldus continued straight down Second without taking in everything around him the way he normally would upon visiting a place for the first time.

Of course, Bethany hadn't described everything in her letters. Most of what she'd written about Corbin was in passing, but Aldus had read her letters in such painstaking detail on so many different occasions that he practically had a map drawn in his head before he'd arrived. When he'd left New York City to travel with Hayes, Aldus quickly learned how very similar many towns were. Not being able to read signs at a glance allowed him to recognize stores, restaurants, and saloons by the sounds coming through their windows, the items on display, or the people walking through their doors. Corbin had all the essential building blocks of most towns. They were just placed in a slightly different order.

Another thing he paid attention to was the faces around him when they arrived somewhere. The folks in Seedley had been quiet and apprehensive. The people he saw now were a mixed lot, most of them either smiling or curious at the small procession making its way through town. Aldus nodded to them without paying close attention. There was only one face he wanted to see, and it was nowhere to be found. Hayes, on the other hand, was in rare form.

The salesman had already set aside the hat with the wider brim meant to shade his eyes while on the trail for the top hat that he'd purchased in New York City a few days before stepping foot onto Aldus's docks. Where Aldus nodded at the folks he passed, Hayes beamed down at them merrily. To anyone who showed more than passing interest in the wagons, Hayes either tipped his hat or removed it in a sweeping gesture accompanied with as much of a bow as he could give while remaining in his seat.

"You putting on a show?" an old man asked from the porch of what Aldus guessed was a dry goods store.

"I am a crafter of exquisite firearms, my good man!" Hayes replied. "Pay me a visit once I've gotten settled to sample some of the finest pistols and rifles you've ever seen." Shifting his gaze to some of the others nearby, he added, "And test your skill in our shooting gallery. There are good times and prizes to be had!"

That promise was met with a fair amount of interest, which Hayes treated as adoration. The salesman was still waving enthusiastically when Aldus came to a stop. Since the two wagons had switched places upon entering town, Hayes had to pull back on his reins so as not to run into his partner.

"What's the matter?" Hayes asked. "I thought you knew where you were going."

"I do," Aldus said.

"Then . . . go."

Aldus had reached the end of Second Street, which meant they were at the westernmost side of town. His eyes were pointed north and his fingers were gripping the reins tightly.

The road had widened considerably since there was only the back end of a few buildings and several lots nearby. Hayes steered around the covered wagon and came to a stop so he could lean forward and gaze in the same direction as Aldus. "What are we looking at?" he asked.

"We can keep going," Aldus replied.

"Ah! Might you be looking at those houses past the next street? Maybe the one with the children playing in front of it?"

As if on cue, the front door of that distant house was opened and a woman took one step outside. She called out but was too far away to be heard by either man. The children playing near that house heard her well enough and dropped what they were doing to run inside.

"Is that her?" Hayes asked.

"Maybe."

"We could go there right now and introduce ourselves."

Pulling his attention back to the road and open ground ahead of him, Aldus snapped his reins. "There's work to be done. Let's get the wagons parked and you can talk to whoever you need to talk to about setting up the gallery."

"It usually is a good idea for me to check to make sure if a particular plot of land is able to be used for our purposes."

"I know. I've been through this once or twice."

After watching Aldus while they drove their wagons side by side, Hayes said, "You seem surly. Well . . . surlier than usual."

"Don't know what you mean."

They didn't have to go too far before arriving at the edge of a wide, open field that was mostly flat and relatively clear of weeds or brush. Both of them set their brakes and climbed down to stretch their legs and work a few kinks from necks and backs before digging into the work at hand.

Aldus put his back to most of the town and stared out at the field. "I suppose the gallery will go here and pointed in this direction so no stray shots hit any windows."

"Well, now," Hayes said with mock enthusiasm. "You truly *have* done this before."

"The answer to your next question is no."

"And which question might that be?"

"Whether or not I'm going to look in on Bethany tonight," Aldus said.

Hayes glanced toward the distant houses. "We'll have plenty of time. Even if I get the proper permission to set up or if I learn we don't need permission to use this spot, we won't put the gallery together until tomorrow."

"I can wait."

The salesman placed a hand on his partner's shoulder. "We've all been nervous about approaching someone special, but we can never become too wrapped up in how we might fail. Instead, we must forge ahead."

Slowly, Aldus turned to look the other man in the eye. "You done?" he grunted.

"Mostly."

"I ain't some nervous kid. I used to wade through blood, plenty of it my own, in bare-knuckle fights. You think I've got my knickers in a twist about this?"

"Well . . . it is quite a big thing."

"I know. That's why I didn't want to run up to that house, pound on the front door, and invite myself in for supper. I'll go tomorrow. That's why I'm here, after all. I've still got a face full of trail dirt and greasy whiskers. Shouldn't I put my best foot forward?"

"Yes," Hayes admitted. "That would be wise. Why don't I just go see who I need to talk to about using this patch of land while you put up the horses?"

"Sounds like a good plan."

Aldus was never really sure where Hayes went when they arrived in a town. Part of that was because Aldus had so many of his own duties to perform that he didn't bother with what the salesman was doing. Another part was that he was simply content to let the other man do his job. Hayes had explained it to him once about how certain fees might need to get paid in order for them to set the gallery up on certain plots of land. Other times a landowner was cut in on a percentage of Hayes's profits while they were in town. Every so often, no fees needed to be paid at all. Aldus never had much of a nose for finances and he'd never wanted one. All he concerned himself with was having enough money to put food in his belly, a roof over his head, and the occasional swig of whiskey down his throat. Everything else was gravy.

He unhitched the horses from the wagons, led them back into town, and found stalls for them in the livery on Third Street. There were two hotels on Garver Street, one north and one south of Third. Aldus liked the looks of the southern one simply because it was farther from the saloon district and therefore a bit quieter. He did run into one problem, however.

"I'll have to ask for one night's payment in advance," said the tall fellow behind the hotel's front desk. He wore black pants, a wrinkled vest, and a crooked smile. Stringy hair grew at awkward intervals from his scalp, making it look as if he wore a poorly made wig.

The moment he reached into his pocket, Aldus realized he'd made a crucial mistake. Instead of bargaining for a smaller down payment at the livery, he'd paid up front. After the robbery in Cedar Rapids and the lack of payment in Seedley, the traveling fund was paltry to say the least.

"Is there any way I can pay you tomorrow?" Aldus asked.

"Afraid not, sir. It's our policy to have partial payment up front."

Aldus wasn't nearly as good at smiling as Hayes, but he gave it a try, anyway. Judging by the look on the clerk's face, the cracked and missing teeth in Aldus's mouth made his grin as ugly as he'd feared. "Any chance you could overlook that policy just once?"

It was plain to see the clerk was about to flatly refuse

that request, but he was suddenly distracted by some commotion from upstairs. At first, it sounded as though someone might have tripped. There was a heavy thump overhead, followed by several loud scrapes. Those were followed by a muffled curse that was still loud enough to be heard by almost anyone within the hotel. What caught Aldus's attention even more was the woman's voice that followed. She laughed and then let out something that was a cross between a yelp and a moan.

The clerk sighed. "I'm sorry about that."

"I . . . didn't know this was a hotel that provided them kind of services."

"Services?"

"Yeah," Aldus replied. "You know. Girls and all."

The clerk nearly jumped out of his skin in his haste to say, "We most certainly do *not* provide those services."

"Oh. Well, I was hoping that this place would be quieter. Maybe I should look in one of the hotels down the street."

Just when Aldus had become convinced the two people upstairs were engaged in their own little party, he heard another thump. When the woman's voice came again, it wasn't laughing and it wasn't anything close to a passionate moan.

"Was that a scream?" Aldus asked.

Now the clerk seemed nervous. "It's room eleven," he said. "Normally I run a clean house that is very peaceful, but he's been getting drunk the last few nights."

"Maybe you should do something about it."

"I will, sir. I assure you."

Every instinct that Aldus had sharpened on the docks of New York was finely tuned to pick up on fear. Sniffing out when another man was afraid was crucial for survival in a fight, and the man in front of him right now reeked of it.

"Who's the woman up there with him?" Aldus asked. "His wife?"

There was another thump and crash as something upstairs was thrown against a wall or door to shatter on impact.

"Not his wife," the clerk sighed. "He's not married. Most likely . . . he brought a woman to his room, although it is expressly forbidden."

Knowing the tall man wasn't about to lift a finger to stop whatever was going on upstairs, Aldus growled, "Yeah, well, someone ought to go up there and remind him of that."

Without checking on what the clerk was doing, Aldus walked over to the staircase and climbed to the second of three floors. At the landing, he stopped and waited. Room number eleven was just down the hall. When the next thump came, Aldus could see that door shaking in its frame. He was halfway down the hall when a man's muffled voice could be heard. Aldus approached the door and pounded his fist against it.

Inside, the man launched into an obscene rant. Now that he was closer, Aldus could hear the woman inside sobbing.

"What's goin' on in there?" Aldus shouted.

Nobody inside responded. The door to room number eight opened a crack, and when Aldus looked over there, it was quickly shut again.

Turning his full attention to number eleven, Aldus placed his shoulder against the door and shoved. The door was sturdy, but Aldus was able to force it open with one more shove.

He stumbled inside, keeping hold of the handle so the door didn't swing all the way inside. It was stopped by a body just inside the room. Directly in front of him stood a man with a solid build, wide shoulders, and thick arms protruding from rolled-up sleeves. A large mouth hung agape beneath a small mustache that formed a straight line on his upper lip. Both fists were tightly balled and sweat rolled down his face. The front of his pants was open, held up, thanks to the suspenders attached to them. "Who the hell are you?" the man grunted.

Aldus eased the door back to get a look behind it. There, on the floor, a woman was curled into a defensive ball. Her dark red hair was a tangled mess, and every part of her was trembling. She looked up at him with one blackened eye, her mouth bloody, and stretched out a hand to shield herself.

"It's all right, miss," Aldus said as he gently took hold of her wrist. "Let me help you up."

She shook her head wildly. "No! No, just leave me be."

The man in the room jabbed Aldus's shoulder with a sharp push. "You heard her! Leave her be."

Ignoring him, Aldus asked the woman, "He did this to you?"

First, her eyes darted over to the man. Then she looked at Aldus for less than a second before letting her head hang forward. "I'll be fine," she whispered.

"You heard her," the man grunted. "She's gonna be fine and this ain't none of your concern."

Aldus straightened up to his full height and wheeled around to face him. The man reflexively flinched backward a fraction of a step before steeling himself and putting the fierce expression back on his face.

"You hit this woman?" Aldus asked.

"Ain't none of your concern, I says."

Having been in so many brawls, Aldus needed to learn to rein himself in. It never paid to fight when angry. Even worse, allowing himself to get carried away when he was hurt or overly emotional only led to him being reckless and making mistakes. However, there were a few things that made him want to kill a man with his bare hands: when that man spat in his face or harmed a woman.

Since Aldus hadn't taken a swing at him yet, the man felt confident enough to step up and glare directly into his eyes. "You'd best turn around and walk outta here, mister," the man said.

"Haven't you been asked to leave?"

"What did you say?"

"I wanted to know if you'd been asked to leave," Aldus said. "By someone from the hotel."

The man spat out a laugh. "What of it?"

"I think it's time for you to go."

"You look like you ain't had more than one thought at a time," the man replied. "Do yourself a favor and leave before I make you even uglier than you already are."

Aldus slowly turned around and offered his hand to the woman.

"Are you deaf?" the man said. "I told you to make yourself scarce!"

Even though the shove from behind hadn't been unexpected, it had enough muscle behind it to send Aldus staggering sideways to bump his shoulder against the wall. The man let out a wobbly laugh as he started shoving him toward the door.

Aldus had been hoping so deeply for the other man to make a move along those lines that he had to struggle to keep from smiling as he planted his feet in the doorway and turned around. The man had a similar build to Aldus, but was all bluster as he puffed out his chest and grabbed the front of Aldus's shirt with both hands.

"You must be deaf," the fellow growled. "Either that or just plain stupid."

He'd barely gotten those words out when Aldus

brought both arms up so they were in between the man's arms. From there, he snapped his arms straight out to either side, forcing the man to lose his grip on him.

"You been asked to leave," Aldus said as he turned the tables by grabbing the other man's collar. "You also need to learn that it ain't right to beat on a woman."

The man tried to answer back, but he had a tough time speaking as he was wrangled out of the room and into the hallway. He pounded against Aldus's arm and even grabbed it, which didn't help in the slightest. When he swung a wild punch at Aldus's face, he still wasn't able to make a dent. Aldus shook off the punch without much of a reaction and then shoved the man's back against a wall between the doors to rooms eight and ten.

"Are you gonna leave on your own accord or do I need to toss you down them stairs?" Aldus said.

The man glanced toward the stairs before staring petulantly back at him. "I'll go. Is that whore somethin' special to you?"

Aldus turned the man toward the stairs and then gave him a push. Once he regained his balance, the man made a show of straightening his shirt and walking to the lobby. Aldus followed him down. Once the man got to the front door, he paused and asked, "You got the backbone to follow me outside or are you gonna run off to hide?"

This time, Aldus didn't try to hide his grin. "I would be pleased to follow you."

The man wasn't wearing a pistol, but he did have a hunting knife hanging from his belt. He strutted outside, walked into the street, and turned around to find Aldus standing less than two paces away from him. Raising both fists in a fighting stance, he said, "Let's see how well you do when you ain't taking me by surprise."

Aldus took one step forward. His fists were held at slightly higher than waist level and his shoulders were stooped forward. The other man came at him with a vicious right cross, which Aldus ducked beneath, and followed up with a left uppercut. Aldus stepped in while bringing his own left arm around to deflect the incoming blow. Having knocked aside that arm, Aldus opened the other man up like a Christmas present and drove a straight right punch into his stomach. The man let out a wheezing grunt that stank of liquor and staggered back. Aldus's instinct was to stay with him and he did so with a few short, shuffling steps.

There were at least a dozen things Aldus could do with his opponent reeling the way he was. Reminding himself that he wasn't in a true fight, he eliminated some of the more brutal options and instead grabbed the man once more by the collar. This time, there was no resistance and the man dangled from his fist like a fish that had been yanked from its pond.

"You . . . you yellow piece . . . piece of . . . ," the man grunted.

Before the insult could be completed, Aldus delivered a quick punch to his face that snapped the man's head back and put him down for the count. Still holding him by the shirt, Aldus lowered him to the ground and said, "The problem with men like you is that you never know when to shut up."

The scuffle hadn't taken long and hadn't been loud enough to draw much attention from anyone other than the clerk from the hotel, who'd come out from behind his desk to watch in the doorway. When Aldus turned and started walking toward the hotel again, the clerk hurried inside.

Aldus didn't say a word to him as he walked to the stairs, climbed to the second floor, and made his way back to room eleven. That door was still ajar, so he eased it open and looked inside. The woman with the battered face sat on the edge of the bed wearing a cautiously fearful expression. She was too tired, however, to do much else than look at him.

"You'd best go," Aldus said as he offered her a hand.

She took it while watching him as if expecting him to pick up where the other man had left off. Once they were outside and she saw the drunk lying where Aldus had dropped him, she walked over and kicked the man solidly in the ribs. Even though the drunk barely even stirred in reaction to the kick, the woman seemed to feel a lot better for it. She had the sunken features and tired eyes of a dove who had been soiled for most of her life. When she looked at Aldus now, some of her sadness disappeared. "Thank you." She started to walk away, but then spun back around to rush at Aldus so she could wrap her arms around him and plant a quick kiss on his cheek. "Thank you so much!"

"It wasn't much, ma'am. You have a good evening, now."

"I will." She put her back to the hotel, crossed over to Douglas Street, and headed toward Second.

Aldus returned to the desk, where the clerk was waiting for him. "So," he said to the tall man with the stringy hair, "you think you can make an exception to that policy of yours requiring a deposit?"

"How many rooms do you need?"

Chapter 19

Aldus returned to the wagons. By the time he'd unloaded the bags with some of their personal effects inside, Hayes was strolling back to him. "Did you find us a hotel?" he asked.

"Yep. The one at the southern end of Garver Street."

"The Kolby Arms?"

"I suppose," Aldus said with a shrug. "We'll need to raise some money pretty quick, though. I used up the last of it."

"You got rooms and put the horses up with what was left?" Hayes asked. "Did you do a few odd jobs to make up the difference?"

"Something like that."

"Well, there's no lot fee for this field, so we can set the gallery up bright and early tomorrow. The man I spoke to about that was bending my ear about hunting geese, so I should be able to sell a few rifles right away. There's a whole group of hunters and trappers coming through here in the next few days! It seems fortune is smiling on us, my friend."

If fortune was smiling, Aldus Bricker was smiling even wider. Hayes winced and then asked, "Is that blood in your mouth?"

After running his tongue over his teeth as if he'd just finished a well-cooked steak, Aldus replied, "Must've bit my cheek."

"Well, keep your spirits up. I have a feeling this is going to be a very profitable place to stay."

"Will you be helping me get the gallery set up?"

"You won't need any help," Hayes said. "Because you'll have the whole day and a little of the next to get it done."

"It'd go faster if you helped me."

"I still need to ride into Omaha to make a delivery that should fill our coffers a bit. It's a one-man job. I'll head out tomorrow and you can get everything set up here. If you get done early, feel free to open up for business."

Surprised, Aldus asked, "Open up without you here?"

Hayes gave him a few friendly pats on the shoulder. "You know what you're doing. You're reliable with numbers. Just don't attempt any repairs until I get back. If any specialized work needs to be done, take appointments at fifty cents apiece. I trust you for the rest."

"I appreciate that, Zeke. Thanks."

"You've earned it. Now I'm going to scout a few of the local saloons. Care to join me?"

"No. I'm going to have something to eat and then get some rest."

"I'll be riding out first thing tomorrow," Hayes said. "If I don't see you, take good care of things while I'm away. And say hello to Bethany for me."

"I will . . . on both counts."

Giving Aldus a sly grin, Hayes headed for Second Street, which would take him into what passed for Corbin's entertainment district. Aldus had only seen a pair of saloons, but if there were any more entertainments to be found, his partner would sniff them out before the night was through. Aldus was left with the bags containing both men's things. Since hauling those things to the hotel was part of his normal duties, Aldus didn't complain before taking hold of them and making his way back to the hotel. The only thing he didn't like was the fact that the drunk had slithered away from the front of the hotel before he could take another crack at him.

The next morning, Aldus slept late. The sun was already burning brightly and there wasn't a hint of dawn's colors left in the sky. There was a small dining room in the hotel consisting of three little round tables that were a stone's throw from the front desk. Aldus wandered down there and took a seat. He waited for a few minutes before a bored girl in her early teens approached him and asked what he wanted to eat.

"Can I have some eggs and toast?" he replied.

"We have ham and potatoes."

"That's all?"

"Yes."

"Then I'll take a plate of that." As the girl started to wander toward a door marked with a sign, Aldus raised his voice to say, "Excuse me."

She turned around as if he'd suddenly become the heaviest burden she could imagine.

"I'm trying to meet up with an old friend," he explained. "Do you know Bethany White?"

"The name sounds familiar."

"So do you know her?"

After thinking for less than a second, she said, "I may have heard her name. Is she the seamstress who works for Mr. Brine?"

"She is!"

"Well, his shop is on First Street."

"Thank you very much," Aldus said. It was fortunate that he could use that little bit of information he was given because the girl who'd given it to him found some-where else to be after handing his breakfast order in to the cook. When Aldus was given his ham and potatoes by an older lady with straight hair kept in a single braid, he wished he'd followed the girl's example. The ham was tough and salty and the potatoes could very well have been scraped off the bottom of a pan after being burned a week ago. Not one to turn down breakfast of any kind, Aldus added enough pepper to drown out the taste and washed the food down with coffee that was strong enough to revive a dead man. A few sips were enough to spur him on, but he drank down the entire cup and scraped every last morsel from his plate before getting up. When he saw the clerk who'd been manning the desk the previous night, Aldus silently cursed himself. Once again, he'd followed his gut instead of his head and or-dered his food without reminding himself that he was almost flat broke. If the meal couldn't be tacked on to his bill, he figured he could pull together enough coins from his pockets to pay for breakfast, but that wouldn't leave him with enough for lunch or anything else.

The clerk was still in rumpled clothes, albeit a differ-ent set than the previous night. He approached Aldus and immediately asked, "Did you pay for that meal?"

"No, sir. Not yet."

"Good," the clerk said through a beaming smile. "Be-cause you can eat for free as long as you're staying here." His smile dimmed a bit before asking, "How long are you staying?"

"Maybe a week or two."

Although the clerk's smile returned, it wasn't quite as bright as it had been. "That's all right. After the way you handled that situation last night, I'm indebted to you. Is there any chance you might be available to handle other situations like that one?"

"You mean if that fella comes back?"

"Yes," the clerk replied with a wince. "Or anyone else like him. I know it's a lot to ask, but . . ."

Aldus slapped the clerk on the back, which caused the tall, gangly man to stumble for half a sideways step. "Anytime you need that fella thumped, I'll be happy to do the thumping."

"That would be great. You see, I'm striving to make the Kolby Arms a more refined hotel than the ones closer to the saloons. I'd like to cater to an upstanding clientele." Picking up on the fact that Aldus was getting lost among so many fancy words, he added, "If I'd wanted men like that in my place, I would have opened a cat-house."

Nodding, Aldus said, "It sounds to me like you're concerned about some other men apart from that one last night."

"There generally isn't trouble here, but when there is there's not a lot I can do apart from fetching Sheriff Dreyer. Naturally, I'd prefer to handle those sorts of things in-house instead of running all the way across town and hoping the law sees fit to respond."

"So you're looking for a skull cracker?"

"A . . . what?"

Back in New York, the man who'd gone out to bring crowds in to watch the fights also had to keep that crowd under control once they got there. With all the betting going on, the drinking, and the ensuing revelry, things oftentimes got out of hand. Skull crackers were the men employed to get things under control or take care of the men who didn't want to be controlled. Usually both tasks were performed with a liberal number of blackjacks applied to the sides of heads. Some of the best skull crackers were former fighters themselves and lived up to their name by wearing large rings that did more damage than a club. One man who stuck out in Aldus's mind had a ring specially made that was just an iron square stuck onto a brass band.

Rather than explain all of that to the clerk, Aldus said, "You want someone to protect your interests at this hotel."

The clerk nodded. "Yes! That's it exactly. In exchange for help on a regular basis, I can offer room and board along with a small payment every week."

"I've already got employment right now, but I can help you out while I'm here. If you need something and I'm not here, I'll be in the field west of town."

"You'll be in a field?"

"I'm here with . . . Never mind. You won't miss me. I'll come around every so often if I'm able. Since I may get busy with my duties, you can keep the weekly payment. Room and board would be enough."

"That's an awful lot for me to provide if you can't even guarantee you'll help when you're needed."

"I'll be the one doing the fighting," Aldus reminded him. "Sparing you one or two of those should be worth the rooms and a couple breakfasts."

"I suppose you're right." After thinking on it for a few seconds, the clerk said, "For now, you've got your room and board."

"For both rooms?"

"Sure. At least for the next couple of days. We can work something out later if you decide to take me up on the original offer. Until then, if you need me, just ask for Edmund."

"And if you need me, I'm Aldus Bricker."

Edmund nodded and shook Aldus's hand, doing a very good job of not drawing attention to the fact that he'd almost walked off without asking for his name. Aldus hadn't signed the register the previous night and hadn't had much of a chance to introduce himself, so he knew Edmund didn't already know it. In his time spent as a fighter, he'd grown accustomed to being known more as a side of beef. Although the men on those docks could rattle off the number of Aldus's wins, losses, and injuries better than he could, they didn't care about such things as proper names. To them, he was the Brick. To Edmund, he was the fellow who could toss drunks out on their ears.

Now that the arrangements had been made, Edmund quickly found other matters in the hotel that required his attention. Apparently he was something more than just a clerk, but Aldus didn't concern himself with that. He had plenty of things on his plate as well.

The first thing he did after leaving the Kolby Arms was to walk straight out to the field where the wagons had been parked. There were plenty of folks around and they all went about their daily business. Shops were opened, horses pulled carriages up and down Garver Street. In the distance, a blacksmith's hammer clanged against iron. When he drew a breath, Aldus could smell the distinctive scents of burning wood and leaves. Autumn was swiftly approaching, which meant the days would become shorter. Unfortunately that also meant he had less time to accomplish his most important job.

Assembling the shooting gallery was twice as tedious as breaking it down. Aldus had a system that seemed almost impossible every time he was about to start it. As soon as he got going, however, one task led to another and the hours melted away. First, he had to remove one set of beams from the wagon. Beneath those, the smaller pieces were kept in boxes or sacks or merely stacked in whatever spaces were available. Such pieces included the pegs and nails used to attach the beams to one another, smaller supports for the structure, and the many targets that had to be put in their proper place. If he had more time, Aldus would have touched up the targets with fresh dabs of paint, but since he just needed to get the gallery up and running, he settled for using the targets as they were.

One by one, he removed the next set of larger beams. When he'd first started traveling with Hayes, this part had required two men to complete. After so much practice, Aldus figured out how to slide the beams partly from the wagon, walk around to the other side, and ease them down. He would then place the beams on a set of thick wooden cylinders that he'd taken from a carpenter's scrap pile in Springfield, Illinois. The beams rolled nicely along those cylinders and could go anywhere Aldus needed them to be as long as he took the cylinder left behind and placed it beneath the front of the beam again. The process involved a whole lot of walking, but it took about the same amount of time as allowing Hayes to carry one end of a beam and shuffle a few steps before having to take a rest.

The skeleton of the gallery was up in a matter of hours and all the pieces were laid out when it was time for Aldus to scrounge for something to eat. Rather than leave everything loose and unguarded, he went to the covered wagon where the scraps of their trail provisions were stored. All he could find was a bag of oatmeal, some sticks of jerked buffalo meat, and just enough coffee to brew one cup. He ate the oatmeal dry, finished off the jerked buffalo, and washed it down with the water from his canteen. The coffee he left for Hayes.

The remainder of the afternoon was spent putting together both ends of the gallery. They were basically two sets of shelves. One in the front was lower and fitted with a rifle rack as well as an open bin to store ammunition. The shelves in the back were for the targets and Aldus put them together with enough time to spare to put both rows of targets in place. The bottles and signs would come later. For now, however, he was finished.

Every step of the way, Aldus had alternated between looking at his work and looking toward the houses where he knew Bethany lived. Even though he'd seen a few children of the right age playing in front of one house, he couldn't say for certain if they were hers. Finally, when he could put it off no longer, Aldus took a deep breath and walked back into town.

A few people asked him about the gallery as he walked down Second Street, and Aldus answered them in as few words as possible. He wasn't even going to attempt to mimic Hayes's boisterous flair, so Aldus settled for being polite and kept moving. He walked up Garver Street and then turned right onto First. Since his mind was filled with all the possibilities of things he could say to Bethany or ways he could make a terrible impression on her, he passed Douglas Street without even noticing how close he was to the tailor's shop.

Thinking back to the few times that shop had been mentioned in Bethany's letters, Aldus tried to figure out exactly where it would be. He found a small storefront on the left side of the street with a sign bearing the name that he'd been looking for. He couldn't read the entire sign but skimmed over it much the same as he would one of the letters so he could pick out enough to give him the general idea. It was a tailor shop and it was named after a word that looked close enough to *Brine* to suit his purposes. Before he could get close enough to see what was in the window, he spotted something that was even more familiar.

Bethany White's was a face that lived in Aldus's thoughts as one of the fondest memories from his youth. Whenever he thought about her smile, his heart ached with the knowledge that he only had himself to blame for not pursuing her. She was a sweet girl who could very well have taken pity on a shy young man, but making his feelings known to her had been too large an obstacle for young Aldus to overcome way back then. She was older now, a woman with all the curves and refinements acquired over the years. Her dress was cut from blue-and-white-checked fabric with a simple lace collar and matching cuffs on the sleeves. Aldus drank in the sight of her all at once, feeling as excited as he'd been before his first fight while also feeling as breathless as he'd been after that same bout.

She was carrying a bag that she held open so she could rummage inside it as she walked. A stout man stood in front of the tailor shop, watching her leave, until Bethany removed something from her bag and turned around to hold it over her head.

"Found it!" she said while waving the small, shiny object.

"All right, then," the man at the tailor shop replied. He was dressed like a businessman without the jacket that went along with the rest of his suit. He waved at Bethany and then turned to shuffle back inside.

Aldus remained rooted to his spot. He didn't even realize he was standing in the street until a man on horseback rode around him. The horse's heavy steps thumped against the ground close to his boots, and the animal's side bumped Aldus like a careless finger knocking over a house of cards. He hopped to one side, turned to see a cart was coming up the street, and then hurried over to the boardwalk before he was trampled.

There was a steady flow of people on the boardwalk. Not enough to swallow him up, but enough to make Aldus feel as if he was effectively hidden within their ranks. From there, he watched as Bethany closed up the bag she was carrying and crossed over to his side of the street. She moved with a spring in her step that made her dark blond curls bounce against the sides of her face and upon a smooth, wide forehead. Whenever she was greeted by someone she knew, she showed the person a wide, if somewhat crooked smile. Aldus couldn't help grinning when he saw that. Bethany's smile had always been one of the warmest, most genuine things he'd ever known.

Although he couldn't do a thing to remove those thoughts from his head, Aldus did his best to put a less conspicuous expression on his face. The one he chose was similar to the blank slate he wore the day before a bout when gambling men would be fishing for signs of weakness in the fighters.

Aldus didn't want to spook Bethany and he most certainly didn't want her to know just how much he thought about her. Even though they'd written so many letters to each other over the last several months, he didn't want to present himself as some steely-eyed predator looking to claim her for his own. Showing up unannounced was risky enough. Figuring out a way to properly introduce himself was—"Aldus?"

The voice that spoke his name was familiar, yet different. Bethany stood in front of him, frozen just as he'd been a few moments ago. So much for a calculated introduction.

He briefly considered passing himself off as someone else. Then he felt a smile take root as he reminded himself of the fact that she'd picked him out so easily from a crowd.

"Is that really you?" she asked.

"Yeah, Bethany. It's me. How have you been?"

Chapter 20

Omaha

Hayes had gotten up before sunrise, packed up what he'd needed, loaded everything onto his horse, and left Corbin as if a tribe of wild Indians were chasing him down. There was no time to lose, especially when dealing with men like the ones who waited for him at the end of his ride. Normally it would have taken him a solid day to make the trip. At least, that's what he'd guessed when studying the maps the night before. But Hayes had his strongest horse beneath him and a good wind at his back. When he arrived in Omaha, the sun was about halfway hidden by the western horizon.

Omaha was a wild place teeming with life drawn by the steam engines of the railroad and merchant traffic along the river. He could find the depot he was after well enough since it was the one surrounded by hotels, vendors' tents of all kinds, and more than enough saloons to fill the Platte River with whiskey. The place he was after catered to gamblers and thieves alike. His clients weren't outlaws, but they preferred to conduct their business in the shadows. The shadows were plenty deep inside the Boxcar Saloon.

Hayes tied his horse to a post outside the place and made sure there was plenty of water in the nearby trough. The brown and white mare had done a superior job and would be treated to the finest greens once the meeting was over. For now, Hayes rubbed her nose and gave her a scratch behind the ear before removing the large bundles that were strapped to either side of the saddle. He cinched the straps up tight, slipped both bundles over his shoulder, and entered the saloon.

This wasn't his first time inside the Boxcar. His face was known well enough for him to make it to the back of the room without being accosted. Even so, he wasn't going to push his luck by being conspicuous. As soon as he sat down, he placed the bundles on the floor and held them beneath his feet. Sitting in that rather awkward position, he ordered a beer from the skinny woman who made her rounds in the place and waited.

The back of the saloon was dominated by a bar that looked solid enough to keep a stampede at bay. It was chipped and notched in many spots but had held up well enough over the years. A broken mirror was hung on the wall behind it, covered partially by shelves of bottles and glasses. The rest of the room was filled with tables and chairs, none of which combined to form one matching set. Hayes had finished about half of his beer when a lean figure strode through the front entrance. There was no door in the frame, which was just as well since the Boxcar never really closed.

Hayes recognized the man immediately, not so much by his sunken features and trimmed mustache, but from the clothes that were wrapped around his compact frame. That man, like the other two who followed him into the saloon, wore a clean black suit and polished boots. The man in front and one of his companions each wore a silver watch with a chain crossing his midsection.

All of them wore gun belts strapped around their waists, and their hands rarely strayed far from the pistols holstered there.

Since getting up would have meant taking his feet away from the bundles on the floor, Hayes waited for the men to approach before reaching up to extend his hand. "Vernon Winter! So glad to see you again."

Vernon didn't so much as glance at the hand being offered and he didn't make a move toward any of the chairs at the table. "Did you bring them?" he asked in a scratchy voice.

Hayes reached down for the bundles and lifted them just enough to be seen. "They're right here."

All Vernon had to do was nod toward the bundles, and both of his companions moved in to claim them.

The salesman wasn't happy to relinquish the bundles, but he wasn't foolish enough to protest when they were taken from him. "There is still the matter of payment."

"Come along with us," Vernon said. "We're not about to settle things in this place."

"It's always been good enough before."

"That was when we were buying one or two pistols. Making a few repairs. This is different. This time, our employer needs a better look at what he's paying so much money for."

Since all three men were armed and had no qualms with putting their guns to work, Hayes stood up. "Lead the way, gentlemen."

Hayes was led to a long warehouse built close enough to the railroad tracks for every rattling wheel and hiss of steam to be heard. Vernon Winter and his two companions rode in a carriage, and Hayes followed along on his horse. Once they arrived at their destination, he was allowed to tie the mare to a post outside one warehouse while Vernon and the men entered another. Vernon came back out to retrieve him and then escorted Hayes to a small room in the corner of the spacious, almost cavernous structure.

Inside the room, there was only a table with nothing on it and a man who stood with his back to the door looking through a window at the adjoining train yard. He was a stout figure and solidly built. His thick arms and heavily callused hands looked as if they'd laid a good portion of the track extending westward into the Great Plains and beyond. After Hayes and Vernon had filed into the room, the man turned around and asked, "Where are the guns?"

Vernon moved to one side, allowing one of his partners to step in and place the bundles on the table.

"They're all there, Augustus," Hayes said.

Ignoring the salesman, Augustus spread out one of the bundles like a bedroll. Inside were rifles held in place by leather loops stitched to the bundle's interior. There were several makes and models of rifles represented there with at least two of each kind, half a dozen in all. On top of that, Augustus unrolled the second bundle to find an identical inventory.

Looking up as if Hayes had just then popped into existence, Augustus said, "You never disappoint, Zachariah."

"That would be bad for business," Hayes replied.

"Are they all modified to my specifications?"

"I worked on each one myself. I fitted them all with my patented sights, filed down the levering mechanisms for quicker reloading, adjusted the tension on the triggers for easier firing, and reinforced the chambers to withstand my upgraded ammunition."

"About that ammunition . . ."

"I brought plenty of it as well. Extra, in fact, than what was agreed upon. Consider it a bonus."

"I'll need to test it."

Sweeping his hands over the rifles, Hayes said, "Be my guest."

Augustus placed his hand on top of one of the rifles, moved it along them all, and then peeled back the top bundle to show the one that had been unrolled beneath it. The rifle he selected was a Winchester. He put it to his shoulder and looked down the top of its barrel through the newer sights. Then he worked the lever to feel the action, which flowed smoother than an overgreased piston. Finally he put his finger on the trigger and dropped the hammer with a flat, metallic slap.

"Touchy," he said.

Hayes nodded. "It takes some getting used to, but you assured me your men know what they're doing."

"Oh, they most certainly do."

"Then they'll find the more sensitive trigger reduces the risk of their shot being displaced as it would when more pressure is required to pull it."

"I'll have one of those bullets," Augustus said as he held out one hand, palm up.

"Most certainly," Hayes replied. He reached for the top bundle, unbuttoned a small pocket, and fished out a single round. "There's not enough room for all of the ammunition, but it's not far from here."

"With your horse?"

"That's right."

Augustus nodded and then fit the round into the rifle. Carrying the Winchester out of the small room, he stepped into the main space of the warehouse, which was filled with stacks of crates and sacks of sugar and grain piled into pyramids that were almost as tall as a man. He

seemed pleased with how the rifle felt in his grasp as well
as how it fit against his shoulder. When the rifle sent its
round flying through the warehouse amid a thunderous
roar and a kick that sent him back a step, he was even
more pleased.

"Very nice, indeed," Augustus said. "Although it will
definitely take some adjustment." He handed the rifle
over to Vernon and strode back into the office. "What
about accuracy? This one was just fine, as I assume they
all are, but what's the effective range?"

"Up to three hundred yards," Hayes told him. "For
maximum effect with the modified ammunition, I'd say
no more than half of that. Those rounds will work just
fine, but you'll lose some of the kick at more than . . .
say . . . a hundred and seventy-three yards."

"When I placed this order with you those months ago,
I half expected you to inform me there would be a delay
in filling it. I even suspected there would be a chance
that you'd back out and keep the advance you were
given."

Hayes looked genuinely appalled. "Back out? I've
never reneged on an order!"

"So it seems. How long before you can make more?"

"How many do you need?"

"Another order the same size as this one. Double the
ammunition as well."

"Give me another few months," Hayes said.

Augustus reached inside his dark suit jacket, which
looked identical in cut and fabric to the suits worn by
Vernon Winter and both of his associates. He removed a
thick envelope from his interior pocket and handed it to
Hayes. "Please count it to make sure it's all there."

"I trust you," Hayes assured him while weighing the
envelope in his hand.

"Don't be foolish, Mr. Hayes. Count it. I'll wait."

Hayes flipped through the cash and added it up in no time. Nodding, he tucked the envelope away into the pocket of his jacket. "How long will you be in Omaha?"

"Just another day or two. After that, we're heading out to make our rounds."

"As will I. So another order of rifles and double the ammunition. I trust I can contact you at the same address to let you know when I'm ready to deliver?"

"Our employer isn't pulling up stakes anytime soon," Augustus said with a shark's smile. "Can I fix you a drink?"

"That would be grand!"

Chapter 21

Corbin, Nebraska

Aldus and Bethany talked while he escorted her home. Although she'd immediately asked how he'd been doing, Bethany did most of the talking as she described how her children were faring in school and all the work that had been piling up at the tailor shop. Once they'd reached the end of Garver Street, she stopped and said, "I've just been chattering on the entire time. How rude of me."

"Not at all. It's wonderful to hear your voice," Aldus said. "I mean, seeing as how we've only written to each other. That is ... if you don't count when we talked all them years ago before I left. Not that that don't count, of course. . . ."

She reached out and placed a hand on his arm. "Don't worry. I know what you mean." Bethany smiled and pulled her hand back. "I ... I'm nervous also. I wish you would have let me know you were coming." Almost immediately, she added, "Not that I'm unhappy you're here!"

Aldus laughed. "All right. We don't have to tiptoe around each other so much. We're old friends, so we can breathe easy and just act like old friends. Agreed?"

"Agreed," she said with a nod. Clasping her hands in front of her, Bethany started walking again. They were at the edge of town where houses were built in small clusters of two or three. Aldus could only see eight or nine of them, but they were spread out as if they'd literally spilled from the main portion of Corbin. Most were two floors high and a few were smaller. Children ran to and fro, playing games and waving to Bethany as she walked by.

"I'm sorry I didn't let you know I'd be coming," Aldus said. "To be honest, it was kind of a quick decision."

She was a full head shorter than him. It wasn't until she looked up at him that Aldus remembered how clear and blue her eyes were. He counted it as a blessing that he'd allowed such a thing to slip from his memory. Holding on to a sight like that while being so far away from her would have been too much to bear.

"So, what was it that brought you here?" she asked.

"Your letters."

Frowning, Bethany said, "I'm so sorry. I haven't had as much time to write to you lately. I hope you didn't think something terrible had happened."

"Oh no. Nothing like that. It's just . . . I . . . read them and it struck me how long it had been since we'd seen each other. My business brings me out to Omaha every so often, so I figured it would be good to come down to Corbin for a switch."

"Your business," she said as her face brightened once again. "You mean your apprenticeship with that gunsmith? Mr. Hayes, isn't it?"

"That's right."

"You'd written about passing through Omaha," she said as she cast her eyes downward. "I . . . wondered why you didn't want to make the ride out here at least once."

"It's not that I didn't want to."

"Oh, I know. I didn't mean it as something cruel or thoughtless. You've got business to tend to and you have to go where you need to go. That was selfish of me. I shouldn't have said anything."

Aldus stopped. When Bethany did the same, he placed a finger under her chin and lifted her face so he could look straight into those bright blue eyes when he told her, "You can say whatever you want to me."

She seemed to look a bit deeper into his eyes as well.

"I mean," he continued, "we've known each other long enough."

"Yes, we have." As soon as he moved his hand away, she turned toward the houses and started walking again. "I remember when we were both still in school. You were always so quiet most of the time. Then again, I also remember how much you used to make me laugh."

Aldus had taken it upon himself to do just that in those days. More often than not, his efforts had gotten him into trouble with the teacher, but he never stopped fishing for just one more smile.

"I'm really glad you decided to come," she said. "So, is Mr. Hayes around? After what you wrote about him, I feel like I know him."

Although he doubted Hayes had written anything other than what Aldus had told him to write, he wondered if a few complimentary embellishments had been made. Hayes wasn't beyond such a thing. In fact, blowing his own horn was more like the salesman's nature.

"He rode into Omaha to settle up some accounts," Aldus said. "He should be back in a day or two."

"Oh. How long will you be in Corbin?"

"At least a few weeks, I'd imagine. Perhaps we could find some time to talk some more?"

Bethany looped an arm around his and led him toward the very house that Aldus had been watching from afar when he'd been working at the wagons. "I've got plenty of time right now. How about you?"

Before he'd taken so much as a second to think about what else he needed to do that night, Aldus said, "I've got all the time in the world."

"What about an appetite? I'm not the best cook, but you're welcome to join us for supper if you like."

"I've always got an appetite."

"Good," she said while grasping his arm a little tighter. "My house is that one straight ahead. Come inside and I can fix you some lemonade."

"That sounds nice."

"Good. And you can meet my boys."

Aldus felt his muscles tense as if in reaction to a punch. Whenever he'd dreamt about seeing Bethany again, meeting her children had been the cold splash of water to bring him right back to real life. It wasn't that Aldus disliked kids. He simply didn't have occasion to be around them very much. The years when he'd been fighting in New York, he'd only seen the occasional blood-thirsty youngster who was brought to the docks by a drunken father. For the most part, he'd treated kids the way he would a hornet buzzing around his head. If he didn't make any moves toward them, they tended to go somewhere else.

Realizing he'd fallen silent, Aldus said, "That . . . that would be good."

"If you'd rather not, I understand."

"Don't be silly! With all I've read about them, I feel like I already shook their hands."

"Wonderful," she said happily. "Because here comes one of them now."

Once again, Aldus tensed. There were several women and children about, either on the porches of nearby homes or running on the grass in front of them. One little boy was running straight for Bethany. He was a little fellow with wide green eyes and a head full of curly, dark brown hair. His little cheeks were red from the run, and dirt was caked onto the front of his dark blue shirt. As soon as he arrived at her side, he reached up for her with both arms and was promptly scooped up.

"This is Michael," Bethany said.

Aldus looked at the boy, and the boy looked back at him while popping his thumb into his mouth.

"Umm ... hello there," Aldus said.

Prompting him with a gentle shake, Bethany said, "Don't be rude, Michael."

"Hello," the boy said. "What's your name?"

"Aldus Bricker."

Michael was more impressed with the taste of his thumb than the man in front of him. Still, he didn't cry in fear or struggle to get away from him as Aldus had imagined.

Finally Michael said, "That's a funny name."

"Michael!" Bethany scolded.

"No, I suppose it is," Aldus said. Leaning in to poke at the boy's stomach, he said, "Maybe I think Michael is a funny name, too."

The boy's face lit up with a smile that he'd been fortunate enough to inherit from his mother. "No, it isn't!"

Aldus smiled, too, and it overtook him until he found himself laughing almost as much as the five-year-old when he tickled his belly.

"Hey! Who are you?"

Aldus looked over to find the voice had come from another boy standing a few feet away from Bethany. He stood between four and five feet tall and had dark blond hair and a face that was so close to Bethany's that someone would have had to be blind not to realize he was one of hers.

"James, this is my friend Aldus," she said. "Remember when I told you about him?"

The eight-year-old took a few cautious steps forward upon long, skinny legs. His front teeth had come in and they stuck out among the smaller ones to make him look almost as awkward as Aldus had felt when he'd been that age. "You're the fighter, right?" he asked.

Aldus nodded. "Used to be. That's right."

"Did it hurt when you got punched?"

"Well . . . it didn't tickle, I can tell you that much."

Michael squirmed in his mother's arms until she set him down. Walking up to stand on Aldus's left foot, he grabbed hold of his belt and stretched his other arm up to point at Aldus's face with one little hand. "Your nose is crooked!"

"Maybe you can fix it," Aldus said as he stooped down to Michael's level.

The boy gleefully grabbed Aldus's nose and twisted it back and forth while sticking his tongue out in concentration. Before his nose was pulled from his face, Aldus stood up and felt it. "Guess it's stuck that way," he said to the child.

Michael shrugged, turned around, and ran for the house.

"Maybe you'd like to try?" Aldus said as he turned to James.

The skinny boy shook his head and stepped away. "That won't fix your nose."

"Guess there ain't no fixing me. It got busted up pretty bad."

James's eyes widened and his mouth fell open. "You mean someone did that to you?"

"Well, it happens in a fight," Aldus said dismissively.

"Did it hurt?"

"Yeah. A lot."

The boy was at a loss for words and he quickly turned away to catch up to his little brother.

Bethany shrugged. "He's afraid of blood," she explained.

"Oh, hell."

"And . . . I'd prefer it if you didn't speak that way in front of them."

Aldus hung his head. "Maybe I shouldn't stay."

"Don't be silly," she said. "Just don't regale them with stories about teeth getting knocked out and you'll be fine."

"You sure?"

She nodded. "I insist."

Chapter 22

Omaha, Nebraska

Hayes had a drink with Augustus and his men, followed by a few more drinks, which led into a poker game held at the back of the warehouse. It was a friendly enough game where Hayes only lost a small portion of what was in his envelope. Afterward, he said his farewells and told them he would go to his horse to retrieve the rest of the ammunition.

"Just bring it tomorrow," Augustus said. "We won't need it until we leave."

"Very gracious of you, sir. I believe I am in need of a few hours of sleep. And so," Hayes said with a flourished tip of his hat, "I bid you adieu."

The men in suits gave him a much less dramatic farewell before going back to their game.

There were plenty of other warehouses in this section of town, most of which were used to hold cargo that had either been taken from or was about to be loaded onto one of the many trains passing through. Some warehouses had horse stalls similar to the one used by Augustus's men, while every other one had hitch rails alongside it. His mare was right where he'd left it. The pair of horses that was tied beside her hadn't been there before, but it wasn't the animals that caught his eye.

His head snapped up and he stopped dead in his tracks.

"It . . . can't be," he whispered.

First, he looked around in every direction. All he found were murky shadows and a few sputtering lanterns hanging from short poles. The corner in the distance was alive with figures darting from one shadow to another, some staggering and some running. The saloons were busiest at this late hour. Hayes's immediate vicinity, on the other hand, only echoed with that activity.

Hayes slowly approached the horse tethered directly beside his own. "Easy, now," he whispered as he got closer. "Just want to get a look."

All of the horses remained calm. The one that Hayes was most interested in looked over and gave him an inquisitive sniff before shifting its eyes back to the trough in front of it. Hayes placed a calming hand on its neck and cocked his head to one side so he could see the rifle in the boot of that saddle at a different angle.

It was a Sharps rifle with a set of modified sights mounted near the firing mechanism. The plate near the trigger guard wasn't original, either. In fact, it was similar to the ones he himself used when putting together one of his specialty commissions. Squinting while leaning in closer, Hayes examined the maker's mark behind the trigger guard.

It was an *H* with a *Z* overlaying it. The rifle was one of his.

"I'll be damned!" he said in a harsh whisper. Reaching for the rifle, he pulled it from the boot so he could get a closer look. Everything from the mark to the custom sights and even the carving on the stock told him it was not only one of his custom jobs, but it was the very

Sharps rifle that had been stolen from him in Cedar Rapids. Just to confirm that, he checked the number near the lever.

Hayes felt his stomach clench as if it were in the grip of an icy fist. When he thought about those outlaws, his first instinct was to take the rifle and use it to hunt them down. They had to be around somewhere. And then, almost as quickly as it had boiled up inside him, the rage abated.

He was no lawman.

He wasn't a fighter.

He was, however, alone.

As his head cleared, Hayes reminded himself that he couldn't be certain the horses he'd discovered in fact belonged to the men who had robbed him. For all he knew, those outlaws could have sold the Sharps to someone else or lost it. That horse could even belong to a lawman or a bounty hunter who had put the outlaws down like the dogs they were. Hayes nodded, silently assuring himself that it was best not to lose his head.

". . . still in there."

Those words drifted through the air from farther down the alley between two warehouses. They were spoken in a quick whisper and followed by scurrying footsteps scraping against packed dirt. Hayes took a quick look in the direction from which those voices came, only to find two hunched figures circling around from behind the warehouse being used by Augustus. He couldn't make out any faces, but a sudden rush of panic coursed through the salesman's body, prompting him to move away from the horses.

There weren't many places for him to go. If he took off running, he would most definitely be seen. If he ducked behind the water trough, he would be discovered by anyone coming for the horses. Since there were two

horses apart from his own and two figures drawing closer
by the second, that hiding spot didn't seem like an ideal
one.

Hayes almost missed the pair of crates stacked against
the wall of Augustus's warehouse. They leaned at a slight
angle to create a dark shadow beside them. Before he
wasted the few seconds he had left, Hayes darted across
the alley, put his back to the wall beside the crates, and slid
down into the shadow. When the top crate shifted as if to
fall onto him, he used the rifle in his hand to prop it up.

He still had the rifle in his hand!

In the excitement to find a place to hide, Hayes had
forgotten about the Sharps rifle he'd been examining. If
he was concerned about the men coming for their horses,
it would have made sense to return the rifle before it was
missed. He clenched his teeth and held his breath. The
mistake had already been made. There was no turning
back now.

The figures slowed and had stopped talking to one
another. Having covered just over half of the length of
the long warehouse, they drew close enough for Hayes
to hear every one of their steps as they came to a halt.

Fast, steady breathing filled the air. Hayes prayed he
wasn't the one making those sounds.

A few more tentative steps were taken.

Rather than move a single muscle, Hayes turned only
his eyes toward the figures. One of the lanterns hanging
nearby cast a weak halo around its post. When one of the
two figures took another step, some of that light fell onto
the face of Wes Cavanaugh.

"Where'd he go?" Wes snarled.

The second figure moved with a slower cadence as he
turned to look all around him while plodding forward. "I
thought I saw someone run toward the street," Mose
said.

"Which street?"

"This one right here," he replied while pointing at the street passing in front of the warehouses.

The men were approaching the horses, which put them at about five yards away from where Hayes was hiding. As the outlaws got closer, Hayes felt more and more as if he were just standing in the open and exposed.

Wes stopped near the horses to reach out one hand toward the saddle with the empty boot.

This is it, Hayes thought. *He'll see the rifle is missing and then find me against the wall near those crates. Odds are, he's found me already.*

"I told you they're all still in there," Wes said. The hand he extended came to a rest on the horse's rump, where he gave the animal a pat before moving on. His eyes were fixed on the corner of Augustus's building. "I saw something move up ahead. Looked like he was headed that way."

Now Mose was near the horses. Unlike the other outlaw, he turned and took a closer look at the tethered animals.

Hayes eased a finger beneath the rifle's trigger guard. The Sharps was resting against the wall with its barrel keeping the upper crate from moving. When he angled his eyes downward, he had a difficult time seeing his own chest, legs, or feet, thanks to the shadows and the dark clothes he wore. As much as he wanted to ease his other hand toward the pistol at his side, he was certain that much movement would give away his position.

"Take a look around the corner," Mose said. "Could be someone heard us out here."

Wes drew his pistol and stalked toward the corner. Actually, he drew Hayes's pistol. The nickel-plated .45 filled his hand, causing Hayes to choke back the impulse to rush forward and reclaim it. As Wes approached the corner, he moved dangerously close to the crates where Hayes was hiding. So close, in fact, that Hayes thought it impossible the outlaw hadn't seen him yet.

A few more steps took Wes past the salesman's position. Hayes got a good enough look at Wes's face to see that his eyes were fixed on the front portion of the building. There were more scraping steps, followed by the brush of a shoulder against the wall.

The next several seconds passed in silence.

Both outlaws held their ground with guns drawn.

Hayes remained so still that his muscles began to ache. The more they ached, the more he thought he might accidentally give himself away with a twitch. He could just make out the outline of Wes through the slats of the crates. Every so often, Wes would lean forward to glance around at the front of the warehouse. Unfortunately Mose was taking more interest in the shadows beside those crates.

The bigger outlaw stood in the light being cast from the lantern meant to illuminate the hitch rail. He squinted into the darkness directly in front of him, his eyes drawing closer to the spot where they would eventually lock with Hayes's.

"You there!"

Hayes almost jumped when he heard that. He might have shifted slightly, but the two outlaws moved a lot more.

The voice had come from the front of the warehouse. When it shouted, "Whoever is there, show yourself," Hayes recognized it as belonging to Vernon Winter.

"It's one of them railroad men," Wes hissed.

Forgetting about the crates, Mose raised his pistol and thumbed back its hammer. "Just one of 'em?" he asked.

Wes waved him back. "There's more inside and they're all loaded for bear. Just keep quiet."

"Where is he?"

The steps that were crunching against the ground from the warehouse's front entrance drew closer. "That you, Zachariah?" Vernon asked.

Hayes could feel beads of sweat pushing through his skin to trickle down the front of his face.

"We may have to take this one," Mose whispered.

Wes hunkered down. "No," he said in a voice that was almost too quiet to be heard. "Just get ready to run back to our spot."

"Who's over there?" Vernon shouted.

Wes stepped back while stretching his free hand behind him to motion to his partner. Mose shuffled into the middle of the alley, his feet making a sound that was like nails on dry slate.

More footsteps came from the front of the warehouse as more men stepped outside to investigate.

"What's going on out here?" Augustus asked.

"I thought I heard someone sneaking around out back," Vernon told him. "They ran off and I think they're down that way."

"Take some men to see what it is. I'll send some more out back."

"We can get the drop on 'em," Mose whispered. "They don't know where we are or how many—"

"No," Wes snapped. "Fighting now will only ruin what we got cooking. We're too close to spoil it now!"

"Should we ride out of here?"

"No," Wes said as he hurried past the crates on his way to the horses. When Vernon and some of the others could be heard approaching the corner of the building, he hissed, "Just run."

And without another word, both men bolted toward the rear of the building. Their steps beat a furious rhythm against the ground. When they approached the other end of the warehouse, more voices called out. Judging by the distance of those voices, the rear entrance was most likely at the corner farthest away from the spot where the horses were tethered.

Hayes was thinking about leaving his shadows when the steps that had been drawing closer rounded the front corner of the building and stormed toward him. Instead, he pressed himself so flat against the wall that he wouldn't have been surprised if he'd burrowed all the way inside the warehouse. Vernon and another man tore down the alley, stopping just long enough to get a look at the horses and the trough. When Vernon turned toward the crates, he sighted along the top of his pistol and moved directly toward the darkest shadows.

Knowing he was seconds away from being exposed, Hayes inched forward.

"Zachariah?" Vernon said. "Why are you hiding there?"

"Two men," Hayes said. "They were just here. They went . . ." Hayes pointed toward the back end of the warehouse just as the men who had emerged from the rear entrance opened fire.

"Go on!" Vernon said to the man with him who'd been playing cards with Hayes a few minutes ago. When the man ran down the wide alley, Vernon lowered his pistol without holstering it. "What are you doing?"

"I was coming for my horse when those two men showed up."

"Who are they?"

Before Hayes could answer that question, Wes and Mose ran back around the corner and into sight. They were all the way at the other end of the warehouse covering their retreat with blazing six-guns. They came to a stop, took a look toward the horses, and spotted Vernon right away.

"Stop where you are!" Vernon said. "What's your business here?"

The outlaws ran in the opposite direction, and like a dog seeing a rabbit scamper away, Vernon raced after them. He was quickly joined by the rest of Augustus's men, who all filled the night with the thunder of gunfire.

Hayes stood where he was, waiting to see if he would need to get on his horse, duck inside the warehouse, or possibly run in another direction. Although the gunmen were a good distance away, Hayes could see one of Augustus's men straighten up and fall back as he caught one of the outlaw's bullets in the chest or head.

Hayes's first impulse had been to take his rifle and leave the gunmen to their work. The more firing he heard, however, the more convinced he became that the outlaws were leading their pursuers on a wild-goose chase. Obviously, they'd been scouting out the area around the warehouses and had been hiding well enough to watch Augustus and the others for some time. If they'd planned that far in advance, it was most likely they'd circle back around to reclaim their horses instead of running into the night like a couple of headless chickens.

After the shoot-out at Cal Overland's spread, Hayes didn't want any part of firing at another human being unless there was absolutely no choice. Then again, after being robbed and having his friend beaten by those outlaws, he wasn't of a mind to just let them go if there was anything at all he could do about it.

When he thought back to meeting Wes and Mose in Cedar Rapids, Hayes remembered one thing above all else. Wes had wanted that rifle so badly he could taste it. Hayes smiled as he dug into his pocket for a small folding knife. When he found it, he took the knife and the rifle to the hitch rail close to where a lantern was hanging.

"If he wants this rifle so badly," he said as he placed the rifle on top of the hitch rail to give him a somewhat steady surface, "then he shall have it."

A pocketknife wasn't much of a tool for working on a rifle, but Hayes wasn't concerned with precision. He stuck the blade into specific parts of the firing mechanism and scarred the work he'd so painstakingly done. He felt like a painter who knew exactly which lines to smudge to make one of his landscapes look especially flawed. Hayes misaligned something here, scratched in a notch there, and tweaked the trigger just a little bit in the wrong direction. He was admiring his handiwork and touching up a few of the more obvious maladjustments when he heard footsteps approaching the warehouse.

Hayes used the tip of his pocketknife to gouge a little deeper into the rifle's innards and then scraped. As his hands worked, his head turned and his eyes darted to find the source of those steps. He couldn't see who was making them, but they were obviously trying to be stealthy in their approach. The gunshots in the distance had tapered off to a sporadic crackle. There were voices coming from that general area, which told Hayes that whoever was firing had lost sight of their intended targets.

Having done as much damage as he could without completely disassembling the Sharps, Hayes reached into his pocket for what would be the icing on the cake. There had been three rounds in the rifle when he'd taken it. There were only two of the modified bullets in Hayes's pocket, but he put both of them in along with one of the original ones. The modified rounds didn't look much different from the others, but the mixture of powder in them was such that it gave a much bigger kick than a typical round. One of those fired from a rifle not reinforced to handle it would cause damage. Considering what he'd done to sabotage the Sharps, that damage should be catastrophic.

The footsteps were drawing closer and Hayes dropped the rifle back into the boot of Wes's saddle. Since there was nowhere else to hide, he simply took off running toward the back of the warehouse. He'd barely taken four bounding steps when Wes and Mose rounded the front corner.

"Don't shoot!" Hayes said as he stretched his hands above his head. "I'm unarmed!"

The bigger of the two outlaws sighted along the top of his barrel, only to be stopped by his partner.

"He ain't one of them railroad men!" Wes snapped. "Just let him go."

"But he could give us away," Mose protested.

"Not any quicker than you would by firing a shot! We got what we needed. Just get yer horse and go!"

Reluctant to make any move that might reverse his good fortune, Hayes crouched down low and eased toward a wall. Although he didn't have anything in front of him that would stop a bullet, he felt better once a wall was against his back and he was no longer in the open.

The outlaws mounted their horses and pointed their noses down the alley. With the snap of leather, they galloped past Hayes and thundered off into the night.

Hayes found himself crouched as low as he could get with both arms wrapped around his head. Once it was absolutely clear that the horses weren't going to turn around, he straightened up and squinted to find them. He only caught a quick glance of movement at the end of the street before they were gone altogether. Although he still didn't have his rifle or the money that had been taken, he smiled with the knowledge that he'd effectively tossed a wrench into the other men's plans whatever they might have been. His only regret was that he wouldn't be there to see how his efforts would pay off.

Once again, the night was dark and quiet. The only commotion he could hear were echoes from Omaha's saloon district. By the time Hayes untied his horse's reins and climbed into the saddle, Vernon and some of the other men had found their way back.

"Did you see where they went?" Vernon asked.

"That way," Hayes replied while pointing in the direction the outlaws had gone. "Do you want the rest of those bullets now or later?"

"Drop them off whenever you like. Just make sure we have them before noon tomorrow."

"All right, then. I'm going to find a hotel in a safer part of town."

Chapter 23

Corbin, Nebraska

The supper Bethany prepared was a simple beef stew served over split biscuits. At least, it should have been simple. He'd tasted worse in his life, but not by much. With liberal application of salt, pepper, and more pepper, it went down well enough. Afterward, the boys ran outside and Bethany invited Aldus to sit with her on the porch. Michael remained close, eyeing Aldus with cautious curiosity. On a whim, Aldus stood up and walked over to him.

"Here you go," he said as he held out his arm and leaned down to the boy's level. "Grab on."

Michael looked up at him and then over to his mother.

"It's all right," Bethany said.

When Michael grabbed Aldus's arm with both hands, Aldus lifted him off the ground and let him swing. "Just like a monkey," Aldus said.

The instant Michael's feet touched the ground, he was reaching for the same arm. "Do it again! Again!"

This time, Aldus held on to both of the little boy's hands and swung him in a circle. James was quick to rush over and demand his turn. Soon they were climbing all over him and laughing every second of the way. Several minutes later, the boys were still raring to go and Aldus could barely catch his breath.

"That's enough, you two," Bethany said. "Go inside and get ready for bed."

Amid a chorus of whines, the boys trudged into the house.

Placing a hand on his shoulder, Bethany said, "I need to get them tucked in. School tomorrow. You can wait here if you like. That is . . . if you don't have anything else to do."

"If you'd prefer to get some rest, I understand," he said.

"It's nice talking to you face-to-face."

"Then I'll wait here. I still need to collect myself after all that roughhousing. I work like a mule most days, but this nearly did me in!"

"You should be here when they're really wound up. Help yourself to whatever you like in the kitchen. You sure you want to wait?"

"I'm sure."

"Then I'll see you in a while."

Aldus sat in a rocker on her porch, looking out at the town that extended to the south and east. In the fading rays of the sun, he could even see Hayes's wagons and shooting gallery. There was paint to touch up, signs to hang, guns to clean, displays to construct, plus any number of odd jobs that needed to be done before the next morning. Still, he remained on that porch and allowed the last bit of the workday to slip from his grasp. He'd come too far to do any different.

Bethany returned several minutes later. The sun had set, the air was cool, and she was wrapped in a shawl as she pulled up the second rocker closer beside him.

"Sorry that took so long," she said. "They wanted two stories instead of just one."

"I didn't mind waiting."

Drawing the shawl in tightly around her shoulders, Bethany stared out at the town's lit windows and watched folks make their way toward the saloons. "Can I ask you something, Aldus?"

"Go right ahead."

"I . . . don't want you to think me rude."

He looked over at her, forming a guess in his mind as to what was on hers.

"Why are you here in Corbin?" she asked. "Or . . . why now when you never made the trip any of those other times you were in Omaha?"

"When I wrote my first letter to you . . . I believe I even mentioned how I could have ridden down here, but I never heard anything from you. Fact is, I didn't hear anything back from my first couple of letters until nearly a year had passed. You were never unkind when you eventually wrote back, but you never really took me up on my offer."

She sighed. "I was afraid of that. I just thought . . . with all the times we've written over the last year or so that it might come up again. I do remember you bringing it up back in that first letter. I was just . . . in a situation where seeing you may not have been appropriate."

"Because of Nate Talbott?"

For a second, Bethany looked surprised. Then she blinked a few times and nodded. "I suppose I did mention his name in my letters."

"Were the two of you together?"

"For a time. Actually," she added, "it was about the same time I got that first letter you sent. Me and Nate hadn't been together for long, but it seemed like we both knew where it was headed. To be honest, I doubted I'd meet anyone who would be interested in me at all."

That made Aldus cringe. The fact that Bethany, of all people, could think something like that made him feel doubly foolish for not having the backbone to tell her how he felt so long ago.

She was gazing up at the darkening sky. "My husband, William, was a good man," she said. "He had his faults, but I thought I could help see him through them. We didn't see eye-to-eye on a lot of things. Even when James was born, he seemed more interested in his work than being with his child or wife."

"He drove cattle, right?"

"Yes. He was gone a lot, but when the rest of the boys from that ranch came home, William would be missing for an extra day or two. I guessed he was out drinking. When he came home, he'd always promise to straighten up and be a better father. He always talked about having lots of children. A part of me thought that he wasn't good enough with the first one, but we decided to have another. Once Michael came along, I thought William would change for the better. He did for a while, but it wasn't long before he started disappearing again. When he took ill, it hit the boys hard."

"Must've hit you as well," Aldus said.

"It did. After he passed on, though, life seemed about the same as it was before. Just me and the boys. Then Nate came along a few years later. He seemed like a good sort. The boys didn't mind him being around and I thought they could use a man to look up to. Also ... I was lonely." She let her head fall forward. "That must sound so pathetic."

"Not at all. You don't have to explain yourself this way."

After drawing a deep breath, Bethany said, "I do, Aldus. It was wrong of me to ignore those first few letters you sent. I felt so bad about it and you deserve to know why. That is . . . if you care about such things."

He nodded. "I care."

Bethany reached over to put her hand on top of his. Rather than let it stay there for long, she patted him a few times and then sank back into her rocker. "I'd just settled in and figured Nate was about as good a man as I could expect. There were times when he seemed similar to William. Other times, he was worse."

Aldus wanted to ask what that entailed, but he allowed her to tell the story at her own pace.

"Nate was settling in, too," she continued. "He mentioned marriage but hadn't really asked me yet. I wasn't anxious to rush to that point, but it seemed good for the boys to have a father again. My mother and sisters visited me about that time and they told me what they thought of Nate. It wasn't much."

"They didn't like him?"

"Not many folks did. I always just thought I could help him become a better man. Maybe smooth out the rough edges. Anyway, I'd come this far already and it didn't seem right for me to just turn around and tell him to go." After what seemed a prolonged absence, her smile returned. "That's when I got your first letter. You were so earnest and so sweet, just like the boy I remembered. You mentioned wanting to see me, and my first thought was to drop everything and run to see you. I mentioned it to Jenny, my older sister, and she said I should do just that. I was so close, Aldus. I almost did it."

Aldus was glad it was dark on that porch because he knew for a fact that he couldn't hide what he was thinking. If she looked at him for just a few seconds, she'd be able to tell he was reflecting on how wonderful it would have been if they'd met. How different everything would have been for both of them. How much better . . .

But it never served anyone to regret where they were or the mistakes they'd made. All that was left to do was find a way to set things right. If there was any reason at all for revisiting painful memories, that was it.

"I should have gone to see you," she said. "At least I should have written you back promptly. The reason I didn't was that I was afraid that I might just . . . I don't know. Maybe having the boys made me more cautious than I should have been."

"By not running off to meet up with a man you hadn't seen for years who'd been fighting on the docks of New York? That doesn't sound too cautious to me. It sounds like you were using your head."

She laughed. "When you say it that way . . ."

"You don't owe me any explanations," Aldus told her. "But it is nice to hear what's been going on."

"You asked about Nate. I guess that was a bit more than you were hoping to hear. I tend to prattle on when I get nervous."

"So, where's Nate now?"

She lowered her head and adjusted the shawl as if hearing his name alone was enough to make her feel colder. "He hasn't been around here for a while."

"In your letters," he said, "you stopped mentioning him." Aldus had to pause so he could remember what Hayes had told him. "Or . . . it seemed he'd left. There was a problem with you and Nate. After that, you seemed sad."

"I did?"

Aldus nodded. "It wasn't so much of what you wrote, but how you wrote it. I could tell there was something different about you. Something just wasn't quite right. It struck me that you were feeling low. Sad, weary, maybe afraid."

Those last few words struck a nerve. The smile on Bethany's face suddenly seemed like a thin coat of paint that fell away as he watched. "Things have been difficult lately. Nate and I have had our rough patches. But you know that because I wrote about it."

Aldus had never cursed his difficulty in that regard more than at that particular moment.

"He'd been drinking more than his fill," she explained. "Staying at the saloons longer and longer until he just stopped coming over here at all. I let it go for a few weeks, but when he started getting cross with the boys, I wouldn't have any more of it."

"What did he do to the boys?"

"They can try anyone's patience just like any child, but he would start yelling at Michael to keep quiet, calling him terrible names. When James told him to stop, Nate pushed him down and would have done worse if I hadn't stepped in."

Trying to contain the rage that was churning in his belly, Aldus told her, "You did the right thing."

"I know. Nate didn't like me reprimanding him in front of the boys and he . . ."

"What did he do?"

"He was drunk. I don't think he knew what he was doing."

Aldus wanted to hear exactly what had happened, but he could tell it would only hurt Bethany again if he pressed her on the matter. Since she was obviously uncomfortable thinking about it, he eased back.

"After that night," she said, "I told him to leave and never come back. Since then, he's come around a few times to try and get back into my good graces. Sometimes he says hurtful things, but I know he'd never act on them."

"Act on them? Has he threatened you?"

Bethany didn't say yes or no. In fact, she remained utterly still before saying, "I can take care of myself and I can take care of my children."

"When does he come around?"

"He's not on any set schedule and it's not very often, as I've said. Besides, all he does is talk." She took a quick breath, blinked, and put her smile back on. It wasn't the beaming one that came from her heart, but it was better than a single coat of paint. "Enough of that. If you thought I was in trouble, I apologize. I am glad you're here, though."

"I'm glad, too. I should have the gallery ready tomorrow afternoon. Bring the boys along and let them take a run at it."

"A shooting gallery?"

"Sure!" Aldus said. "The young'uns love it."

"I don't know if I want my boys shooting a gun."

"They'll need to learn sometime. Besides, it's not like I just hand them a pistol and tell them to go to work. I've been doing this for a while. Ain't nothing gonna happen to them."

"Will I get to meet your friend Zeke?"

"He should be back soon," Aldus said. "Probably the day after tomorrow. He's always in a hurry to get to Omaha, but he's never in a rush to leave. Know what I mean?"

"Oh yes," she chuckled. "We get plenty of rowdies either on their way to Omaha or staggering away from it." After a moment, Bethany said, "I suppose I can bring the boys over to see the gallery. I'm sure they'd enjoy it."

Aldus stood up and stretched his back. "And I guess I should be going. Thank you so much for the meal, Bethany."

She stepped up to him, placed her hands on his face, and gave him a kiss on the cheek. "And thank you for coming here. It's good to make up for a bit of lost time."

There were plenty of things Aldus wanted to say to that. Before he made a fool out of himself, however, he nodded quietly, put on a shaky smile, and walked back to the Kolby Arms Hotel.

Chapter 24

After seeing Bethany the night before, Aldus woke up bright and early the next day. While that wasn't a surprise in itself, he felt ready to run everywhere he needed to go. He had a large breakfast at the hotel, which tasted even sweeter because it was free. There were already a few locals poking about near the wagons and gallery when he made his way to the field outside town, and Aldus talked them up as he made his final preparations. He wasn't sure what he said since the words just spilled out of him, but the folks nearby laughed and waited anxiously for the gallery to be opened.

Aldus had heard Hayes's first-day speech every time they entered a new town. Even though many of the folks in the towns they frequented had heard it several times as well, Hayes still recited it word for word as if it was a beloved tradition. Now it was Aldus's turn and he spoke those words with as much flair as he could muster. He knew he wouldn't be able to fill his partner's top hat, but he drummed up enough interest to form a line at the gallery and sell a good number of tickets.

The first few shots that were taken rattled Aldus by reminding him of the confrontation in Seedley. It wasn't long before he'd boxed up those gruesome memories and stored them in the back of his mind along with the other unpleasantness that would surely pay him a visit through dreams and lonely echoes. His spirits were truly lifted when Bethany brought her sons along to get a look at the town's newest attraction.

Michael was frightened by all the noise, but refused to look away as bottles exploded and targets were knocked down.

James couldn't get his hands on a gun fast enough. The disappointment on his face was palpable when Aldus handed him a skinny little .22-caliber rifle.

"I don't want that one," the boy whined. "I want one of the big ones. Or a pistol! Like a real gunfighter!"

Aldus stepped in front of the display of Hayes's modified Winchesters and buffalo rifles to block them from view. "How about you start with this one? It's a lot like the one I used to shoot squirrels when I was your age."

James's eyes grew big as saucers and when he twisted around to look at his mother, Bethany told him, "I will *not* have you shooting squirrels!"

Although the boy was clearly disappointed, he felt better once he had his hands on the rifle. Aldus showed him how to hold it, helped him sight down the barrel, and pointed him at the row of bottles at the opposite end of the gallery. James fired and yelped at the sound without sending so much as a chip of glass into the air.

"My fault," Aldus said. "I forgot to tell you one very important thing. You gotta squeeze the trigger, nice and slow. Don't pull. You hear me?"

James nodded as if he'd just received one of the universe's biggest secrets. After taking several moments of intense concentration, he took his shot and clipped one of the bottles well enough to send it wobbling off its perch.

"I did it!" he shouted.

Aldus was quick to take the rifle from the excited boy's hands before clapping him on the back. "Nice job. Wild Bill couldn't have done any better."

"You knew Wild Bill Hickock?"

"Well, no. It's my guess he started off with a rifle just like this one, though."

"I want to fire a pistol!"

"You'll have to ask your ma about that."

James turned to Bethany and proceeded to jump and beg until she finally gave in.

"All right," she said, "but only if Mr. Bricker helps you."

"Is it all right, Mr. Bricker?" James asked. "I'll do just what you tell me."

"Only on one condition. No more Mr. Bricker. Ain't nobody calls me that. Just call me Aldus."

James grinned and nodded. His grin became even wider when Aldus went to the covered wagon to retrieve his gun belt and buckle it around his waist. Then he drew the Schofield from his holster and held it down low so James could get a better look.

"Oh boy!" James said. "You ever killed a man?"

Bethany started to scold her son, but Aldus quickly said, "No harm done. I've been in plenty of fistfights, but I'm no gunman."

"Fistfights?" Michael asked from where he stood hanging on to his mother's skirts.

Seeing the exasperated look on Bethany's face, Aldus tousled the smaller boy's hair and said, "Remind me to tell you about that some other time."

"I'm sure he will," Bethany sighed.

Aldus stopped himself from digging in any deeper by showing James how to fire the Schofield. It was a quick lesson since genuine customers were getting anxious to have their turn, and James mostly wound up holding on to the pistol while Aldus placed his hands over the boy's and took a shot. When the bottle at the other end of the gallery exploded, James puffed out his chest and beamed with pride.

"That was fun," Bethany said, "but I'm sure Mr. Bricker has customers to tend to."

"Just call him Aldus, Ma," James scolded.

"I'll be sure to remember that." Looking up at Aldus with a warm smile, she said, "Thank you for this. Do you have any plans for supper?"

"Not at all," he said.

"You can come by again if you like. It'll be nothing fancy, but you're more than welcome."

"Sounds terrific. I'll be there."

After saying good-bye to her and the boys, Aldus watched them leave. When he turned toward the wagons to see if anyone seemed interested in doing anything more than looking, he found one of the locals leaning against the wagon with the locked drawers containing Hayes's tools and ammunition. It was the man Aldus had tossed out of the Kolby Arms, and although he seemed much more sober than he'd been that night, he wasn't at all happier.

Aldus walked over to him and stood just within the big man's reach. "What are you doing here?"

"I was about to ask you the same thing," the man growled.

"What does it look like I'm doing?" Aldus replied while holding his arms out to encompass the wagons and gallery. "I'm tending to my business. Perhaps you should go tend to yours before that face gets any messier."

The man took a step forward and glared at Aldus. "No. You're tending to *my* business. Leave them alone."

"Who?"

"You know damn well who!"

Some of the others near the wagons were taking notice, but Aldus didn't care about that.

"Them kids ain't yours," the man said. "And that woman sure ain't, neither!"

"You're Nate Talbott," Aldus said as his entire body became numb. It was the same feeling he would get when he was seconds away from a fight that he knew was going to be drawn out and bloody. He wanted that fight to commence more than anything when he saw the smug grin on Talbott's bruised face.

"You got that right," Talbott said. "And I staked my claim long before you showed up. I don't care who you think you are, you ain't about to roll into town and take what's mine."

Aldus had his hand around Talbott's throat in the space of a heartbeat. "Bethany don't belong to you or any man," he said. "Neither do them boys. I heard about what you did to them."

"Did you?" Talbott spat. "That ain't your concern, mister. If anyone steps out of line, I'll knock them back where they need to be. That goes for . . . goes for you, too."

Even though Talbott was having trouble speaking because of the tight grip around his neck, he kept his head high and venom pouring through every word. Even when Aldus slammed him against the side of the wagon, he couldn't wipe that smug, arrogant confidence from the other man's face.

"You won't hurt them no more," Aldus said.

"I'll do what I please."

When he tightened his grip, Aldus was ready for Talbott to defend himself. Not only was he prepared for a reprisal, but Aldus yearned for one since it would allow him to unleash what he had in store.

Instead, Talbott merely grabbed hold of Aldus's wrist and squirmed against the side of the wagon. "I ain't afraid of you," he wheezed.

"If you had one lick of sense," Aldus growled, "you would be."

While Talbott might not have had much sense, he had enough to know to keep his mouth shut at that moment. Even after Aldus let him go, Talbott stepped away and didn't do anything to provoke him.

"You steer clear of her and them boys," Aldus said.

"Or what?" Talbott asked now that he'd put some space between himself and Aldus. "You'll run and tell her about me and that whore over at the Kolby Arms?"

"This is between me and you from here on. You start anything else around that family and I'll finish it. You hear me?"

Talbott nodded as he continued to back away. "Yeah. I hear you. Just be sure to watch your step."

"I'm watching it right now," Aldus said as he stepped closer to Talbott. "You want to put this to rest right here? That suits me just fine."

Talbott made a show of looking around to all the others gathering around the potential fight even though he was plainly concerned with only one man. He laughed unconvincingly and walked away.

Aldus's blood was surging through his body. He felt heat flowing just beneath his skin, and his fists were clenched tight enough to whiten his knuckles as he watched Talbott's retreat. If not for the hand that came to rest upon his shoulder, he might very well have run to catch him.

"That one's a snake," said the man who'd caught Aldus's attention. "Let him crawl back under whatever rock he came from."

"You know that fella?" Aldus asked.

The local man waved him off. He was well dressed and looked to be somewhere in his forties. "Just one of the dregs that spends his nights drunk and trying to act like a bad man. I'm sure you know the kind."

"Yep."

"How about giving me a look at one of those Winchester rifles you have on display? I've been meaning to get me one of those."

One of the many things Aldus had learned as a fighter was how to pick his moments. Now was the time to conduct the business of selling guns, so he got back to it and allowed his blood to cool down.

Business thrived for the rest of the day. Hayes never showed up, but neither did Talbott. Bethany did a passable job of roasting a chicken for supper, and they spent another night talking on the porch. This time they discussed simpler, happier matters. It was the kind of night that made every moment of the ride to Corbin worth the effort and ended with a kiss. Their lips touched and Aldus got to wrap her in his arms. The worst part of that entire week was letting her go.

Chapter 25

Hayes came back to town the following day. He arrived well past noon and was pleased to find a fair number of patrons at his wagons. Reining his horse to a stop, he looked down at Aldus and called out, "You seem to be doing well for yourself!"

"I made a few sales," Aldus replied. "Two shotguns and a Winchester."

"With ammunition to go with it?"

"Naturally."

"Good man," Hayes said. "I'm famished. Have you eaten yet?"

"Yes, but I could eat again."

"Then meet me at the hotel. I need to bring my things to my room after putting my horse up."

"We can eat there for free if you like," Aldus said.

"You're treating me to a meal? What's the occasion?"

"No. We're both eating for free. I'll explain when I see you there."

Never one to question a free meal, Hayes pointed his horse toward Third Street and flicked his reins.

Aldus finished up what he was doing and put away the sample rifles before walking over to the Kolby Arms Hotel. He could see Hayes settling in at one of the tables in the dining room, and before he could join him, Edmund came down the stairs and caught his attention.

"I'd like to thank you for what you did," the lanky hotel manager said.

"Haven't done much," Aldus replied. "Not around here, anyway."

"Oh, but you did. We have a regular group of blowhards that come here every so often, and ever since you put that one man out on the street, nobody else has been willing to step up."

"That's good to hear. What do you know about that man?"

"Just that I don't want him around my hotel, and thanks to you," Edmund added with a grin, "he won't be darkening my door anytime soon."

"Glad I could help. By the way, my friend and I will be having something to eat."

"Whatever you like!"

Aldus shook Edmund's hand and stepped into the next room to join Hayes.

"You've covered a lot of ground in a short time," the salesman said.

"I do my best. How did things go in Omaha?"

Hayes took most of the meal describing his exploits in vivid detail. Even knowing his partner's penchant for drama, Aldus couldn't help being impressed.

"So, did they catch them robbers?" Aldus asked.

"Who? Augustus's men?"

"Them or the law."

"I don't know," Hayes said.

"And . . . you let them keep the rifle?"

"After what I did to that rifle, he'll wish he'd been shot."

Aldus didn't know as much about the inner workings of firearms, but he'd seen enough to know what kind of damage could be done by a faulty one. "I suppose that should teach them a lesson. Would've been easier just to turn them over to the law."

"The law's after them, don't you worry," Hayes said impatiently. "Now please tell me you gathered enough courage to speak to Bethany."

Smirking, Aldus nodded. After a bit of prodding, he gave a quick account of how he'd spent the last couple of nights. It wasn't long after that, while the two of them were walking down Garver Street after finishing their meal, that the conversation drifted in another direction.

"How is she feeling?" Hayes asked. "Were you right in thinking she was troubled about something?"

While Aldus had been more than happy to tell his friend about the good times he'd had with Bethany and her sons, he hadn't told him everything. She hadn't said it outright, but Aldus knew a good portion of what she'd told him regarding Talbott was only meant for him. Still, Hayes had played a large role in bringing Aldus this far and had always proven to be a valuable ally.

"I was right," Aldus said. "Nate Talbott was courting her. He turned out to be a skunk who hurt her . . . and the boys."

"There's nothing worse than someone who would stoop so low. Have you met this man?"

"Yes. I just about wrung his neck the other night. Put on a bit of a display at the gallery when I did. I didn't mean to act that way there, but it just happened."

After considering that for a moment, Hayes asked, "Has it affected sales?"

"I don't think so."

"Then good for you!" the salesman said as he put up his hands in a flailing attempt to mimic a boxer's style. "I only wish I was there to see it. By the way, do I get the honor of meeting the delightful Miss White?"

"She works as a seamstress at a place on First Street."

"Let's pop in and say hello. After that, I've got a lot of work to do and I don't know when I'll get a free moment again."

"I suppose it couldn't hurt."

The two of them swapped some more stories about what they'd been doing over the last few days, which was more than enough to occupy them during the short walk to Brine's Tailor Shop. It was a small place. Small enough for Aldus to see just about everything and everyone inside after taking one step through the door.

"What can I do for you gentlemen?" asked a short man who'd been sitting on a tall stool behind a wide table covered with various shapes cut in fabric. "Looking for a nice suit or perhaps a jacket for the coming winter?"

Even though he could see the short tailor was the only other person in there, Aldus asked, "Is Bethany around?"

"No, her boy came in here looking for her and she went home."

"Was it anything serious?"

"The boy was worked up, but that little fella's always worked up about something or other."

Aldus's mind was racing as he turned around and started hurrying down First Street.

Racing to catch up to him, Hayes asked, "Did we miss her?"

"Looks that way. Something's wrong."

"Another instinct or something worse?"

"More than instinct," Aldus said, "but I hope it's not too bad. I need to make certain, though."

"I'm with you, Aldus."

"It might be best if you stayed behind. Things may get rough."

"In case you haven't noticed, things have been fairly rough ever since Cedar Rapids. Besides," Hayes added, "I'm invested in this, too, and I want to see it through. What kind of friend would I be if I turned tail just because things may get rough?"

Aldus could already see the houses at the northwest corner of town. His eyes locked on Bethany's place and he said, "All right, then. But if I have to get my hands dirty, you just stay out of my way."

"No argument there."

They arrived at Bethany's house in a rush, but there wasn't much to see. Aldus put his hand on the Schofield at his hip and shouted, "Bethany? You in there?"

No sound came from the house. There also wasn't anyone else nearby for him to ask. There was, however, a horse tied to a nearby fence post.

"M-Mr. Bricker?"

Aldus looked around for the source of the squeaky little voice and felt a surge of relief when he saw Michael crawl out from beneath the front porch. "Come here, little man," he said as he dropped to one knee. Michael ran at him and wrapped his arms around Aldus's neck. Although the boys had taken to him, Aldus was surprised by the overwhelming display.

"What's the matter?" Aldus asked.

"James is in trouble. I went to fetch Ma, but she went inside and didn't come out."

"What trouble is James in?"

"Mr. Talbott was here when we come home from school. He yelled at James and told him to get in the house. When James said no, Mr. Talbott hit him and knocked him down. That's when I went to fetch Ma."

"She went inside to help your brother?"

Michael nodded. "I heard shouting."

Every one of Aldus's muscles tensed. He looked at the

front of the house but couldn't see a hint of movement behind any of the windows. Holding the little five-year-old by the shoulders, Aldus said, "You stay out here with my friend. I'll go in and see about your brother and ma."

Michael looked over to Hayes and then back to Aldus.

"It's all right," Aldus said as he stood up and walked toward the house. "He'll take care of you."

The little boy stood in his spot until Hayes stepped up to take his hand. "My name is Zachariah. Let's just stand over here and wait for everyone to come back out."

The two of them spoke a bit more, but Aldus was only concerned that Hayes keep Michael out of harm's way. He approached the front door and almost knocked out of habit. Instead, he drew a breath, placed his right hand on his Schofield, and used his left to test the knob. It opened with a creak that raked against Aldus's ears like rusty nails. Knowing it was too late to regain any element of surprise, and not exactly certain what he'd do with it if he could, Aldus entered the house.

The front room was empty.

There was nothing moving on the stairs, and Aldus couldn't see anything stirring at the top of them.

When he heard a few scuffling steps from the kitchen, he said, "Bethany? You in there?"

He got no reply.

"James? It's Aldus. Come on out now."

More scuffling came from the kitchen, so Aldus cautiously moved in that direction.

"Who's in there?" Aldus asked, even though he was already fairly certain of the answer.

The kitchen took up most of the back portion of the house. It was also where Bethany and her family ate their meals. The door leading into it, however, only looked into a small portion of the left side of the room.

Most of what Aldus could see from the hallway was a row of cupboards against the left wall and the potbellied stove in the back. Since he knew his view wasn't going to improve on its own, he eased forward another couple of steps and then stopped himself before charging blindly into the unknown.

Aldus leaned over to look into the largest section of the kitchen and found James cowering under the dining table as a wide-shouldered man stooped down to try and pull him out. Bethany was crumpled in a corner, unmoving.

"Hey!" Aldus barked.

Talbott wheeled around. His pistol was already in hand, and he fired a quick shot at the kitchen entrance. The shot was wild and drilled through a pile of plates stacked on a shelf at Aldus's chest level. "Leave us be!" Talbott shouted.

Pressing a shoulder against the wall, Aldus drew the Schofield and held it at the ready. "What are you trying to do, Nate? Kidnap the boy?"

"Ain't kidnapping him! He's mine! He's mine and so is the other one. So is Bethany!"

"You don't own anyone. That ain't how a family works." Aldus peeked into the kitchen. As soon as he got a glimpse of where Talbott now stood, another shot was fired at him, which hissed past Aldus's head and punched a hole into the hallway behind him.

"They ain't your family!" Talbott said.

"And they're not yours, either. Just leave 'em be. You had your chance with Bethany and made a mess of it. You don't get another one."

"Oh, you'd like that, wouldn't you? That's why you came to town in the first place, ain't it? To steal them from me!"

Aldus could feel the seconds ticking away. Every one

that passed where James and Bethany were trapped in there with a crazed gunman hammered against Aldus's heart. "They ain't property!" he shouted. "Men like you don't deserve to be with good folks like these. This right here proves it!"

"Yeah?" Talbott grunted. "Well, if I can't be with 'em... nobody can."

At that moment, Aldus knew he'd run out of time.

Chapter 26

All Aldus could think about when he charged into the kitchen was keeping Talbott's aim focused on him instead of James or Bethany. He rushed through the door, wincing as another shot was fired, half expecting to drop after taking a bullet. Fortunately he made it across the room to a narrow space between the stove and a tall cupboard. Sucking in his stomach wouldn't help much since he was somewhat exposed, but he did it anyway as Talbott fired at him. Glass shattered and splinters fell onto Aldus's hat, but he was otherwise unharmed.

Aldus thumbed back the Schofield's hammer and leaned away from the cupboard to line up a shot. James was still hunkered down on the floor and Bethany had yet to stir behind the boy, so Aldus kept his aim high and squeezed his trigger. When the window at the far side of the room shattered, he knew he'd pulled his aim a bit too far in that direction.

"You thought you were such a big man embarrassing me in front of the whole town!" Talbott said. "You think you can just whip a man like a dog and get away with it?"

"If that's what this is about, then why are you bothering with the boy and woman?" Aldus leaned out again to get a look and wasn't fired upon. Either Talbott was listening or he was aware that he only had a couple of bullets left in his cylinder.

"I heard what you said about this family," Aldus continued. "But I'm here now. And as for whipping you like a dog and getting away with it . . . I haven't seen one thing to make me think I couldn't."

Talbott's face was flushed with anger and the gun in his hand was trembling. "I'll kill you, too, while I'm at it. That'd show Bethany what kind of weak fool you are."

"You've already shown her what kind of man you are," Aldus said in a voice that was as steady as his hands. "Since her boy is here, I think it'd be good for me to whip you again so he can see."

One skill that helped any fighter didn't have anything to do with his fists. It was the fine art of baiting another man to charge recklessly into a brawl. Anger might have put some power behind his swings, but an enraged man's thoughts were scattered and every movement he made was wild. The only problem with that strategy was that if that angry man got a hold of the fighter who'd taunted him, the bout would most likely be over.

Aldus knew what he was doing when he'd spoken those words, and the cruel smirk he wore when saying them was more than enough to push Talbott over the edge. He flew at Aldus while firing his gun, but his target was already on the move. Aldus ran away from the stove and toward the middle of the room before circling in to charge at Talbott. His ears were ringing and his heart was beating so fast that he lost track of whether Talbott's gun had been emptied or not. He swung the Schofield at Talbott's head, hoping to knock the man out with one blow, only to have the pistol knocked from his hand.

Rather than try to retrieve the firearm, Aldus fell back on what he knew. His hands balled into fists and he drove a few straight, chopping blows into Talbott's ribs.

When he saw Talbott bring his gun around, Aldus reached out to grab his wrist in his left hand and pull it across the front of his body. That took Talbott off his balance, but not completely. Aldus hung on to Talbott's wrist with both hands and jammed his back against the other man's chest. Pulling Talbott's arm down while bending forward, Aldus lifted him from his feet and flipped Talbott onto the floor. From there, Aldus twisted Talbott's hand as hard as he could until the man beneath him let out a yelp and dropped his gun.

"Get out of here, James!" Aldus shouted.

The boy was terrified but managed to pull himself up. He stopped and looked over at his mother. Bethany was coming around and pulling herself to her feet.

"Go!" Aldus shouted. "I'll see to her!"

James rushed over to his mother so they could both hurry toward the door.

Dropping to one knee, Aldus put his left hand flat on Talbott's chest and dropped his right fist down like a pickax. His knuckles thumped solidly against Talbott's face, opening a cut that had been put there when he'd hit him outside the Kolby Arms Hotel. Talbott's arms flailed wildly, catching Aldus in the stomach and ribs in a series of thrashing punches. Aldus didn't feel any of them land. He was too angry and too intent on putting his opponent down for the count.

"Give it up, Nate," Aldus said after he delivered a jarring blow to Talbott's jaw. "This ain't gonna end the way you want it. Just give up before things get any worse."

Talbott looked up at him wearing an expression that showed he was beyond the capacity of rational thought. Suddenly he smiled through the bloody mask covering his face and said, "Worse for you is more like it."

Aldus felt a punch skim across his midsection. A biting pain followed the brush of knuckles, causing him to recoil reflexively and grab at the stinging section of his stomach. Warm blood spilled across his fingers, confirming that the wound across his belly most certainly hadn't been put there by a punch. Looking down, he saw a hunting knife clutched in Talbott's hand. Sometime during the struggle, the man on the floor must have snatched it from the scabbard hanging from his belt.

Aldus clutched a hand to his gut and put some distance between himself and the blade as Talbott climbed to his feet. There wasn't a lot of blood soaking into Aldus's shirt, and a few quick glances down told him that the cut wasn't very deep. It ran across most of his stomach just beneath his breastbone, which meant he could have been gutted if Talbott had had a bit more strength in that arm.

"Come on, big man," Talbott said, sneering. "Get a little closer so I can finish the job."

Aldus came at him like a bull with head down and legs pumping for all they were worth. Whether it was a good idea or not, he didn't have many options. Talbott cocked his arm back for a powerful stab, but Aldus got to him before he could follow through. Grabbing hold of Talbott's shirt with both hands, Aldus swung him around and slammed him against the table. Talbott managed to keep from falling down by reaching back with his free hand to brace himself. Pushing off from the table, he slashed with his knife while spewing obscenities like so much poison.

Waiting until another swing came at him, Aldus stepped in and wrapped an arm around Talbott's arm to stop the knife from coming any farther. He cinched in his grip and almost snapped Talbott's elbow, but the crazed man still didn't relinquish his weapon. Even after Aldus pounded his fist into Talbott's body and head, the blade still remained where it was. Aldus was about to try to take his opponent down once more when Talbott swung his knee up to slam into Aldus's stomach. Not only did the impact force a good portion of the breath from his lungs, but Aldus was overcome by scalding pain from the cut across his stomach. His knees buckled and he couldn't do anything but drop.

Talbott grabbed a handful of Aldus's hair and pulled his head back to expose his throat. Grinning triumphantly, he raised the knife in preparation for the killing blow.

A gunshot blasted through the kitchen, causing Talbott to look toward the doorway. Aldus took that opportunity to grab both of Talbott's ankles and flip his legs out from under him. Standing up, Aldus reached down and took the knife from Talbott's hand.

Standing in the doorway, Bethany had one hand on James's shoulder and the other holding Aldus's Schofield in a shaky grip. Both she and her son were white as ghosts.

Aldus pointed toward the door to the next room and said, "Get out of here right now, you hear?"

"Aren't you gonna finish him off?" James asked.

"He's already finished. There's nothing to be gained by kicking a man when he's down."

When he heard movement behind him, Aldus twisted around to face Talbott. The fallen man was crawling on all fours toward the pistol he'd dropped. Walking straight toward him, Aldus brought the hunting knife down to place it on Talbott's throat. "You touch that pistol and I'll put an end to you," he said.

Talbott looked past him to James and Bethany.

"I'm trying to set a good example for that boy by not killing you," Aldus said as he scooped up the pistol Talbott had dropped. "Why don't you set one by owning up to the mess you made?"

Talbott drew himself up onto his knees. His head hung low as if everything that had happened suddenly fell onto his shoulders. When Aldus told him to get up, he didn't protest in the slightest.

Bethany's eyes were bloodshot and rimmed with tears.

"Best take James outside," Aldus told her.

Talbott smiled and stretched out both arms. "It ain't too late, darlin'. I love y—"

She pulled her trigger and the Schofield sent a round blazing through Talbott's shin. He spun around like one of the targets in Hayes's shooting gallery and flopped onto the floor.

"Don't you ever speak a word to me again," she said. "And don't show your face around here or to my boys for the rest of your days."

Lifting Talbott to his feet, Aldus held him upright as he hopped around and wailed in pain. "This is all your doing," Aldus said. "You'll take your medicine."

Talbott hung on to consciousness by a thread as Aldus helped him out of the kitchen. Before they got too far, the front door busted open and two men stormed inside. "Raise your hands! Drop your guns!" the man leading the charge said.

Bethany moved past the other two. "It's all right, Sheriff! It's over."

"There were shots." Glancing down at Talbott's leg, the lawman nodded. "Did this one cause the trouble?"

"Yes. I can tell you everything that happened, and my boys are witnesses," she said. "Mr. Bricker here kept Nate from killing us."

"If it's all the same to you, I'll have everyone tell me what happened. My deputy here can keep an eye on Nate. First off, I'll need those guns."

As the lawmen collected the guns along with Talbott's

hunting knife, Hayes poked his nose inside. "Thought you could use a hand, Aldus. I wanted to come in and help you myself, but I thought fetching the law might do more good."

"You did the right thing," the sheriff said. "Now, how about you bring Dr. Fagan out here? His office is at the corner of Second and Douglas not far from mine."

Before he made a move, Hayes looked at Aldus and asked, "You need anything?"

"Go on and get the doc," Aldus replied. "I got what I need."

Chapter 27

Sheriff Dreyer was a soft-spoken man who knew Nate Talbott all too well. He listened to Bethany tell him about how Talbott had forced his way into her home and frightened her children. Michael had slipped away, fetched her from the tailor shop, and brought her back to the house. Before Aldus showed up, Talbott had been ranting about reclaiming what he thought he owned, and when Bethany took a stand against him, he knocked her out. Aldus told the sheriff about the ensuing scuffle as Dr. Fagan wrapped up Talbott's leg well enough for him to be moved directly into a jail cell.

"What will happen now?" Bethany asked.

The sheriff scratched his head. "I'll keep hold of him until Judge Stephenson can preside over a trial. From what I heard, he shouldn't have to wait long before being carted off to the prison out near Lincoln."

She nodded and the lawmen started filing out of her home. Without another word, Aldus walked over and wrapped his arms tightly around her. Bethany kissed him deeply and when she finally pulled away, she whispered, "Thank you."

* * *

A few days passed and Talbott had already been taken to Lincoln, where he was to stand trial. Night was approaching, Hayes was taking inventory, and Aldus was touching up the paint on the targets in the shooting gallery.

"I'd say it's about time to move on," Hayes announced. "The sales here were better than expected, but there's bigger stops to make."

"You pulled in a good amount from those railroad men in Omaha, didn't you?" Aldus asked.

"Yes, indeed. They're always wanting better rifles. I hear Augustus and those men of his guard a mighty big sum of money that's used to pay Union Pacific workers from here all the way out to California! Once they see how well those Winchesters work out, they'll be back for more. Until then, I say we head back down into the Kansas and Missouri circuit."

Aldus leaned in so he could make sure every inch of the little iron circle in front of him was coated in bright red. "I believe . . . I'll be staying here for a spell."

"All right, then. I can pay you your percentage of what we made here, which should give you a good start."

Setting his brush down, Aldus straightened up and turned to look at Hayes. "That's it? I didn't expect tears, but . . ."

Hayes walked toward him wearing a wide grin. "I've seen you with Bethany. She's a fine woman. I've also seen you with them boys. If you didn't decide to stay after all the time and effort it took for you to get here, I would have cursed you for having rocks in your head."

"Can't argue with you there."

"So, what's the plan? Are you going to settle here for good? Build a house? Marry that sweet woman and live in hers?"

"I don't know," Aldus said earnestly. "All I'm certain of is that I'm supposed to be here. I can't change what happened before, so I'll take what I was given now and run with it as far as I can."

"What will you do to earn a living?" Raising his bushy eyebrows, Hayes added, "You could always take up the firearms trade."

"Edmund over at the Kolby Arms offered me a job there making certain none of the customers get out of line. The owners of the two biggest saloons here in town made me pretty good offers for the same kind of work. That should see me through for a while."

"Thought you'd had enough of earning with your fists."

Aldus shrugged. "It's what I'm good at. Doesn't have to be forever. You could always settle here as well, you know. Every town needs a blacksmith or two."

"I'll consider it," Hayes said. "Mind if I check in on you whenever I'm in the area? Perhaps call on you for some help in a circuit that won't take you far from home?"

"I insist on it."

"Why don't we have one last drink before we start breaking down the gallery? I assume you won't leave before you help me with that at least."

Aldus winced. "Of course, but will you be able to do that without me later on?"

"There's always able-bodied men to hire for that sort of work. I did manage to function before you signed on, you know."

"Right," Aldus said as he looked toward Second Street. Bethany and the boys were standing there waving at him. Their smiles could be seen from a distance, and hers shone brighter than the setting sun.

"We don't have to start on the gallery now," Hayes said. "Go on and enjoy your evening."

"Why don't you join us for supper? Bethany's not the best cook, but her food's better than what they serve at the hotel."

"I wouldn't want to be an imposition."

"Nonsense! Come on. The boys will get a kick out of seeing you do some of your pistol-spinning tricks."

Hayes brightened immediately. "Well, I may be out of practice. Of course, who am I to deny such an eager audience?"

As Aldus strode toward them, Michael and James came right up and climbed all over him. Picking up Michael was almost as easy for Aldus as picking up his hat, although he did wince at the jab of pain from his bandaged midsection. He held on to the little boy while giving Bethany a lingering hug.

"What did you learn in school today, boys?" Aldus asked.

Michael was first to say, "I'm learning how to read! Want me to show you?"

"I would. In fact, I'm sure you could teach me a lot on that subject."

Ever since he'd sent his first letter to Bethany, Aldus had imagined plenty of ways for their reunion to turn out. This wasn't exactly one of them.

It was far, far better.

Chapter 28

Kearney, Nebraska

The town of Kearney had seen better days. So had Wes Cavanaugh. Empty storefronts lined most of the main streets, scattered in among businesses that were struggling to stay afloat. While such a downturn didn't do anything for local commerce, it gave Wes plenty of choices when he was searching for a rooftop overlooking the train station. He settled on the shell of a feed store as his post, and he crouched behind its warped old sign as Mose tried to look inconspicuous near the platform.

After nearly getting caught while scouting in Omaha, Wes had been prepared to take the Union Pacific payrolls down at his first opportunity. Unfortunately the armed guards became skittish after that night and closed ranks until the train steamed westward.

Wes had paid too much for his information and he'd be damned if he was going to let his biggest robbery slip through his fingers. So, instead of allowing the number 24 train to go about its way, he and Mose rode after it. They'd done enough scouting to pick up on patterns within the rotation of the guards and the habits of the men on board. If they could wait until the train made a

stop and let enough of its men off to stretch their legs
and make their rounds, Wes figured he and Mose could
still blast their way on board and ride away with more
than enough to make the venture worth their while.

Five of the ten men had stepped off the train, escort-
ing two small strongboxes bound for parts unknown.
Wes didn't care where those boxes were headed. There
were only five men left on the train, and they looked
bored. Two of them wandered toward a saloon across the
street from the station, giving Wes the chance he'd been
waiting for.

"Here we go," he whispered as he sighted along the
top of the stolen Sharps rifle. The outlaws had been so
busy trying to escape Omaha and then keep up with
number 24 that Wes had almost forgotten what it felt like
to heft the fancy rifle. He worked the lever and noticed
it felt a bit strange. There were a few rough spots around
the trigger as well, but he chalked it up to the Sharps being custom made. Wes was used to models that came
straight off the shelf, and he'd fired this one enough times
before getting to Omaha for him to be plenty comfortable with it.

Before he could fidget with the rifle any further, he saw
one of the three remaining gunmen step onto the balcony
behind the third car. As luck would have it, the man was
Augustus himself, leader of the gunmen hired by Union
Pacific to safeguard the payroll shipment across the country.

"Kiss it good-bye, railroad man."

The shot was lined up.

Wes squeezed his trigger.

The hammer dropped a bit sooner than he'd expected
and the gun in his hand exploded.

Wes hollered as he turned away from the edge of the
rooftop. His eyes burned and there were fresh cuts on his

hands and face. He was deafened by a loud ringing that filled his entire head. On the platform below, Mose stuck to the plan by charging at the train as soon as he heard Wes's gunshot. Unfortunately Augustus was not only alive and kicking but alerted by the misfire.

Augustus drew his pistol and brought it up before Mose could figure out things weren't going as he'd hoped. Men swarmed from the train as well as from the saloon across the street. In a matter of seconds, all five of the remaining Union Pacific gunmen had converged on the platform.

"Now, what did you intend to do here?" Augustus asked. "Might you be Mose Robins?"

Mose's eyes widened and he nodded as if he'd just witnessed a miracle.

"So that would mean the man up there is Wes Cavanaugh," Augustus said. Pointing toward the rooftop of the old feed store, he looked over to one of his men and said, "Get up there and see what all that screaming is about. Sounds to me like he might have hurt himself."

Two men rushed toward the building where Wes was cursing up a storm.

"H-how did you know us?" Mose asked.

"Friend of mine told me you'd be coming. Name's Jimmy Stock out of Cedar Rapids. He knows an awful lot of things. Good fellow, too. A real straight shooter."

"That's the man who told us about this train!" Mose snarled. "I'm gonna kill that two-timing snake!"

"I doubt you'll be doing much of anything. I been told you and Wes Cavanaugh like to rob banks. That's the sort of thing that gets you locked up for a real long time. Come on, now. Let's get you fitted for some shackles and leg irons."

Wes and Mose wound up getting a real good look at the inside of number 24 when they were chained and tossed into one of the cars by Augustus's men. The outlaws were left with the U.S. marshals in Cheyenne. After that, the only glimpse of a train they got was when they spotted smoke on the horizon from the small square windows of their federal prison cells.

Jimmy Stock received a healthy reward for providing information that prevented railroad money from falling into the wrong hands. It wasn't a fortune, but he still retired from selling good information to bad men and became a partner at Tennison's Saloon. He wasn't certain it was a wise thing to do, but it felt right. In the end, that was the only choice worth making.

Read on for an excerpt from another
rip-roarin' Western

Ralph Compton
The Hunted

A Ralph Compton novel
by Matthew P. Mayo

Coming from Signet in August.

"That's what you got for me? That?" The dealer nodded toward the cards laid before him. His words came out too loud, and as if he'd been waiting long minutes to say them. The thin man with oiled mustaches, black visor, and arm garters shook his head and winked at the gawkers gathered about his table.

Across from him, his customer sighed and closed his eyes for a moment. He was a mammoth man with a broad back turned to the rest of the room.

The dealer and the others clustered by the table flicked eyes at one another, then settled back on him. The player's rough-spun coat, the dark color of axle grease, strained across the shoulders as he brought a hand up to scratch the stubble on his face. "I'm out," he said quietly, nodding toward the table.

"You about were anyway." The dealer shifted his cigarillo to the other side of his slit mouth and winked at the watchers. Their soft laughs chafed Charlie, but he'd earned them. Coming in here half lit and feeling as if he knew more about playing blackjack and bucking the tiger than any man alive. Heck, three hours and he'd spent more time running from it than wrangling the tiger, and what did he have to show for it? A whole lot of empty in his pockets.

He had his emergency five-dollar piece in his vest and that, plus his mule, Mabel-Mae, and his meager kit, was about all he had in the world now. Three hours earlier he'd been halfway to owning a sizable chunk of land in a pretty mountain valley. Now he'd set himself back by two years—that was how long it had taken him to earn that two thousand dollars. Those two years had all but killed him, he'd worked so hard. And now? Now he was two years older, and as his father used to say of his family's lot in life, he was poorer than an outhouse rat.

"Hey, how about letting someone else take up space in that chair?" The dealer squinted one eye against the slow curl of silver smoke rising up the side of his face from the cat-turd cigarillo. Charlie wanted to smear the smugness off his face, but he'd avoided jail for too long now to cozy up to the idea of being near broke and tossed in the calaboose in Monkton, Idaho Territory.

He pushed away from the table, the chair squawking back on the boot-worn boards. He kept his eyes on the dealers the entire time he stood, taking longer than he needed to. It wasn't much, but showing off his height was about all he had. It worked. The dealer's grin sagged at the corners and his cigarillo drooped as his eyes followed the big man's progress upward.

He'd not been there when Charlie sat down at the table, so he didn't know how big the fellow he'd been mocking was. And what he saw was a giant of a man, closer to seven feet than six. He was wide enough at the shoulder that by now, at thirty-eight years of age, he naturally angled one shoulder first through doorways and ducked his head a mite. It didn't guarantee he'd not rap his bean on the doorframe—there weren't too many weeks of the year when he didn't have a goose egg of sorts throbbing under his tall-crowned hat.

Charlie's stubbled jaw—he'd not taken time to clean

up before hitting the saloon for the first time in many months since he'd sold off his latest claim—was a wide affair beneath a broad head topped with brown curls, tending to silver, forever trapped beneath his big hat. It added nearly another foot to his height, but he didn't mind. It suited him somehow. His hands too were wide, callused mitts with thick tree-branch fingers more suited to dragging and pounding and stacking than tapping out cards. He should have known better than to think he could best the house.

The dealer eyed Charlie's hands covering the entire top of the now-wobbly wooden chair he'd been seated in. He swallowed once, began to speak, gulped again as the big man took his time straightening his coat, squaring that mammoth hat. The big man still didn't look away from the dealer's face.

The dealer finally managed to whisper, "Thank ... thank you for your patronage, sir."

Charlie nodded once, turned, and heard the dealer let out a stuttering breath of relief. Despite his new financial situation, Charlie half smiled. At least he had his size. It wasn't worth much, but this big body could, by gum, still earn him a day's honest wage most anywhere labor was needed.

The big man strode the length of the narrow room, making the long walk toward the front of the saloon, the floor squeaking and popping under his weight. Everyone he passed gave him the hard stare. He felt certain they all knew he'd lost all but his shirt.

Midway to the door he passed a cluster of men at the end of the bar. He felt relief that they were chattering among themselves and not concerned with him. Then he heard a voice that about stopped him in his tracks.

"Shotgun? Why, by God, it is! As I live and breathe, it's my old friend Shotgun Charlie Chilton!"

Though it had been many long years since he'd been called that, Charlie's step hitched, as if out of dusty reflex. He paused right there in the middle of the room and closed his eyes. He knew a couple, three things: He should have kept on walking, he'd never had many friends and most of them had died away in the war, and the man who all but silenced the room with his drunken shouting was no friend. Anybody who called Charlie by that old name was no one he wanted to know anymore— and should by all rights be dead by now anyway.

Charlie knew he should have kept right on going out that door, headed to the livery where he'd intended to bed down for the night in the stall beside Mabel-Mae, his old mule. And then come tomorrow he'd lick his wounds out on the trail, put some distance between himself and the town of Monkton. And once he did, he'd cipher out a way to earn money again, make up for the last couple of years' wages he'd blown at the faro table.

Though Charlie knew all these things and thought all these things, he still opened his eyes and slowly turned to face his past. And that's when what had begun as one of the best days of his life, which had gotten pretty bad, got a whole lot worse.

For who he saw annoyed him to no end. Jacob "Dutchy" Erskine. They had called him Dutchy because he looked as though he might be a Dutchman, though he wasn't any more Dutch than Charlie was the king of China. But the fool was grinning at Charlie, and judging from his rheumy eyes and leering mouth, his boilers looked to be half-stoked with liquor too.

Charlie turned back to the door. He hadn't gone another step before the voice stopped him again. All eyes were on them both now. Even the lousy banjo player in the corner had stopped.

"Shotgun Charlie, as I live and breathe!" Dutchy slid

away from the elbow-smooth bar top and stumbled the few steps toward Charlie.

The drunk man was still a good couple of strides away when Charlie held up a hand. "I . . . I don't know who you are, nor what you're after, but you've mistook me for someone else."

The man halted, weaving in place, his smile drooping. "What? Charlie . . . aw, you're funnin' me."

Charlie pinned a broad forced smile on his wide, windburned face. He looked left and right, nodding and smiling at the staring faces. Seemed as though there were a whole lot more people in here than when he'd come in. He felt his cheeks redden even more. Curse Dutchy for a fool.

"I'm telling you . . . fella," he said in a lowered voice, "I ain't never seen you before. Now do us both a favor and back off."

"No, no, I ain't neither. Come on over here and meet my new chums. You can buy us all a drink with your faro winnin's." Dutchy's smile turned pinched; his wet eyes narrowed. "Unless you'd rather reminisce all about the old days right here in the middle of the bar." He raised his arms wide to the room.

Charlie saw the two missing fingertips on Dutchy's left hand. They had healed poorly after they'd been shot off long before Charlie ever knew him. The hard pink scar nubs looked like pebbles or warts, and Charlie had always wanted to pare them off with a knife. If they had been on his fingers, he'd not have been able to live with the look, nor, he suspected, the feel of them.

Dutchy giggled, looked around at the silent, expectant faces. "Maybe you'd like to tell 'em all about the last time we seen each other. Wichita, wasn't it? Something about a lousy Basque, wasn't it? All them sheep running all over the place, and Charlie here, he . . ." Dutchy stopped and leaned forward. "What's the matter, Charlie? You look like you seen a ghost. Maybe one of a little girl? One who's been all trampled by a . . . horse?"

It had been a long, long time since Charlie had dreamed of the little girl. But it hadn't been any longer than that afternoon that he'd thought of her. He'd been walking on into town leading Mabel-Mae when he'd seen the children playing before a white-painted schoolhouse a few streets away from Monkton's main street. He thought of her every day, in fact, and this man, this damnable Dutchy, was fixing to rip it all wide open again.

Big Charlie Chilton had tried hard since that accident to make sure he was slow to start a thing. But once he set to a task, he dedicated himself to it and rarely gave it less than his all. But when his great ham-sized right fist drove like a rock hammer square at Dutchy's grinning face, Charlie hadn't known it would happen. Like the old days he'd worked so hard to put behind him. No warning, just action. He hated the fact that it felt good when his tight knuckles jammed hard against Dutchy's leering face.

The strike happened so fast that the entire room was still silent, listening with rapt attention to the drunk's account. The next thing they all heard was a muffled snap and Dutchy's head whipped to one side as if he were gawking at a passing bullet. His body followed suit and spun in a dervish dance before slamming into the bar leaners behind him. They parted fast and let Dutchy drop, his head clunking against the mud-scraped brass rail.

The early gasps had given way to scraping chairs and now yammering as standing people leaned, trying to get a look at the collapsed victim.

"He dead?" someone asked.

As if in response, Dutchy groaned and rolled his head to and fro, the left side of his face already swelling and purpling.

An old man with a cob pipe leaned close over Dutchy. "Naw. It was his jaw that cracked." He plucked the pipe from its customary spot in his mouth, the groove worn by it in his teeth. "He ain't dead, but he ain't gonna be right by a long shot for a long time to come, mark my words. . . ."

That was the last thing Charlie heard as he bulled his way through the double front doors, the glass panes rattling as he pawed them shut behind him. His big granger boots punched squelching holes in the slushed mud of the early October street as he stepped off the sidewalk. The livery. That's where he had to get to. Had to get on out of here before someone set the law on him.

Charlie didn't hear the doors open and close again behind him, fast footsteps hammering the boardwalk in the opposite direction, toward Marshal Watt's office.

Also available from

National bestselling author

RALPH COMPTON

"A writer in the tradition of Louis L'Amour and Zane Grey!" —*Huntsville Times*

Available wherever books are sold or at
penguin.com

S543